I0686909

ANGIE'S PROMISE

Alma Chronicles III

Toby Fesler Heathcotte

Mardel Books

Angie's Promise is a work of fiction. Names, places, and incidents either are products of the author's imagination or are used fictitiously.

Angie's Promise ©2004 by Toby Heathcotte

First edition released in USA in 2004 by Wings E-Press

Re-released in 2009 by

Mardel Books
6145 West Echo Lane
Glendale, Arizona 85302
mardelbooks.com

Second printing 2009

All rights reserved. No part of this book may be reproduced or transmitted in any form or by any means without the written permission of Mardel Books except where permitted by law.

Cover design by Zanne Kennedy
Author photo by Dennis Habbershaw

ISBN: 978-0-9819961-2-7

In a vision, Angie sees her fiancé's plane crash in 1987 in the American Southwest. She begs him not to leave, but he ignores her warnings, takes off in the plane, and dies before her eyes. Angie refuses to accept a future without her love. When lucid dreaming fails to keep his spirit near, Angie searches for a chink in the barrier of death. And she finds one.

"Angie's story gives readers a chance to come to terms with their own losses."
Regan Taylor

"Suspense, psychic phenomena and tons of emotion, a top notch author."
The Romance Studio Four & One Half Hearts

"For anyone that has lost someone dear *Angie's Promise* offers solace. For those who have not yet lost someone, it offers hope."
Love Romances Five Hearts

"Though not a romance, *Angie's Promise* is a love story that extends through the ages"
Romance Reviews Today

"Angie must face one obstacle after another in this compelling read. Her psychic powers work for and against her as she fights to rejoin her true love."
Romantic Times Four Stars

"I absolutely loved the book. I read it in ONE day and that's not too easy to accomplish with 12-year-old twin boys and a nine-month-old baby girl. I truly couldn't get the characters out of mind and certainly laughed and cried."
Cindy Anstett

"Just finished *Angie's Promise*. In case you can't see the tears I'm crying like a baby. What a wonderful book."
Sherry Wille

For my sons

"Nothing is at last sacred but the integrity of your own mind."

Emerson

The Alma Chronicles

Incarnations of the Souls

50-10 BCE England	1700s CE England, Scotland, & Maryland Colony	1900s CE Arizona, California, & Afghanistan	2000s CE Arizona and California of Greater Hispania
Alma	Alison	Angie	Angela
Taliesin	Thomas	Ty	Todd
Lugh	Lainn	Luke	Luke (living)
Morfran	Mac & Megan	Melinda	Melanie
Caitlin	Catherine		
Kegan	Colin	Karim	Kendall & Kegan
	Henry	Hank	
	Emily		Euphoria
	Judith & Jeannie	Jillian	Janice
	Aaron & Donnie	Aaron	Aaron (living)
Emmons (in Afterlife)	Emmons	Emmons (in Afterlife)	Emmons (in Afterlife)

One

Drowning in Ecstasy

Late May 1987

The hull of the sloop *Destiny* glittered cool white against the seamless blue of ocean and sky. Eight hours out from Catalina Island, weary from the sun and the long day's sail, Angie Brock headed toward San Diego Bay with the man she would marry the next Saturday. Relaxed against the smooth curve of fiberglass behind her back, she watched her beloved grasp the wheel with wind-weathered hands.

Tall and suntanned, Ty Beckman scanned the ocean with cobalt eyes. He had a cleft chin, and his unruly black hair streaked with gray blew in the wind as they tacked southward.

"Want me to steer?" Angie hoped he would say no. A delicious laziness from the launch's ceaseless rocking consumed her.

"Not just yet." Ty grinned and checked the gauges. When he adjusted the sails, they luffed momentarily then sighed like a lover as they swayed across the bow to port.

Tucking her hair into a captain's hat, Angie stretched out on the leather-padded bench. With one arm for a pillow, she pulled over-pink legs up and inhaled the fresh-scented breeze. The cloudless sky looked as empty of birds and planes as the sea was of other craft.

1

Eyes heavy, Angie struggled to focus on a tiny object far away. She could not identify it as bird or jet. What else could hover in the sky?

Lines, like flashes of light, fanned out. A phantom airplane materialized from nowhere, suspended before Angie's vision. As she lay transfixed, the plane grew larger, taking shape with an ominous quality. Ice-white with Navy blue lettering on the side, it hung in the air like an ornament swaying on a Christmas tree branch.

Distant screams came from within the plane. Passengers? Their fear infected her. Angie wanted to help—warn someone, tell Ty, but she could neither move nor speak.

The ghostly plane exploded. Shafts of orange and gold shot out in all directions. Popping sounds reverberated through the still sky. Crackling flames seemed to reach out to scorch her face and hair although she remained untouched.

Urgency in Ty's voice jarred her out of the trance. "Take the wheel," he commanded, "I need to check that halyard."

"What did you say?" Angie gasped. Sweat beaded on her forehead, her breath came in shallow bursts, the skin prickled on the back of her neck.

"Sorry, didn't know you'd fallen asleep, but I need your help for a minute." Ty looked worried. "Take over for me."

Straightening her red tank top, Angie scooted behind the wheel and glanced at the unbroken calm of the sky. Maybe she had fallen asleep and dreamed the exploding airplane.

Ty trod across the cabin cover, swung around the mainsail, and grabbed the jib stay. Squinting against the fierce, late afternoon sun, he pointed to the west. "Fall off! We've got company. Be careful!"

2

Another sloop passed close by, and Angie focused on steering clear. She resolved to tell Ty about the dream or vision, or whatever it was, later.

"That halyard won't take much stress without snapping." Ty returned to the wheel. "Wish I'd replaced it in Catalina. I'll have to do that before I sign over the pink slip."

"A sale?" Angie scowled. "What're you talking about?"

"A guy at the club made an offer on the *Destiny*. I decided to sell her."

"You can't be serious." Angie chuckled at how easily Ty could always get a rise out of her by teasing.

A pleading look crossed his handsome face. "She's too much work, Angie."

"You mean you've already decided? That's it? No discussion?" Angie felt an old tightness in her solar plexus, like when her mother had made decisions with no regard for their impact on Angie's life.

"Having a sailboat was fine when I was single." Ty squeezed her shoulder. "But now that I'm going to have you around all the time, I've been thinking I should get rid of it."

"What kind of crazy logic is that?" Pulling free of his arm, she tried to keep anger out of her voice. "You love this boat. I do, too. We should keep it. At the very least, we should've talked it over." Angie sighed. "You've got an equal partner this time whether you want one or not. I can't be any other way. Not after twenty years as a single parent."

"Angie, for God sake. What's the matter with you?" Ty took the helm, and she backed away. He bit his lip with an indulgent look. "I'm sorry, but it isn't the end of the world. We'll buy another one if you want to."

"I don't want another one, dammit. I want this one." Angie needed to calm down and took a deep breath, searching for a way to convince him. "You used to daydream about owning a sailboat when you were a kid. Remember how you drew boat pictures on your school papers?"

A wide smile crossed his face. "Old Maid Ellington used to take my sketches and throw them away." His deep tone pitched higher as Ty imitated her scratchy voice. "'If you keep daydreaming around about sailboats, you'll never amount to a hill of beans, Tyler Beckman.'" He laughed. "Remember how she always used both of my names? Mom said the old lady didn't like boys. Probably did like them. Maybe that was the trouble."

Remembering their former teacher's great size, lumbering gait, and perpetual hair net made Angie laugh. That the old woman had any sexual feelings at all seemed preposterous. "You think she had the hots for you?"

"Could be." Ty tickled Angie's chin. "You did."

"Still do." Angie could see her charming teenage boyfriend again in the lifted black eyebrows and knowing look on Ty's face. The argument was finished. His thoughts had turned to lovemaking. Raising an eyebrow, Angie caressed his bare leg.

"We'll get to that later." Ty gave her a quick kiss and nodded toward the line secured in a winch. "Pull in that jib just a little."

Angie tugged on the line to tighten the sail. The winch caught in a peculiar way that she did not recognize.

"That's the third time we've had to adjust the tack." Ty wiped his forehead and surveyed the rigging. "Should still be on a run, but we're practically close-hauled we've pulled the sails in so tight."

"What do you think is wrong?" Sky, wind, water—everything seemed the same, but Angie felt an eerie sensation.

"Prevailing wind's supposed to be from the northwest."

"The wind feels different." Angie shivered despite the warm air.

"It's changing direction." Ty looked worried.

Although they sailed straight toward San Diego, the land mass lay far beyond their view. The ocean looked the same in all directions.

Ty touched her arm. "Look, babe, about selling the boat, I've been alone for so long, I've filled my life with stuff to do. All I want now is to make up for what we've missed. I want to spend all my time with you." He faltered. "Twenty-five years is a hell of a long time apart. I don't want to have to leave you whenever a sail needs repair. Or that damned halyard." He pointed to the mast.

Angie knew he had trouble with the words. In spite of the strong Navy officer image, he needed her and tried to tell her so. It took strength to do that. She laid a hand against his cheek. "Don't worry, love. I'll always be with you." The relief in his smile touched her. She kissed him. "Nothing can ever separate us again. I promise."

Waves slapped against the side of the boat.

Tensing, Ty broke away. "Wind's really picking up." He reached for the mainsail line. "Turn on the radio and see what they're saying."

While descending the galley steps, Angie looked to the west. On choppy water, a lone sailboat bobbed up and down against the brilliance of the sinking mango sun.

Even though not certain whether the boat approached or headed away, she felt less alone with its presence. Relief swept her at the sight of land, darkly outlined far in the distance.

Hot wind blew. Angie fished in a shorts pocket for a knitted band and quickly pulled her hair back into a ponytail. Sweat dampened the tank top as she hurried into the galley. Loose apples rolled around in the stainless steel sink, and a cooler slid back and forth in the aisle. Wedging a sea bag between the cooler and the bunk solved that problem.

Bracing herself on the railing, Angie turned on the radio, flipped through the channels, and listened to the weather station. She stepped onto the shiny, teakwood stairs, halfway out of the cabin. "They're reporting cirrus clouds, sixty-eight degrees, and moderate breeze—twelve knots."

"Damn!" Ty strained forward, gripping the wheel and studying the rough water. The same sky, still cloudless blue, framed his head, but the wind blew stronger and hotter by the minute. "They've had the same damn report on all day long. They're supposed to change it every three or four hours."

"I know the message is wrong." Angie watched the sails billow and snap. "The wind's whipping up."

"Come and check the jib." Ty's voice took on the crispness he used with naval aides.

Angie sat to his right and stuffed the jib winch into its slot. She remembered how it had caught earlier. The sails sagged and flapped. "Ty, I think there's—"

"Shit. Pull that jib in tighter."

Angie wished for enough sailing knowledge to understand their predicament. Although she trusted Ty's skills and judgment, her skin prickled like it did when things were about to go very wrong, the way she had felt the morning her uncle had died. Remembrance of the mysterious plane in the sky shuddered through her.

"Barometer's falling," Ty shouted. "Take the helm."

The winch appeared to be holding so Angie slid behind the wheel and wiped perspiration from her upper lip. She struggled to stand against the rushing wind and unsteady boat.

Ty turned the mainsail winch. Both sails filled. "What's the wind speed?"

"Thirty knots per hour. God!" Angie reread the gauge to make certain. Going from twelve to thirty was not good—too fast.

Ty went below and returned with two orange life jackets, handed one to her, and donned the other.

Angie looked at the life jacket with distaste. "It's going to be intolerably hot with this on."

"I don't care. Wear it." Ty took the wheel. "We're in deep shit."

Before she had the life jacket fastened, sweat trickled between her breasts. "It's like being in Phoenix in August—oven-hot air." She pointed to the east. "It's coming from there."

"Desert heat. Santa Ana." Ty slapped a thigh with his palm. "That's it!"

"What's it?"

"A wind inversion. Hot air from the desert blows up fast. We could be in for some real trouble. I'll take the sails down, then I'll start the engine. Here, take over." Ty said something else as he turned away, but Angie did not hear him in the tearing wind. He scrambled onto the cabin cover and started to down the crackling mainsail.

The wind gusted and pushed Angie onto the seat, and she struggled to see. Her arms felt like rags from fighting the wheel. "Can't hold on much longer."

Ty must not have heard her because he did not respond. Angie glanced at the wind speed—thirty-five knots. Jagged waves surged up and down, creating pale froth. Her stomach knotted. As the unfettered mainsail flapped on the cabin cover, the mast made loud cracking noises.

Clinging to it, Ty yelled at her. His face fierce, he pointed toward the east. He wanted her to do something, but what?

At the same moment, the jib line flew through the winch. The jib billowed out like a huge seagull taking off. Angie let go of the steering wheel and lunged for the line. The nylon rope ripped through her palms.

Momentum jerked her over the starboard side and out of the boat. Her body seemed to hover in the air, as if in slow motion. Ty's face contorted and he stretched both arms toward her. His lips shaped the word "Angie." She heard nothing except the wind moaning like a foghorn.

Angie hit the water on her side, and the force pulled her knees up. The wave was cold and hard as pavement. Her arms shot overhead. As she went down, the roaring water rushed into her ears. Water clogged her nostrils and stung her eyes. Her sunglasses flew off, then the headband. Water billowed her shorts and shirt. The life jacket felt like a clamp around her chest, its straps slashing her face. She felt assaulted. No breath. No air. Her screams made no sound. Water gushed into her mouth.

Determined not to die, Angie threw back her head, kicked her legs, and stretched up. Her head popped out of the water. Her heart hammered against the life jacket as she sucked in breath and frantically tried to tread water. The waves karate-chopped her. She gasped hot air.

A huge wave ran toward Angie, crested over her, and rolled her under again. Stinging water ripped along her face and body. She kicked up and prayed to break the top of the wave. Her head popped out. Hot wind struck her face. "Ty! Help!"

About twenty yards away, the *Destiny* rolled back and forth, its broken white wing flapping out to the side. Ty leaned over the stern and threw something into the water. A safety ring bobbed several feet away.

When Angie tried to swim toward it, she panted, and water filled her nose and mouth. Ty yelled, the wind howled, the waves slapped her. She could not sort the sounds.

Silhouetted against the burning sun, Ty stood in the boat facing her, his face dissolving in the shadows as he motored away.

"Don't leave me!" Angie screamed. The life ring drifted farther and farther from her. A wall of water rose up in front of her. Something smacked against her foot. Sharks? Oh God. She did not want to die.

Two

Of Promises and Prophecy

Angie bobbed upright in the churning water as the wind beat her face and blew matted hair in her eyes. She huddled her arms across the jacket and shivered. In the distance, the *Destiny* turned in a small circle, came about, and headed into the wind. The remaining mainsail luffed, and the boat swayed in front of Angie.

"Hold on, hold on, I'll get you," Ty yelled as he lashed the wheel and threw a red and white line to her. He strained out over the hull, calling her name over the din of wind and waves.

When the rope floated about six feet from her, Angie lunged for it, missed, and cried out in frustration. Pain rolled through her stomach, and she thought she would vomit.

"Take it easy, Angie." Ty reeled the line in and threw it back, but she missed again and frantically searched the waves for sharks. Taking aim, he threw the rope once more. It landed within her reach.

Holding her breath, Angie lunged for the lifeline, caught and squeezed it against her chest. As Ty pulled the rope toward the boat, she skimmed along the agitated waves toward him, exhaling a high-pitched laugh. Her breaths came sharp and fast. Nearing the boat, she realized Ty was saying something and focused on hearing him despite the howling wind. Looking scared, he hung over the stern, pointing down. Waves slapped his face and shoulders.

Fumbling for the steps, Angie submerged with the rocking boat. Finally, she felt Ty's arms under her shoulders. Her feet flailed as she tried to put her weight on the steps, but she fell back, and his hands left her shoulders. For an instant, she hung unsupported in the air. Then he captured her waist, lifting her up and into the boat. They fell together against the wheel.

"Thank God. Thank God." His ragged voice sounded magical.

Angie tried to thank him, but could only pant and shiver.

Ty carried her down into the galley and set her down on a berth. He grabbed a blanket from the hold and swaddled her, then ran to the head, calling, "Damn it, where's a towel?"

Although she remembered packing towels in the sea bag, Angie could not respond because her teeth chattered so.

Ty pulled up the end of the blanket and ruffled her hair, then rewrapped her snugly. "Got to get us outa here, babe." He flipped on the running lights and ran up the steps.

Drawing her swathed legs up to her chest, Angie squeezed her shoulders and rocked back and forth, trying to control the shivers. She could not see Ty's face through the cabin door, only his legs were visible between the spaces in the wheel. His arm reaching down to adjust the gears reassured her. The vibration of the engine and the warmth of the blanket lulled her. She came alert with a nervous twitch then dozed.

"Wake up, Angie, we're back in Harbor Island." Ty's gentle voice sounded far away.

The wind had fallen to a comfortable breeze as the sailboat glided between rows of parked launches to the yacht club dock. Occasional laughter and bits of conversation from people on surrounding boats broke the evening stillness. Angie felt safe but too exhausted to get up.

After Ty docked the boat, he came down to the cabin, found a dry sweat suit, and helped her dress. He supported her during the walk to his restored 1969 Mustang and tucked her inside the car. As he rolled down her window and closed her door, Ty said, "Let's run by the base hospital before we go home."

"No, that's not necessary." Shuddering, Angie remembered waiting in cold corridors, anxious to know her son Luke's diagnosis and condition. She hated the sterile superiority of hospitals.

"It can't hurt to get you checked over." Ty sounded confident she would capitulate to his reasoning. He thought she always should.

"I'm fine, really." Angie smiled in a way that she hoped he found disarming. "I don't need a doctor to tell me."

"How can you know that?" Leaning through the open car window, Ty looked surprised.

Angie shrugged. "I can sense when I'm sick. Right now I'm fine. More tired than I've ever been, but okay."

"You sure?"

The disbelief on his face annoyed Angie. He expected her to reaffirm her words, a doubting attitude no one exhibited in the other parts of her life, as mother and teacher.

"Just take me home," Angie said, her tone final. "I want to sleep for a week."

"Okay, but I don't like it."

Throwing their gear into the car trunk, Ty drove the few blocks to his bungalow on a quiet, shady street in Point Loma. He left their luggage in the car and carried Angie inside the dark house. When she protested that she could walk, he laughed and only set her down after he reached the bathtub. Ty pulled off their clothes and steadied her under the shower spray. The warm water relaxed their weary bodies. He dabbed the water from their skin with a towel. They lay down naked on the bed, kissed, and fell asleep, cuddling.

The next morning Angie awoke to sunlight pouring through the window from a bright blue California sky. Sleeping peacefully, tousled hair limp on his forehead, Ty lay uncovered. His tanned skin glowed against the dusty rose sheets. She stretched and yawned lazily, wondering why she felt achy before she recalled going overboard.

Slipping into an emerald green gown, Angie padded barefoot on cool tile to the tiny kitchen. She made coffee, cut lemon Danish into small squares, and carried the food on a pewter tray to the bedroom. Sitting on the bed, she sipped coffee, joyful at being alive to hear Ty's bathroom sounds.

Wrapped in a white terry robe, he returned, face freshly shaved and hair combed. "Morning."

"Thanks for saving my life."

"I was afraid I'd lost you." Ty looked vulnerable as he sat beside her. Taking her cup and setting it on the tray, he laid her back on the pillows then kissed her cheek and neck. "I never knew how much I loved you until yesterday."

Angie glanced at the LED light on the clock radio, nine a.m. "What time does your plane leave for Long Beach?"

"One thirty." Ty opened his robe and dropped it on the floor. "Plenty of time."

Sighing, Angie traced the line of his thigh gently with her fingertips. She trailed her hand slowly up the length of his arm and caressed his smooth cheek. Letting her fingers linger in his hair, she raised her head and mouth to his and whispered, "Kiss me again. Don't stop, ever."

"I won't." He opened the buttonless negligee and kissed her mouth, her thigh, her knee, her toes.

The sweet taste of his tongue lingered in her mouth. She breathed in Ty's scent, the combination of skin, soap, and aftershave faintly reminiscent of cherry blossoms in an Indiana springtime. Angie surrendered to the delight of his lips. She existed only in this moment—no past, no future— only now, for his touch.

He stretched out beside the length of her body and pulled her to him. Angie could feel his urgency pressing against her. They kissed, long and open. He caught his breath as she took him in her hand and caressed him lovingly.

"I want to be inside you," Ty whispered, rose up, and entered her. He thrust harder and faster then stopped momentarily.

Sensing that he was looking at her, Angie opened her eyes. For a brief moment, she imagined many different faces gazing at her, but somehow it was always Ty's that came into focus. Those intense eyes bore into her, claiming her as his own. Her voice broke. "I love you so. I can't imagine life without you."

"You won't have to, babe." Ty hugged her tightly, thrusting rhythmically and more rapidly. "Nothing will ever separate us."

"Not even death?" Nearly crying, Angie spoke the words.

Ty paused mid-thrust, desire making her breathless. They both trembled as he seemed to consider. "Not even death," he said with finality and sank into her.

Angie pressed against him, matching his rhythm. His low moan triggered an exquisite ripping through her. She arched up with the delicious feel of her release.

"Don't worry, darling." Ty lay back, his voice husky in the quiet sunlight. "I'll never leave you."

"I would find you again, even if you did. I'd make a doorway through the worlds if I had to."

With thoughts of their tender lovemaking earlier, Angie pulled the rose coverlet up to make the bed.

Precisely at noon, Ty paused in the doorway. "Ensign Porter's here. You ready?"

Nodding, Angie dropped a pillow against the headboard. "My bag's packed."

The starched white of his shirt and dress slacks shouted official Navy captain, but the way the uniform clung to Ty's backside as he bent to pick up her suitcase rekindled the morning's desire. Angie doubted she would ever get enough of his delicious body.

A thought nagged her. There was something she needed to tell him, but she could not remember what. Could that be a sign of aging already, at forty-five?

"You look great." Ty strode down the short hallway.

"Thanks," Angie called but disagreed. The pink silk blouse accentuated the vestiges of burn no amount of sun block seemed to prevent. Her heels clicked on the tiles as she followed Ty out the front door of the bungalow. Palm trees lined the curb on both sides of the secluded street.

A white four-door sedan lettered U. S. Navy stood parked in the driveway. Ensign Porter, tall, blond, and built like a football player, sprinted from the trunk to the driver's side. Efficient and loyal defined the ensign, Ty had remarked many times.

Climbing in the back seat, Angie sank into the stuffy, beige leather interior. Ty followed her and rolled down the window. The breeze felt good during the brief drive through downtown San Diego. She ignored the sights, explaining details of the next weekend in Phoenix.

Angie felt overwhelmed every time she thought of the plans they had made—the church, the caterer, the florist, hotel reservations, California, Indiana, and Florida flights on which family and friends should arrive. So much could go wrong, and she wanted everything to be perfect for their wedding. Thank heaven she had her son, Luke, to help, or she would not have gotten through the last three weeks of preparation.

"Did I tell you?" Angie asked. "Luke's going to pick up the tuxes for the ushers on Friday morning, but I have to turn in my grades and check out at school. I really need you to meet the caterer at noon. Otherwise, there might not be any food for the rehearsal dinner."

"Don't worry, Angie." Ty laughed and squeezed her shoulders. "I'll be there."

"That's not what I'm worried about. Once my mother arrives, she'll consume everyone's attention. You know how Barbara is. I hope your brother-in-law doesn't show up at the last minute. I made a reservation for your dad and sister together, but none for him."

Chuckling, Ty drew her into her arms. "I'm very proud of you. You've managed to coordinate far more than a wedding. This is a major troop movement. You should be the Navy captain, not me."

Although pleased, Angie blushed. "Organizing thirty high school sophomores for a fifty-five minute class is pretty good preparation."

The car sped onto the Coronado Bridge, arching in silver splendor across the bay. Angie loved the view. If not for passing cars, she could imagine herself suspended between sea and sky in a magical, exhilarating place.

Below, the tiny town of Coronado looked more like a Monopoly game than a real city—a mere circle of land, filled with houses, motels, streets, trees, tourists on bicycles, all surrounded by bay and ocean. Disney could not have created a quainter place. North Island Naval Air Station filled a whole section of the fanciful game board, with tiny boats at anchor and toy airplanes parked behind low, sand-colored buildings.

Today the planes looked different. One stood out, magnified a thousand times in her imagination. The memory of the phantom plane Angie had imagined at sea filled her mind. With it came an incredible sense of foreboding. "Oh, God."

"What's the matter?" Ty turned his gaze from the window. "Something else you want me to do on Friday? I'd better take notes."

"I intended to tell you yesterday." Angie glanced at Ensign Porter who appeared intent on driving but no doubt could hear every word said in the back seat. Hesitating at the idea that the young man might find her foolish, she decided the stakes were too high to remain quiet. "I saw a vision from the boat. An airplane accident."

"What do you mean? I didn't see anything."

"It was just before the winch broke. In the excitement I forgot." Angie's sense of impending danger grew. "I was sort of dozing, not really asleep. An airplane seemed to materialize out of nowhere, then it exploded."

"What kind of plane?"

"I don't know." Angie shuddered. "A small one. I think it was a warning."

"Are you afraid to get on your flight? Because, if you are—"

"Me? No. Maybe I should be, but I'm more afraid for you."

"Why me?" With a sudden movement, Ty straightened, looked out the window, and rolled it up.

"The plane had Navy markings. I think it's a warning for you." Goose flesh rushed down her neck and arms, evidence of the truth Angie spoke.

"Oh, I doubt that." Ty cracked the knuckles of first one hand then the other. "I fly all the time. You're just tired or excited about the wedding, maybe."

Angie covered his long fingers with her own sunreddened ones. "You could be right. I wish I knew for sure."

"You're probably nervous." Ty smiled and put his arm around her. "Hell, that's understandable. Maybe you'd feel better if you didn't fly to Phoenix today. Ensign Porter could drive you."

"I don't know." Angie closed her eyes, unable to picture the image again. "The explosion was clear. I'm not sure of the meaning. I wish I knew what we should do."

"Didn't you tell me once you saw the winning numbers on a lottery ticket?"

"The numbers I saw weren't winners. I lost five hundred dollars worth of tickets." Angie blushed at her own gullibility. "But it was different when Uncle Manny died back in Indiana. I knew it at that moment, like he came to tell me good-bye."

"My grandmother used to say she had premonitions." Ty's tone carried disbelief. "But they never came true. I think she was just lonely."

The sedan stopped at a traffic signal. Angie lowered her voice, hoping the engine's idle would cover her irritation. "I'm not some old farmwife trying to get your attention."

Ensign Porter gazed ahead. He appeared to pay his passengers no heed.

"You already have my attention." Ty kissed her behind the ear.

Angie pulled back. He had chosen the wrong time to tease. "We have to do something. Otherwise, why would I have the vision? Let's play it safe and stay on the ground. You could drive to Long Beach, and I'll ride with the ensign, okay?"

"I understand how it might scare you to see something like that, but I think it's just your imagination." Ty patted her knee.

"Don't say that. I wish I knew the reason for these experiences." She looked into his eyes, hoping to find an answer. "They've got to mean something."

"Damn it, Angie, this isn't logical, and you know it."

Angie failed to mask a sarcastic tone. "What's logic got to do with it?"

"Everything. I'm a captain in the Navy with a job to do. I have to do it if I intend to keep on being a captain. I'm flying to Long Beach today to inspect a squadron of jet fighters, like I do every month."

His certainty caused her to doubt herself. Had the vision warned of danger? Maybe it only dramatized her fear of losing him. She touched his cheek. "I love you so."

"Angie—"

"Hi, Corporal," Ensign Porter spoke through the front window to the sailor at the entrance to the base. When the guard saluted, the ensign glanced at Angie with a hint of veiled curiosity on his clean-cut face then focused on Ty. "Beg your pardon, Captain, we'd better go straight to the plane now if we're gonna keep your schedule."

They sat in silence while the ensign drove the short distance to the airstrip. Angie searched Ty's face for some sign that he took her seriously. He glanced at her, and they exchanged awkward smiles, then he squeezed her shoulder. Surely, he did not think she hallucinated the plane crash. He had not hinted she was demented, only too anxious, but thoughts of her instability might cross his mind. She said a silent prayer that Ty would heed her warning.

When the car stopped, the ensign leaped out and opened Ty's door.

Ty took Angie in his arms and held her. "I'll say good-by here." He kissed her mouth then both her eyes. "I'm glad you worry about me. That lets me know you love me."

Inhaling his fresh fragrance, Angie murmured, "Never doubt it."

"Have Ensign Porter drive you home." Ty stepped out of the car and turned back to her. "I'll call you tonight."

Angie refused to watch him leave. Leaning back in the seat, she closed her eyes and calmed herself, trying to reconstruct the vision.

The plane reappeared in her mind's eye, a white shape hovering in a blue expanse. As she focused on the image, numbers came into her awareness—forty-

seven... three... twenty-seven... three... or maybe eight.

The sound of the car ignition brought her to wakefulness. Ensign Porter drove the sedan in an arc, turning around the way they'd arrived. The pilot, in a black leather flight jacket and goggles, passed near the car and waved to her. Beyond him a white, single-engine aircraft sat on the tarmac. Cessna—USN No. 47-3278 was painted on the body in Navy blue.

"Oh, God, that's it. Stop the car!" Angie dashed out of the sedan and ran after Ty. "Don't go... don't get on that plane... you'll die if you do."

He turned back toward her. "Angie, please stop." His ragged voice caught.

"Take a different plane," she cried, clutching his arms. "What would it hurt? It might save you."

"This is pointless." Ty looked toward the Cessna as his pilot climbed over the wing.

Angie dug her fingertips into the backs of Ty's arms. "You can't go. I won't lose you. Not again. I won't."

"I've told you over and over. I'm not in any danger." Words that might have comforted sounded angry over the engine's roar. "You aren't going to lose me!"

"If you fly out of here, you'll have to kill me to do it."

Her hair blew as Angie ran around the Cessna and fell in front of the wheel. The pilot, already in his seat, watched her. Breathless, she wedged her hips under the airplane wheels and lay on the tarmac, hot from the sun, willing her outrageous act to force Ty to give in. The air reeked of rubber and gasoline.

Face set with anger, Ty strode toward her. "Goddammit, Angie, you're going to get hurt." He knelt beside her and pulled her up into his arms. "You can't do this to yourself. Or to me." He cradled her, rocking gently.

"I saw this very plane." Angie searched his face for acquiescence. "The numbers were the same. How could I know?" Struggling to convince him, she started again. "I saw it. White with Navy blue letters! It exploded in midair. Believe me."

"I do." A look of infinite sadness spread over his cherished features.

"Then you won't go?" Gulping, Angie touched her hand to her breast. "Oh, thank God."

"Darling, I believe you saw the vision." Ty patted her tangled hair. "But I've got to do my job."

"No, Ty." After all this, did he still not believe her?

"If we're going to be married, you've got to accept what I do. Flying is part of the job."

"I do accept it. But this is a warning." Angie shouted, hoping volume might persuade him when logic did not. "The plane is defective."

"Calm down, Angie. It's been checked out. That's routine procedure."

Ensign Porter ducked under the wing. Angie read confusion and perhaps pity on his face but did not care. She would risk any shame, any disgrace to keep Ty off that plane. "I won't let you go."

"I'll be careful." His love for her visible in his expression, Ty held her face between his hands. "There's nothing else I can do."

"You can't go." Her voice rose in terror. "You'll die."

"Ensign..." Ty called to the young man who stepped behind her then told Angie, "I'll see you Friday in Phoenix. On Saturday we'll be married, and this will be behind us. I promise." His voice sounded controlled with a trace of a plea. He kissed her quickly. "I love you."

"Please believe me." Angie despaired.

"I hate to leave you this way, but I have no choice." Ty grimaced as if trying to keep back tears. He pulled her up from the tarmac with him and transferred her into the arms of Ensign Porter. "Hold her. Don't let her follow me, whatever it takes."

"Aye, aye, sir."

Ty turned and sprinted around the wing.

Angie struggled against the young sailor. "Let go of me."

"Please calm down, ma'am." Ensign Porter's hold tightened even though he looked very uneasy.

Ducking inside the plane, Ty reached out, waved, and closed the cockpit door. The roaring engine drowned out her cries. Angie writhed in the ensign's arms. Her back against his chest, she felt his arms like a vice around her waist as he pulled her up so high her feet left the ground. She screamed for him to let her go and grabbed his wrists, trying to pry them apart. She kicked his shins and felt her high heel dig into the flesh of his leg. He wailed, relaxed his grip, and she broke free.

Angie ran behind the plane as it taxied down the runway. "Stop, Ty, come back!" Screams rasped from her throat and drowned in the roar of the plane's liftoff. She longed insanely to reach up, grab the plane out of the air, and set it safely back on the earth. Scrambling past parked planes, she stumbled when a heel broke off one pump. She kicked off the other and chased the plane, ignoring the rough pavement, hot on bare feet.

No longer thinking at all, Angie reached the end of the runway and fell. Her arms supported her as she looked up, gasping and crying.

The plane climbed higher and farther away. It banked and circled back over the airstrip. The ensign and two other crewmen ran down the field toward her.

At a popping sound like a cheap aluminum toy breaking, they stopped and looked up, shielding their eyes.

For Angie, time stopped. Like back on the boat, a static image in the sky claimed her attention. A sense of unreality froze her.

The ice-white plane hovered momentarily in the still blue air.

Shafts of orange and gold flame shot out. The screams of the two helpless men inside rose above the engine's roar.

The blazing Cessna dropped to the tarmac with a deafening boom, bounced once, then lay crackling in a pool of hot tar and flaming gasoline.

Angie scrambled toward the plane. They had to get Ty out right away.

"Captain Beckman... oh, my God," Ensign Porter yelled and ran behind her. He grabbed her shoulders, throwing her off balance.

Together they fell, and Angie felt a sharp pain along her leg. Not caring, she tried to break free, but the ensign held her tight,

He shook her and shouted into her face. "You knew. How did you know?"

"Let me go. We've got to save him."

"You can't go over there."

Sirens wailed all around them.

Tipped on a twisted wing, the downed plane burned in the summer sunshine, wheels crunched into its under-belly, flaming scraps of metal strewn about the pavement.

Sailors ran from all directions, filling the field. Two olive-drab crash rigs clamored up. Medics ran out, shouting instructions.

Crewmen in silver reflector suits dragged thick hoses and spewed liquid foam on the burning wreckage. They sprayed small fires breaking out all around the aircraft. Two crewmen crawled onto the damp wing, slipping on the foam as they struggled with the cockpit door.

Slumped on the pavement fifty yards away, Angie clamped her hands over the lips he had kissed only moments earlier. The scent of cherry blossoms still clung to her clothes from his arms around her as she watched flames consume the cockpit where he sat. Those crewmen had to get him out of there. He would die. He could not breathe in the fire.

The door gave way, and the two crewmen lifted someone out of the cockpit. The victim's dark head flopped awkwardly, his suit scorched and blackened. Gently, the crewmen laid their burden on a stretcher. Medics bent over him. One fastened straps across his body, the other covered his face with a white cloth.

Sweat beaded on Angie's forehead, and bile rushed up her throat. They were to be married on Saturday. Nothing could change that. She had loved him all her life. Now that she had found him again, she would never give him up. That would be too cruel to even consider. Only this morning, they'd promised never to abandon each other.

Scrambling up, Angie ran to the stretcher, dropped beside it, and tugged the cloth away. The empty stare of death gazed back at her from Ty's burned and blistered face.

As if from a great distance came a long, moaning keen then another. Angie wondered who cried so piteously, but her head would not turn so she could see. Surprised, she realized her own hands held the sides of her head. Her jaws opened and closed in a spasm of grief. Rocking back and forth, she wailed Ty's name over and over. The sound reverberated through her being.

Hands grabbed both her arms and propelled her through space. Angie did not know what was happening to her body and did not care. She let go of consciousness and floated gratefully into a dream.

Three

I'll Find You Someday

At five the next morning, Luke Brock strode impatiently out of the elevator doors into a gleaming white corridor of the Naval hospital. A rumpled purple Phoenix Suns shirt covered his stocky, muscular body. He itched to do something. Sitting in the car all night on the drive to San Diego had made him tired, tense, and irritable.

He hurried to the nurses' station where a middle-aged nurse sat with her back turned, her rear end hanging off both sides of a rolling chair. Luke drummed thick fingers on the counter. "Excuse me, what's Angie Brock's room number?"

With a bored expression, the nurse turned the metal registry file and glanced at it. "Sorry that information is restricted."

Luke wondered why but did not want to take time to ask. "How is she?"

"I can't give you that information." The nurse expelled a long breath, almost flattening chubby cheeks.

"I'm her son, just arrived from Phoenix." Standing on tiptoe, Luke clenched the counter edge so tightly his knuckles turned white. He wanted his scowl to intimidate without his actually making a threat. "Tell me where she is."

"I'll have to call Doctor to get authorization." Her voice carried an officious tone. Fast for one so large, she whirled in the chair and dialed the phone.

Stretching over the counter, Luke flipped the pages on the card file. "Room four-oh-seven."

"Stop." The nurse covered the receiver with her hand and gave him a dirty look.

Luke sprinted down the corridor, reading the numbered arrows painted on the wall.

The officious nurse shouted, "You can't go in there."

Luke opened the door of 407. His mother lay on the bed, crisp sheet pulled up to her chin. Tendrils of black hair crept out of a plastic cap. With her hands folded across her stomach, she looked as fragile as a porcelain doll. An IV monitor beeped, dripping fluid down a plastic tube.

His tough act dissolved and Luke leaned over, speaking softly, "Mom?" When the nurse entered, he whispered, "She gonna be okay?"

"Doctor said it's all right for you to be here, but visitors are restricted because of the... uh... situation." The nurse checked the IV, pulled up one of Angie's eyelids, then turned back to Luke, speaking much more politely than she had earlier. "She's in shock. We just have to wait and see. Don't stay long." The nurse closed the door behind her.

Pulling a chair up beside the bed, Luke sat beside Angie and rubbed his eyes with the backs of his fists to ease the ache.

What a hell of a deal! He could hardly believe his ears when Admiral Mahoney called and said Ty had been killed. Luke grieved that he had lost his only chance for a father, just when the two of them had gotten really close. Now his mother might die, too. Luke wished he could protect her.

Angie grimaced and caught her breath.

Bending over her, he touched her hand. "Mom, it's me, Luke. I'm here with you."

She sobbed and mumbled something.

"What'd you say?" Luke kissed her cheek

When she failed to respond, he put his cheek to her mouth, relieved to feel her breath, then sagged back onto the chair. Only a few days ago, he'd had an epileptic seizure and she had come to his rescue. At the time, he had felt guilty because he didn't know how to return the favor. Now, it looked like the tables had really turned.

Enough of this wallowing in self-pity. There were other ways to help her. Funeral plans to make, wedding plans to cancel. When Angie awoke, he would have it all handled, and she would not have to worry about a thing. Ty's family might not know yet. Luke would call them, as well as friends in Phoenix and Grandma in Florida. This would take some delicate explanation, with everybody expecting to attend a wedding next weekend but having to come to a funeral instead. Angie's address book was the place to start.

Opening closet and cabinets, Luke looked for her belongings but could find nothing, not even her clothes. He hit the nurse's button.

The bored voice finally came across the speaker. "Nurse Boles here. Whatcha need?"

Luke fingered the plastic tubing that ran down from the glucose bag. "Do you know where my mother's purse is?"

"Didn't have it when she was admitted." The nurse hesitated in her annoying way of seeming to enjoy withholding information. "Confiscated, maybe."

"Confiscated? What the hell are you talking about?"

She took a long breath. "I'll get Doctor for you."

The nurse's responses were off. Luke fought an urge to scoop Angie up and run out of the hospital.

Sluggishly, she moved her lips.

"What is it?" Luke bent his ear to her mouth.

"...should've convinced him... my fault..." Angie sobbed. "Why... didn't he listen?"

"You're not to blame." Luke put his arms around her and cradled her to his chest. Her head sagged, and he supported her like a baby. "It's okay. Everything's gonna be all right." How could she blame herself? A lot needed explaining around here.

Angie seemed to relax, and he laid her back on the pillow then searched in his pocket and found a wadded scrap of paper. Whatever was going on, Admiral Mahoney would surely know. Luke dialed the phone and waited impatiently through several rings until the admiral answered and Luke identified himself.

"Hello, glad you got here." The admiral sounded older than he had yesterday. "How's your mother?"

"Not doing very well." Luke thought she got paler by the minute.

"I'm sorry to hear that." The man on the other end of the line coughed.

"Admiral, I need your help." Luke wished his voice sounded more professional, less like a panicky son.

"Just name it."

"Mom's purse is missing." Luke opened the drawer beneath the bedside table, but it only contained a bedpan wrapped in plastic. "I need her address book. There are a lot of people I have to contact. The nurse here seems to think the Navy has her belongings."

"Well, uh, Luke..." The admiral sounded too hesitant. He probably knew exactly where they were.

"Her purse has got to be somewhere. Ty's car, maybe. Or on the airfield?"

"I'm sorry. Wish I could help but I've got to keep a low profile till the investigation's over. You know, being Ty's friend and all." The admiral laughed a little phony laugh. "Puts me in a delicate position. You understand, I'm sure."

"No, I don't. Tell me what's going on."

"Mrs. Mahoney says she wishes Angie a speedy recovery." The phone clicked.

Admiral Mahoney knew a great deal he was not telling.

A well-scrubbed Navy medic came into the room, nodded to Luke, and took the chart out of the slot at the end of the bed. After reading briefly, the middle-aged doctor turned to

Luke. "I take it you're Mrs. Brock's son? Would you come outside with me? So we don't disturb her."

They stepped into the hallway, empty except for a thin, balding man in rimless eyeglasses and Navy whites. He slouched against the wall.

Luke tousled his hair with nervous fingers. "She'll recover, won't she?"

"I hope so." The doctor looked grim. "Shock's difficult to predict. We have to wait till she decides whether she wants to wake up or not."

Luke's stomach knotted. Needing action, he paced down the hall and back toward the doctor.

"Here's Captain Jamison," the doctor indicated the other man, who came to attention and strode quickly toward Luke. "He's been waiting to talk to you." The doctor nodded to Jamison then walked down the hall into a patient's room.

"Lucus Brock, I presume." Jamison extended his hand. "Like to ask you some questions, if you don't mind."

The listless handshake perturbed Luke. He needed some answers of his own. "Regarding what?"

"Just routine." Jamison took a spiral notebook from his shirt pocket and opened it.

"Whatever that means." Nothing about this place seemed routine to Luke. "I'd like to get my mother's belongings back."

Jamison glanced at the notebook. "Your mother Angela Brock?"

"Yes." Luke scowled. If she were in real trouble, somebody had better start explaining. "What's the purpose of your investigation?"

"Born Medfield, Indiana," Jamison slid the glasses down his thin nose and read, "nineteen forty-two?"

"Yes." Luke barely controlled his temper. This jerk was deliberately stalling.

Jamison spoke softly in an affected way as if his authority could not be challenged. Luke had to lean forward to hear. "Scheduled to marry Captain Tyler Caldwell Beckman, USN?"

"That's common knowledge." Legally, Luke had to answer the questions but disliked Jamison's manner more each moment. "Where are you going with this? I'm her lawyer."

"She knew in advance that he was going to die?" The Navy man pushed the glasses back up and gave Luke a quizzical look.

"Did she? Sometimes Mom does know things in advance."

"How?" Jamison spoke almost in a whisper.

"I don't know. Psychically." Luke saw no comprehension on the irritating captain's face. "Paranormally?"

"Mrs. Brock had prior knowledge of a defect in the aircraft." Jamison cleared his throat and pushed the glasses down again to read. "It has come to my attention that Captain Beckman recently named her as beneficiary on a sizable insurance policy."

"If my mother is under suspicion, tell me. I'm her legal counsel." Luke wondered whether there were any precedents in law for investigating psychic knowledge.

"Her father died under suspicious circumstances." Jamison wet his thumb and turned pages. "Wiley NMI Brandon died in the line of duty, Carswell Air Force Base, direct result of refueling tests to establish procedures for inter-continental flight. December twentieth, nineteen forty-eight."

"What does that have to do with anything?" Luke stopped trying to disguise his anger.

Jamison looked self-satisfied and held out his hand for another perfunctory handshake. "I'll be in touch."

Though they were the same height, Luke outweighed the asshole by forty pounds. There would be no problem taking him down. Luke ignored the proffered hand and took an aggressive step toward Jamison. *Did everyone around here respond only to threatening behavior?* "Tell me what's going on."

"Thank you for your cooperation." Jamison spoke on the run, his head bobbing as he hurried down the hall and turned the corner.

"We want her things back. You've no right to keep them."

Jamison pushed the elevator button and called without looking back, "They'll be sent." When the doors opened, he stepped inside, turned with military briskness, and focused on a spot over Luke's head while the elevator doors closed.

Striding back into his mother's room, Luke fumed. That little twit Jamison thought his mother had sabotaged the plane. *He must be nuts.*

There seemed to be no change in Angie's condition. At least she had not had to endure Jamison, but Luke wished she'd awaken. He rubbed her too cool hands.

While Luke paced back and forth at the end of the bed, he realized he had to go into action. This waiting was too punishing. So much needed doing, and he doubted his restlessness helped Angie any at all. The problem of the phone numbers plagued him until he remembered her friend, Jillian, had a key to their house. She could get the numbers for him. He kissed Angie's pale cheek and said, "Be right back."

On the way to the elevator, he leaned over the counter and gave the fat nurse his most charming smile. "I've got to find a hotel and call my family. Would you check on my mother every few minutes?"

The nurse curled her lip. "What do you think? I don't do my job?"

"Not at all. You look very efficient, and I trust you to take good care of her."

The nurse flushed. "Well, thanks."

Unwilling to come into waking consciousness, Angie recognized a recurring dream and entered it.

Daddy stood beside a bi-plane, smiling and waving. He wore a round hat with a strap. She tried to run toward him, but tall wheat surrounded her, closing her in. Falling on her back, she watched Daddy jump in the plane, which streaked high into the sky.

Longing to go with him, Angie scrambled up and ran, leaping to clear the wheat. The force of her lunge propelled her into the air, as if she had no weight, and she flew with her arms outstretched. Daddy's plane dipped beneath her, and she leaped onto the wing. Her brother Bobby sat inside, a little boy again.

Daddy swooped and dived, making the airplane do tricks, and they all laughed and felt happy together again. Daddy had come for her. She felt safe, at last.

Angie opened her eyes to unfamiliar white walls. Vertical blinds clanked shut then someone walked toward the bed. Angie did not recognize anything and did not care. Hurting all over, she gazed at a woman's face hovering above her. The woman said something unintelligible.

"Leave me alone." Angie turned her head.

"Well, I think we're coming out of it." The nurse had an annoying voice. She picked up the IV then dropped it. The sliver of plastic tubing swung to and fro. "Did you know you've been here over twenty-four hours? Uh-huh. It's Monday afternoon."

Angie barely heard the words or felt the touch. Images flashed through her mind—the plane bursting into flames and falling, foam spewing everywhere, Ty's head flopping to the side while the crewmen carried him.

31

Why had he not listened? What could she have said to change his mind? If she had been able to persuade him, he would be alive now. Her darling. She could not bear to imagine the agony he endured. Angie did not want to live without Ty.

The intrusive nurse raised the head of the bed then listened to Angie's heart. "You're doing fine. I'm going off my shift now. You have a good day. Drink lots of fluids and try to rest." She set a paper cup on the bedside table. "I know you're upset, but the Valium should take hold soon."

When the door clicked behind the nurse, Angie rolled over on her stomach and let out a long wail, clinching the pillow in her arms. She felt abandoned by everyone. Daddy died when she was six. Her mother, Barbara, had left her and Bobby in the orphanage for two years. Angie's husband deserted her, leaving her to raise their sick child alone. Bobby had died not long ago. Now this?

Angie could never accept such injustice. Ty would not abandon her. He loved her too much. If she could not trust in his love, she could not trust in anything.

The memory of flying with Daddy in the dream returned. *Was it really a dream or something more?* Had Daddy come for her? She wanted to go with him and die, too.

Angie squeezed the pillow and cried. Her shoulders shook as the sobs raced through her. Throwing the pillow on the floor, she rolled onto her back, covering her eyes. The IV pricked her arm as she flipped the tubing out of the way. Tears ran down her cheeks and into her ears. Although she gasped for each breath, still the tears fell. Her hand quivered as she tried to draw it across her brow.

Finally, lying still as the afternoon faded into twilight, Angie felt empty, unfocused, and without volition. She gazed at the unbroken whiteness of the room.

At a point where the two smooth walls connected to the shiny white of the ceiling, she noticed a faint unevenness of color. Still transparent, something opaque, almost blue, formed there.

After a moment, Angie could no longer see the corner because an image floated in front of it. Peering intently, she saw two eyes emerge. They looked like Ty's. Faintly against the paleness of the wall, the rest of his face appeared—high cheekbones, cleft chin, dark curl on his forehead. His features took on depth, color, and energy. His face resembled a three-dimensional movie projection, a hologram, but alive and aware of her.

A wash of love flowed through Angie. Her breast expanded to receive the adoring warmth pouring in. Her arms and legs tingled, and her head buoyed up with the intensity. She felt reassured, bountiful, sated from the filling. Ty's image floated above her. He was really there, not a projection of her desire.

His soft voice filled her heart. "I will love you forever. Even death can't keep us apart."

Joyously, Angie willed her adoration to flow back. The air glowed pink as she cried out, "I'll find you, my darling. Someday, somehow! I promise."

He seemed content, and his eyes crinkled into a smile. His image dissolved in the fading light of evening.

Ty had heard her and wanted to be with her. That's why he had come—to let her know he was alive, to reassure her their relationship would go on. Nothing could stop it.

Some people said they communicated with the dead. Why not her? Grandma used to tell of seeing the little people who carried messages from the other world. Whenever somebody was about to die, she saw a banshee, a woman dressed in black, walking back and forth on the sidewalk in front of the house. Others might think them family myths, but Grandma always told the stories for the truth.

In memory, Angie saw her grandmother—ninety pounds, four feet, ten inches tall, white-haired, spectacles too big for her happy face. Angie could almost hear the pert voice, saying, "Don't fret yourself, sweetie, the departed know the netherworld far better than we. They know how to traverse it to come to you. They'll let you know what they want you to know when they want you to know it."

Angie knew she would find Ty because he would help her. What was more, Grandma had said it could happen. Now, Angie had a reason to live. She felt peaceful about making the promise even though she did not know how to keep it.

Four

Suspicion Exploding

The following Saturday

A white Navy limousine stopped in the circular drive of Pointer's Funeral Home, the red brick facade embellished with pillared portico. An ensign held open the back door.

In a khaki raincoat, Angie took the sailor's hand and stepped out on the curb. Adjusting a bouquet of bitter-smelling sunflowers, stems wrapped in green tissue paper, she climbed the steps and pushed down on the gold-plated handle of the mortuary door.

Why was the door locked with only an hour before the public was to arrive? Luke had scheduled the motorcade to leave for the cemetery directly after the visitation. Just the same way, he had organized the shivaree for her wedding that would never take place.

A spasm of grief threatened to overwhelm Angie's composure. She pressed the doorbell button. Surely someone would answer. Ty lay inside, and she needed time to say good-bye to his physical body.

Angie felt in sympathy with the overcast sky. "June gloom," Ty had always called these days with a sky so full it seemed about to cry.

A short young man with heavy blond eyebrows, opened the door. He carried his gray suit coat hooked in his elbow and hastily began putting it on. "Yes?"

"May I come in? I'm Angie Brock."

"Hello, Mrs. Brock. Your son said you'd be arriving, but we weren't expecting you for another hour." The funeral director held the door as she passed through then closed and locked it. "We aren't quite ready."

"I'd like some time alone with Captain Beckman."

Glancing at his watch, the funeral director mumbled, "Let me see. The florist's finished. Admiral Mahoney ordered the guard posted at one-thirty. You could have... thirty minutes?"

"That'll be fine."

Nodding, the self-important man dashed soundlessly along the vestibule and through a door at the end.

Laying the flowers on a table, Angie took off her raincoat and left it on a chair. She smoothed the skirt of the royal blue dress Ty had bought her last Christmas. He had loved for her to wear his favorite color, and she wanted to please him, especially today—their wedding day.

Bouquet in hand, Angie walked across the marble floor, heels clicking. She clutched the handle of the viewing room door, filled with dread. Would her courage fail her? Only his body lay in there. His spirit lived somewhere, waiting for her to find him. Several deep breaths gave her the strength to turn the knob.

Inside, sweeping peach and gray drapery folded along the walls. Beethoven played softly through the sound system. Ty's cherry wood coffin stood on a catafalque on the opposite side of the room, flanked by U. S. and Navy flags. Baskets of flowers tiered along both sides.

The acrid sweet scent of many varieties of flowers assailed her—the funeral stink she hated. Struggling against her impulse to run away, Angie trudged across the gray plush carpet. The heaviness in her neck and shoulders shuddered through her whole body. Today, she should have been wearing her wedding gown, gliding down the church aisle toward her handsome groom with his welcoming smile.

Here, only his photograph smiled from atop the coffin. A sense of unreality seized her. This could not be true. It all happened so fast.

She placed the flowers gently across his feet and stared into her shadowy reflection on the cherry wood. Ty's scorched and blistered face lay beneath, damaged beyond the mortician's ability to repair. Angie caressed the gleaming wood then kissed the place she guessed his mouth would be, trembling when she pressed her cheek against the cold, hard surface.

"My love... my... Oh, Ty... I can't let you go." A sob clutched her throat. This hurt too much. The coffin contained only his body, but she loved it so. Longing to feel his caress in return, she rubbed her hand along the coffin, remembering his pleasure in her touch. "My darling, I can't bear to say good-bye."

Surprisingly, the sound of her own voice comforted her. She brushed her hair back and scanned the draped wall. He was out there somewhere, and she would find him. The physical relationship could not be the same as before because his body had been destroyed by the fire, but it could be good between them again. Sniffing, she whispered, "Help me... find you."

Tears fell down her cheeks as Angie picked up the picture and touched his glorious face, eyes bright beneath a blue and gold braid hat. He had scrawled, *Love you always, Ty,* across the bottom and sent the picture on her birthday. She had packed it last week on what she had thought an illogical impulse, never imagining she would put it to such an awful use. She stared at his image, sobbing.

Why had he not listened to her? It was like he had to die. What good did it do for her to see the vision? Even while they sailed, she sensed something bad would happen and felt powerless to intercede.

Wiping her cheeks and nose, Angie gazed into the photograph and remembered Ty's wind-weathered face as he had scanned the ocean just a few days ago. "There's so much I don't understand... but I will. There's got to be a reason why I'm alive... why you could save me... but I couldn't save you."

Angie clutched the photograph, knelt, and prayed to believe. Her mind skidded off that empty place where faith languished. She had to trust that something would help her recognize his spirit. Otherwise, she would end up in a sanitarium.

"Mom? Are you okay?" Luke stood in the doorway. "Everybody's waiting outside to pay their respects. Can we come in?"

Angie tenderly set Ty's photograph on the casket. This public day would be difficult to endure. She determined to focus her mind and control her emotions. She had to maintain the decorum expected of a Navy wife. Never would she behave like her mother, who collapsed mentally after Daddy's death, so incapable of coping that she had put her children in an orphanage. Years later, when Bobby died, Angie had handled everything because Barbara went to pieces again and had to remain sedated, unable to attend her son's funeral.

Today Angie would stay strong for Ty's family and the guests who had so kindly come to pay homage. Luke had made most of the arrangements, and she would get through this day and make him proud. Quelling tears, she concentrated on keeping her chin from trembling, composed her face, and turned away from the coffin. "I'm finished now."

Luke, handsome in suit and tie, put his arm around her. "You okay?" Love shone from his glistening brown and green-flecked eyes.

Nodding, Angie pressed against his sturdy body, gaining strength from his familiar presence. "I can do this."

The funeral director propped the double doors open and quietly spoke to two sailors, who marched across the room and stationed themselves at both ends of the coffin. Looking forlorn, Ty's father and sister entered the room.

Samuel Beckman resembled an exhausted, old Ty. Angie remembered as a child feeling afraid of Samuel. Although he stooped now, then Ty's father stood so tall and straight that he towered above her. When the Beckmans arrived at the hotel yesterday, Samuel had held her for a long time, unable to speak. He had not asked about the funeral arrangements and even now seemed overwhelmed.

Tearlee, Ty's sister, was so much younger Angie only remembered her as a little girl. It seemed strange to think of her as a wife and mother. Tall, like her father and brother, she wore a pink suit. Framed by short brown hair, her pretty face looked drawn and tired. Her husband and children had not flown out with her, though she did not seem to mind, more concerned with her father's grief than with her own.

Holding Samuel's arm, Tearlee bore much of his weight as they prayed before the coffin. Samuel's shoulders sagged. The funeral director waited respectfully behind them till they finished then deftly indicated a place a few feet to the left of the coffin. Samuel and Tearlee followed his direction.

Admiral Mahoney, a short, balding man, came through the double doors in an impeccable full dress uniform. He surveyed the room with a critical glance. He strode toward Angie with arms outspread and swept her into them. "My dear, Angie. I'm so sorry. I hope all the arrangements are satisfactory. Trust that I wanted to make them myself, but I was unable... uh... I couldn't."

The compassion in his wrinkled face told Angie he grieved for his friend of many years. Relieved to finally see the admiral, she took his hand in both of hers. "I'm glad you're standing beside me in the receiving line today. Ty would want you here."

"It's the least I can do." Admiral Mahoney cleared his throat. "I'll miss him."

Angie squeezed his hand. "I know."

"I wanted to be with you and comfort you." The admiral seemed distracted and glanced away. "So did Mrs. Mahoney. But with the investigation going forward, we felt this was best. I'm sure you understand."

What was he talking about? Luke had insisted on following the doctor's advice for Angie to remain in the hotel until today. Her son had even answered all the phone calls. She sensed he had tried to protect her. *But from what?* She wanted to ask Mahoney to explain, but he turned to speak to a sailor in the line.

Whispering softly, military and civilian visitors poured into the room. The funeral director efficiently guided them into a line to file past Tearlee, then Samuel, the admiral, then Angie, who stood to the left of the coffin.

At first, Angie felt surprised by the number of visitors but realized Ty had become as popular in the Navy as when they were kids in school.

"Be right back." Luke cleared his throat and scowled at Mahoney before stepping into a curtained side room.

An old Chinese man and woman stopped in front of Angie. They nodded, bowed their heads, and said condolences. She remembered when Ty picked up his shirts at their laundry.

The admiral greeted a young naval officer and his pretty red-haired wife, who murmured kind words. Angie had never seen them before now.

The young woman stepped past the admiral and said to Angie, "I'm so sorry, Mrs. Beckman."

If only that were her name, Angie thought, realizing with a pang that now it never would be.

"I didn't know the captain," the Navy wife continued in a sympathetic voice, "but my husband has told me what a wonderful man he was. This is such a loss to everyone."

"Yes, it is. Thank you for coming." Angie smiled and shook the husband's hand. "Thank you, too."

As the two moved past Angie and stopped before the coffin, the wife whispered, "Where's the man we saw on television?" Her husband looked around and shrugged. "She doesn't look like one! Suppose she really knew?"

"Shhhhh," the officer said with a quick glance at Angie. He steered his wife away.

As the couple headed toward the vestibule, whispering together, Angie felt certain she was the subject of their conversation. They could not know about her vision, could they? The television in the hotel room had not been on for the past few days because Luke had said Angie should rest. What news had she missed?

A middle-aged woman moved through the line. Tall and attractive, with shiny brown hair and an elegant suit, she patted Ty's father's arm as he bowed his head. Murmuring to him, she moved to the admiral, who spoke to her softly. The woman started crying, and Admiral Mahoney hugged her. After shaking hands with Angie, the woman moved on quickly without making eye contact and leaned against the coffin, sobbing and dabbing her face with a handkerchief.

Fearing the woman might lose her balance, Angie put a supportive arm around her.

"I can't bear to think of him dead."

Angie stroked the woman's hair. "I loved him, too."

"Thank you." After touching a kiss to Ty's picture, the woman turned away.

Tearlee moved in beside Angie and tapped her on the shoulder. "You know who that was?"

"No," Angie said, feeling great compassion, "but I can fairly well guess."

"Jean... his first wife!" Astonishment filled Tearlee's voice.

"Yes, that's what I thought." Angie felt a peace and connection with the woman.

"God, Angie, aren't you jealous?"

Angie shook her head. "Ty always spoke kindly of her." He never resented Angie's ex-husband either. Had she and Ty always known their true passion resided in each other? Her eyes misted. "We were so good together."

Squeezing Angie's arm, Tearlee said, "Why don't you let me take over for a while?"

"No, I'm okay." Angie blinked back tears, straightened her shoulders, and took a deep breath. The thought of sitting in the curtained family corner and drinking coffee depressed her. She could not control the tears there. Standing in the receiving line with people to greet gave her strength. Angie smiled at Tearlee. "Why don't you fill in for your dad? He looks like he could use a break."

With a glance at Samuel, Tearlee changed instantly from busybody sister to compassionate daughter. She went to him and hugged him. Samuel slumped away, and Tearlee greeted another sailor in front of her.

Luke returned and took his place in the receiving line between Angie and the admiral. After giving her a hug, her son turned to the next mourners, greeting them warmly, seemingly comfortable in his role. He had arranged for Ty's family, brought her from the hospital to the hotel, canceled the wedding plans, and handled the funeral arrangements. He had even phoned his grandmother and asked her to fly out. She had refused, of course.

Angie appreciated Luke's allowing her to depend on him. She sensed he would never again doubt himself or take a risk with his life, as he had when he stopped taking his epilepsy medication and provoked a seizure. It seemed impossible that only a week had passed since that had happened.

"We need to talk as soon as this line slows down," Luke whispered.

"What's going on?"

"Mostly stupid stuff. Don't worry." Luke turned to the next person in line, and his warm smile dissolved. "Oh, it's you."

Ensign Porter acknowledged Luke with a furtive nod then clasped Angie's hand tightly with both his large, sweaty hands. "I can't tell you how sorry I am, Ms. Brock."

The sound of the ensign's voice propelled Angie's thoughts back to the airfield. The last thing she could remember was his screaming at her. The reality of Ty's death came thundering down on her, and she staggered back.

"Are you okay?" Ensign Porter sounded so solicitous that Angie recovered herself.

What must he be going through after seeing his commanding officer die? Angie said, "Yes... yes. Thank you, Ensign."

"Call me 'Mike.'" Big, timid eyes stared down at her as he squeezed her hand.

Ty's diamond dug into her skin, and Angie pulled free of the ensign. "Mike... I wanted to tell you... thank you... for helping me when... the other day..."

"No problem." Mike blushed. "Uh... look. About the television interview. Things just kind of got out of hand. I couldn't believe what I'd said when I saw myself on TV. The reporters confused me with their questions."

"What are you talking about?" Angie asked. Mike's manner, combined with the admiral's vagueness, meant something was wrong.

"I guess I was in shock, too. I just wanted you to know. I'm sorry." Scarlet-faced, Mike scurried away.

Luke's eyebrows furrowed, a clear indication of his anger, and Angie asked, "Luke, what's wrong?"

"There's lots of talk about the explosion, due mostly to that son-of-a-bitch. He got on television and said you knew the plane was going to explode."

"Well, I did," Angie felt confused. "I told you I saw a vision of it. What could be the harm in Mike's saying what's true?"

Encircling her waist, Luke pulled her back from the receiving line and guided her into the curtained room that smelled of roasting coffee and stale cigarette smoke. He whispered, "An investigator came to the hospital. At least the doctor had sense enough not to let him talk to you."

"Is that who kept calling at the hotel?" Angie read tension in the lines of her son's face.

Luke nodded. "I said you couldn't talk to them until we get back to Phoenix next week."

"Why? What do they think I've done?" The extent of Luke's concern worried Angie. She had never been guilty of anything worse than a parking ticket.

"They don't know." Luke's voice carried contempt. "They're just fishing for answers."

"I saw a vision of the crash." Angie sucked in a breath and put her hand to her breast. "They think I caused it?"

"I'm gonna take care of this. Don't you worry." Luke guided her to a chair and sat with her.

"God, this is tough." Her mind raced with anger and shock. If only Barbara were here, but Angie and Luke would have to go it alone, like they always had. "Thank God for you, honey," she said and kissed his cheek.

Luke rubbed her trembling hand. "You know what? I'm proud of you today." As the funeral director moved toward them and cocked an eyebrow, Luke said with great gentleness, "It's time to go, Mom."

Donning their raincoats, Angie and Luke went outside where the motorcade waited. They sat together on the back seat as the limousine wound through the streets of Point Loma and out the narrow inlet to the gravesite. Two sailors guided them to seats on the front row.

The sky threatened bleakly, a puffy gray, laden with unpoured rain. The wind blew damp ocean air across the drawn faces of the mourners as they emerged from cars and limousines.

Naval officers carried the coffin to a platform under a loose, black canvas canopy. Its edges whipped and cracked with the gusting wind.

"We are gathered here," the preacher intoned, "to put to rest the mortal remains of our dear friend, co-worker, son, and brother, Captain Tyler Samuel Beckman, USN."

Angie could not bear what she heard—words so quick and final. A preacher should be saying, "Dearly Beloved, we are gathered here today in the sight of God to join together this man and this woman..."

Past the endless rows of white crosses, the leaden sky merged with gray water on the sunless horizon. A distant foghorn moaned, and a beacon winked faintly, warning ships away from the craggy bluff.

Ty had loved this narrow peninsula, bounded on three sides by ocean and bay, his home for twenty years. Angie chose the spot so he would be near his favorite sounds—the ocean's waves and the roar of airplanes taking off or landing across the bay.

The crowd of mourners, in somber blue, gray, and olive, huddled together, the long tails of raincoats tucked under their chairs, not the bright clothes they planned to wear for the wedding and dinner dance.

Did they all suspect her of murdering their beloved Ty? She wanted to scream and beat her fists against the coffin... against Ty for dying... against people's ugly thoughts. But, she sat with hands clenched in her lap and watched a sailor place a folded American flag into Ty's father's hands. Samuel's head drooped and his shoulders shook as he hunched over the flag.

Struggling to walk across the damp ground on swollen feet, Angie went to Samuel and put her arms around him. She had no words to say. None would do.

The gun-metal gray vault holding Ty's mangled body slowly descended into the open trench.

Only her promise to find Ty again consoled her. Could he come to her? What must she do to find him? Wondering how to even begin, she felt as if she stood at the edge of an abyss.

Nothing but suffering had come from her visions—Ty's death, a promise she did not know how to fulfill, jeopardy with the Navy, and suspicion all around her. Why did she see visions if nothing positive ever came from them? It seemed pointless to talk about them.

Angie could no longer hold back her tears. It did not matter anyway. Nothing mattered. Ty was dead. She covered her face and wept.

Five

Home to the Empty Heart

With rain spattering the windshield, Luke drove his turquoise Trans-Am over the jagged, fog-shrouded mountains east of San Diego. Angie lay asleep in the passenger seat beside him, still drugged by the Valium he'd insisted she take after they left the cemetery. Reacting to a strong gust of wind, he pulled the wheel back and slowed to forty-five miles per hour on the steep downgrade.

At the mountain's base, the rain stopped, the sun shone, and the road straightened out. The blue desert sky he loved widened before him. Relieved, Luke pressed the accelerator. The speedometer read eighty as they entered the arid expanse of scrub desert.

Luke felt anxious to get back to Phoenix and put this wretched day behind him. Acting polite and compassionate in the receiving line had strained him. He did not know any of the people passing through or how they felt. He'd wondered if they grieved for Ty or felt fascinated by the sensationalism of the crash and Angie's vision. Maybe they had real concern, but probably they wanted some clue about whether Mom was under suspicion for sabotage or murder. If only that bastard Porter had not shot off his mouth.

What would the Navy decide to do about the investigation? Luke hoped Jamison did not turn up in Phoenix to ask questions. God, how could he even entertain the idea that Angie had tampered with the plane? With no evidence, he would surely come to his senses and end this craziness. Her visions had sure caused a flap.

47

Ty's death seemed awful, but Luke did not quite know how he felt about it. No one he cared about had ever died. Uncle Bob, the only real corpse he'd ever seen, had looked like he was sleeping. With Ty's coffin closed, Luke figured the guy looked a lot worse with his burns and all. No point in wasting any time imagining the gruesome details.

What Luke really cared about was getting Angie through all of this. Her hospital stay scared him, but she seemed to have everything under control at the funeral home. In fact, he'd been proud of her. But, when she went to pieces at the graveyard, he felt helpless, a disgusting emotion.

With no cars in front of him or behind him, Luke sped up to ninety and enjoyed the engine's hum. Angie had wanted to stay in San Diego with Samuel and Tearlee, saying she should help them close up Ty's house, but she had given in easily when Luke insisted she go back home with him. He liked that.

Silvery green sage with tiny purple flowers grew in profusion on each side of the road. Brown dirt and scrub plants stretched out for miles. Far in the distance, mountain peaks, shaded in muted tones of red-brown and gray-green, looked like they'd been sketched across blue paper.

Luke loved the wildness of the desert, more beautiful because it seemed unconquerable, satisfying something in him he wished he could describe. Ever since his stint on the high school newspaper, he'd needed to write his thoughts and emotions down on paper. That made them real.

"Where are we?" Angie's sluggish voice startled him.

"Just about to Yuma. Wanta get some coffee?"

"I don't care." Her pretty features looked as if they had fallen down her face.

"I think I will." Luke twisted his neck and back to encourage circulation. "I'm tired of sitting."

"Maybe I should drive for a while."

"Oh, right!" Luke grinned. "My mother, the doper, is going to get behind the wheel."

"The other drivers wouldn't have a clue how much danger they were in, would they?" A tiny smile almost slipped into her haggard expression.

"Guess we should put a sign on the car." Luke hoped to encourage her good humor. "Mad mother at wheel. Beware." Suddenly, she turned from him, covering her face with her hands. "Mom, don't cry... Mom..."

"Oh, God, how am I going to live without him?" Her words came out muffled.

Luke felt at a loss to know how to console her. "Try not to think about it."

"It hurts so much... I just can't tell you."

As they passed a stand of date palms surrounding an abandoned campground, Luke remembered a game they used to play on the road, guessing the dates of origins of cars and buildings. "I'll bet nineteen forties," Luke said. "What's your bet?"

She did not answer.

"Mom... play the game with me." He indicated the campground. "Nineteen forties?"

Still no answer.

"There's our road." Luke pointed to a sign that read Brock Research Center Road.

Angie gazed out the window and shrugged. "I can't play, honey... I'm sorry."

Luke bit his lip and kept silent through the high, barren sand dunes and across the curving bridge over the Colorado River into Yuma. He pulled into a restaurant parking lot and got out. On the other side, he opened the passenger side door and waited, but she sat still with her head in her hands. He asked, "You coming?"

When she shook her head and lay back against the seat, Luke shrugged, slammed the door, and wished he did not feel annoyed. He did not understand how to deal with her mood changes and needed her to return to normal. He felt ashamed for not showing more support.

Once inside the fast-food restaurant, Luke ordered two sandwiches and drank coffee while he waited.

Ty would have known what to do to help Angie. Luke already missed the guy. These past two years had given him a glimpse of what life might have been like with a father. Luke admired the way Ty had always called his mother babe, and she seemed to like that a lot.

Supermom had done great by herself, but he could not deny he'd yearned for a man to bounce ideas off, about women and sports and college—especially women. Doc Gutierrez had been that kind of buddy once in a while, but Luke always wondered if the doctor did it more because he could not cure Luke's epilepsy or maybe because he just liked Angie. Doc had always seemed fascinated by her.

The hamburger, when it came, tasted like wood. He left it half-eaten, picked up the toasted cheese he thought Angie might like, and headed to the car.

Smiling, she accepted the sandwich, nibbled a bite then dropped the rest back in the bag. "I just can't believe he's dead. It's like a nightmare. I don't want to face it. Wish I could fly away from here."

"Yeah, I know what you mean." Forlorn, Luke drove onto the highway and sped through the scrubby countryside as day faded into evening.

After a long silence, Angie sighed. "I tried to fly out of the orphanage when I was little. The matron made Bobby carry his sheets after he'd wet the bed. All the kids laughed, and he cried. He was humiliated. I hated her. So, I built a makeshift airplane to fly us out."

"Did it work?"

"The airplane didn't. But the old bitch moved Bobby's bed close to the bathroom and left the light on, like Mother used to do." Angie cradled her head as the desert passed by them. "Wish leaving the light on would make this pain go away."

"Why don't we call Grandma and ask her to come out?"

"No point. She wouldn't come to the funeral when you asked, would she? Besides, she thinks the visions are a sign I'm crazy." Angie chuckled. "How's that for irony?"

"You need somebody."

"I need to be alone." She covered her eyes with her arm.

Angie grimaced. Why had she said that? When had she ever been anything but alone? Raising Luke by herself after his dad left. Wishing things had gone differently in her relationship with Ty years ago. She remembered Ty's shocked expression when she had broken their first engagement long ago. He had had a fling with a WAVE and she could not forgive him. Afterward, he had dated lots of Navy women, but he said no one interested him until he met Jean, with her cultured speech and refined style.

Ty soon decided nothing could replace the passion he had shared with Angie. He and Jean divorced by mutual agreement. Angie had married Russell by then, so Ty immersed himself in his career.

How Angie had longed for him during those years after she divorced Russell and moved to Arizona, not knowing Ty was free, too. If Ty had not heard of her brother Bobby's death and come to the funeral, they might have lived out their lives, yearning for each other.

They had both underestimated the power of their young love, Ty toying with it and Angie letting pride end it. But, the years of separation had nurtured their passion. The past two years together again taught them the meaning of joy. She remembered the delight of their lovemaking on that last morning.

Now his beautiful body lay inside a coffin, sealed off from her forever. Her promise to find him again seemed outlandish. What had she been thinking? Perhaps the

Valium had caused delusions in the hospital when she imagined Ty came to her.

Angie doubted either of them could find a way to cross the barrier of death. Joining him would be better than this anguish.

Fumbling in her purse, Angie retrieved another pill and swallowed it.

Luke and his lethargic mother arrived home close to midnight. As he dumped their suitcases inside the door, she wandered through the downstairs.

"Hey Mom, you want a glass of wine?" Luke called from the refrigerator then got a beer and turned to walk toward the living room.

Angie came close to him, putting her hands on his shoulders like she used to when she gave him behavior talks. Then, he had been shorter. Now she tilted her head up to look at him. "I want to tell you something, honey."

"What?" Her tone made him antsy. He hoped she was not going to get too mushy on him.

"I love you very much." Angie looked tired and drawn. Her lip quivered. "I always will."

"I know that."

"No matter what happens, just remember, okay?" Turning, she trudged up the stairs.

"I will." Although Luke wanted to hug her, he decided against it. She had an air about her that he did not recognize. "It'll be all right, Mom," he called up after her, wishing his words rang truer.

When Luke heard her bedroom door close on the second floor, he flipped on the television and popped open the beer, welcoming its cool, tangy taste. The familiar room, with its floppy pillows, flowered couch, and blue walls, made him glad to be home. He put his feet up on the coffee table and relaxed, laughing at a late night comedian's skit.

Angie's Promise

As part of Angie and Ty's wedding plans, they had expected Luke to continue to live in his mother's house so they could stay with him when they came into town. That would've been a real money saver while Luke salted away his salary for an investment nest egg. He had daydreamed of a happy bachelor life. He could think of several ladies he wanted to entertain and hoped to get to know better. He also intended to invite golf buddies over to tip a few.

Now, everything had changed. No reason for Angie to move to San Diego. Maybe Luke should get his own apartment. After all, he had already celebrated his twenty-fifth birthday. But, what would happen to her if he left?

Draining the beer can, Luke leaned back and closed his eyes, exhausted. He'd just watch this program, then go up to bed.

The ringing of the doorbell jarred Luke, and he jumped up, disoriented. Sunlight streamed through the living room windows, and a morning TV show blared its theme song. He leaned over the back of the couch and looked out the front window. A Navy man waited at the door—Jamison. Damn! Luke rubbed his head and opened the door.

"Mr. Brock, I'd like to speak with your mother." Jamison, hat in hand, wore a summer white uniform. Perspiration beaded on his bald head.

"Damn it." Luke planted a hand on each side of the doorjamb to bar the bastard from coming inside. "Why don't you leave her alone? You know she didn't have anything to do with the accident. How could she?"

Jamison squinted, probably thinking that made him look tougher. "I have some questions to ask her. I can get a formal authorization, if you insist."

"It's okay, Luke. Let the man in." Angie stood in the hallway, wearing a housecoat, her eye sockets hollow, hair hanging loose. She carried an aqua dress over her arm.

"Thank you, ma'am. I'll be brief," Jamison said.

Luke rolled his eyes and moved aside. The three stood in a semi-circle beside the open front door, morning sun dappling their faces. Luke felt awkward but was not about to offer a seat. He wished he could prevent the interview but knew the law allowed it.

"We have several reports, Mrs. Brock, that you knew in advance Captain Beckman's plane would crash." Jamison drew a notebook out of his pocket. "Would you please explain that for me?"

"I saw it in a psychic vision." Angie's voice sounded flat but all right.

"When was that?"

"The day before..." She bit her lip, breathed in, and set her jaw. "...before the accident."

"You were quoted as saying..." Pushing rimless glasses up the bridge of his nose, the Navy man studied his notes.

"Quoted by whom, Ensign Porter?" Luke regretted he'd not beaten the hell out of Porter. This guy wasn't much better. All so self-serving with their prattle about doing their duty.

With a dismissing glance at Luke, Jamison continued, "Your words were 'The plane is defective.' Please describe the defect to me, Mrs. Brock."

"You don't have to answer that question, Mom."

Walking to the middle of the living room, Angie closed her eyes and a look of calm crossed her face. She waited a moment then spoke softly. "Wait... I'm seeing it now. There's a problem... a leak in the gas tank... something about a memo... somebody knows what happened."

"Beg your pardon?" Jamison said as Luke hurried to turn off the TV.

"Somebody knows... knew about the problem." Angie sounded distant and confused. "I see words about the gas leak printed on paper."

"Mrs. Brock," Jamison said, following her, "I'm trying to conduct this interview with sensitivity to your great loss and grief. However, that may be impossible if you keep interjecting the... ah... paranormal."

Angie's eyes popped open. She seemed surprised by Jamison's presence, like she had gone out of focus. Luke thought she had probably seen something psychically.

"You are the beneficiary," Jamison said, "of a sizable insurance policy. Captain Beckman had already named you before the wedding."

Fighting the urge to solve the Navy's investigation by taking this investigator out, Luke closed his fists.

Angie's voice sounded level. "I knew he intended to buy a policy although I didn't realize he'd done it." She cocked her head and stared at Jamison for a moment with a wry little smile curving her lips. "So is that what this is all about? You think I murdered my fiancé for insurance money?"

Now that's the old Mom back again! Relieved, Luke relaxed his hands.

"Mrs. Brock, I never implied such a thing."

"If there was a saboteur," Angie said, gesturing with the dress, "you'll have to look elsewhere, Captain. I loved Ty." Her eyes filled with tears. "Yesterday should have been our wedding day."

"... uh, I have more questions."

Smoothing the fabric of the dress, Angie murmured under her breath, "I might be better off if I joined him."

"Mom!"

Jamison cleared his throat. "I understand your father died under somewhat similar circumstances."

Angie squinted at the Navy investigator. "This interview is finished." Her voice brittle, she shook her head and started up the stairs.

"You heard her, Jamison." Luke grabbed the doorknob and gestured for him to leave. "If you want to talk to her again, it'll be in court."

After the investigator hurriedly left, Luke slammed the door shut. *What kind of talk is this. Suicide? Good God.* He should have knocked Jamison out.

Six

What Might Have Been

Five weeks later

The ringing telephone jarred Angie from sleep, her body damp with sweat. The air conditioner pumped out hot air. Maybe it had overloaded from battling one hundred and ten-degree temperatures all through June.

Without opening her eyes, Angie rolled over and fumbled for the receiver, attempting to answer without rising. Unable to reach the phone, she raised herself up groggily, surprised at being sideways on the bed. She could not remember falling asleep. "Hello."

"Angela, how're you doing?"

"Okay, I guess." No one called her Angela anymore, but she did not recognize the voice on the other end. "Who is this?"

"It's Samuel."

"Samuel?" The sun had set, leaving the room in shadows. Crawling off the bed, Angie went to the window and opened the Venetian blinds.

"Samuel Beckman, dear," came the tremulous voice of an old man. "Are you okay?"

"Oh, hi." Angie struggled out of a Valium-laced haze into clear focus. "So good to hear from you. I think of you a lot these days. How are you doing?"

"Well, that's why I called... not very well."

"Why? What's the matter?" Falling back on the bed, Angie wondered what else might have gone wrong in Ty's family.

"Just old and tired, I guess, and... not very well at all, dear." Samuel cleared his throat.

"I'm sorry to hear that." Angie wondered what he was trying to say, perhaps he was just wanting a bit of sympathy.

"Doc says I've got some kidney problems. Nothing serious—just have to watch it. Lumbago acts up a lot, too. And, uh. Tired more than I used to be."

"Sorry." Probably the old fellow was not really sick, just giving up. Angie could not blame him.

"Know I shouldn't ask you, Angela." A tapping sound came over the wire, as if Samuel were pecking the receiver with a pencil.

"How can I help?"

"Can't get too far from the doctor at my age." Laughing weakly, Samuel sounded embarrassed. "Could you take care of Tyler's things? His house and car and... uh..."

"I'd be glad to help." Poor old guy. His grief must be unmanageable. Angie had always thought the death of a child the worst tragedy imaginable, unable to conceive of her devastation if Luke died.

"I know I'm asking too much of you." The speed of Samuel's words picked up, as if, relieved of the burden of having to ask, he could relax. "But I'd be very grateful. I wish I didn't have to ask. I know how upset you are."

Rising, Angie unwrapped the belt of her chenille robe and shook it loose. "Of course, I'll do it."

"It's a terrible burden for you." A bit of a whine came into his voice.

"No, it isn't. I could jump through the phone and kiss you for asking. Finally, something I can really do for Ty."

"One more thing, dear. That Navy investigator asked us if you ever had... uh... unusual experiences. Tearlee told him you or Tyler had never mentioned them. She said all we knew was what we heard at the... at the funeral. Hope that was okay."

Would Jamison ever ease off? Angie hung up with assurances that she would stay in touch by phone. Happily, she flipped on the overhead light, revealing a pile of clothes flung on the rocking chair. She pulled her suitcase down from the closet shelf, set it on the unmade bed then chose several blouses and pairs of slacks, as well as a blazer for cool evenings on the bay.

After the slam of the back door, Angie heard Luke throw down his keys and bound up the stairs. *Would he enter the house like a teenager until he was a hundred years old?* She tried on a sports skirt and looked at her image in the cheval mirror. The skirt set low on the hips and hung slack on the rear. Her depression had driven away her appetite.

Luke stopped at the doorway and looked in. "What's goin' on here?" Whether in suit and tie for work or in ratty cutoffs and T-shirt like now, he always looked dashingly handsome with his short, muscular build, curly blond hair, and startling moss green and brown eyes. Some girl would be incredibly lucky someday to marry him.

Luke smiled broadly at Angie's news of leaving for San Diego. "Want me to order a pizza again tonight?"

It would probably be a relief for Luke to have her gone for a while. Angie asked, "How about we go out for steak and lobster? My treat."

"All right!" Raising his arms in the air, Luke bowed three times like a Moslem novitiate. "Thank you, thank you, Samuel Beckman, for rescuing me from a pizza overdose."

The next morning at six Angie drove onto the freeway, refreshed from her first good night's sleep in over a month. Although she had hardly used her car, Luke had kept it clean and the gas tank filled.

Remembering how she had walked the floor at night, grieving, depressed, exhausted, Angie feared she had taken advantage of her wonderful son this past month. He had done so much, encouraging her to eat, holding her while she cried, but still going to work every day and never complaining. It must've been hard for him. "World's best son," he would say. Luke seemed more mature these days. This crisis in her life had brought out the best in him.

Suicide had come to her often as an option. The idea of her own death held no fear. On the contrary, death seemed alluring, allowing her a chance to join Ty in a tangible existence. Angie wondered what being dead was like and if she had the audacity to take her own life.

Only the thought of leaving Luke alone stopped her. The memory of her days in the orphanage filled her with a raw hopelessness, unhealed by the passing years. Never would she cause her son to experience the anguish of abandonment or the anger toward her that Angie had felt toward her own mother. Luke had suffered enough already with epileptic seizures and his father's desertion. Even as a grown man, Luke deserved at least one functioning parent.

Pressing the record button on the voice-activated cassette, Angie began dictating a things-to-do list: "Call a realtor. Go through Ty's papers for his lawyer's name. Call Admiral Mahoney. Get packing boxes. Get some quotes on painting the interior."

Alive again and nearer to Ty with each mile, Angie vowed to handle the grief. Maybe this trip would help her keep her promise. Although she had wanted to search for him, sorrow had sapped her energy, not leaving enough reserve to meditate or visit a medium. Whatever it took—psychically or physically—she felt ready for the next step. *What better place to begin than Ty's own home?*

After a month of mulling the episode over, Angie again believed Ty had been there in the hospital room with her, his mind alive behind the image, his thoughts speaking to her. By contrast, the earlier experiences of communicating with Uncle Manny and of seeing the airplane explode had come from a static place, like looking at a picture or reading a book. It might not be too scientific, but Angie felt encouraged. The love she and Ty felt for each other still lived and would soon express itself in a connection.

The desert gave way to mountains, more desert, then the verdant swells and valleys east of San Diego. It seemed only an hour passed rather than six before she descended the last range of peaks into the metropolitan area. Her stomach growled, and she started watching for an exit with a restaurant.

Feasting on fettuccine and garlic bread, Angie smelled, tasted, and let each bite rest in her mouth, relishing the flavors. She had forgotten how good food could taste. At three in the afternoon, no other customers remained in the place to hear her sigh while she savored a hot fudge sundae.

Leaving the restaurant, she smoothed down her skirt, confident she would fill it out smartly before long. She smiled at the way Ty had always admired her figure. After a stop at a convenience store for milk, wine, potato chips, and ice cream, Angie pulled in Ty's driveway.

Nervously, she wavered at the front door, not having been inside the bungalow since that last morning. With her bags packed, she had gone from the airport to the hospital, to the hotel, then back to Phoenix. How would the house affect her now?

Unlocking the door to the mustiness of damp adobe, she walked hesitantly across the Mexican, burnt orange, terra-cotta tile. The late afternoon sunlight reflected off the shiny oak finish of the antique dining room table where Samuel and Tearlee had stacked the unpaid bills.

Ty had meticulously refinished all the wood pieces in the house himself, proud of creating just the right ambiance to entertain naval officers and their wives while still maintaining a homey air. Angie loved his taste, a combination of mid-western rustic charm and sleek Spanish style. Though not the blues and greens she would choose, Ty had a good eye for color. Yellow and rosy beige echoed through the floors, the upholstery, the walls, and the vase of silk sunflowers standing on the floor beneath a skylight.

With a sigh of relief that the electricity was still turned on, Angie stashed the groceries in the kitchen and walked into the bedroom. Everything looked the way they left it that last morning. In her haste to catch the plane in time, she had pulled up the covers after they made love, leaving one rose-colored pillow untucked. Memories of Ty's touch flooded her mind.

His terry cloth robe hung over a side chair. Holding it to her face, she caught her breath at the faint fragrance like cherry blossoms still clinging to it. Although wanting to fall over the bed and sob, Angie forced herself to hang the robe in the closet and bring her suitcases in from the car.

Unpacking calmed her, so she resolved to stay as busy as possible. Giving way to tears robbed her of the strength she needed to put Ty's affairs in order and to discover a way to find him. Perhaps a psychic or some other kind of spiritual counselor would give her suggestions.

To help herself focus, Angie transcribed the recorded list into a stenographer's notebook, which she had laid on the bedside table, available for recording dreams. How unusual that she had forgotten to pack it. Even stranger, she had not missed having the dream journal until now. Her dream recall had dropped to nothing since Ty's death, so she had not missed the journal. Now, on the path to finding him again, Angie resolved to write in the journal regularly in order to record each step leading back to her lover.

Settling into Ty's bed felt unnatural and lonely. The oak posters, taller than in memory, cast oval shadows from the moonlight. Longing to feel his arms around her and his body against her skin, Angie mulled over those last few moments of his life for the thousandth time.

What could she have said to keep him off that plane? If she had acted coy, Ty would have seen right through her phoniness. Claiming illness might have worked, but the idea had not occurred to her at the time. Telling the truth failed her completely. Would it have changed his mind if she had told him she saw the number on the plane? Did she, in fact, tell him? She could not even remember what they had said to each other.

Why did she have visions if she could not change the outcome? It seemed she had no choice in any part of the experience. Why have such a gift? Maybe the ability should be called a curse, instead. Wryly, Angie wondered if answers would ever come, or if she would drive herself insane with asking.

Sleeping fitfully, she got up at two to drink milk. At three she thought she heard a noise outside and checked the door locks. Awakening a third time with a scrap of a dream in her mind, she reached for her notebook and jotted it down quickly.

...dreamed of Ty, walking something like a horse, but not a horse.

Not much, a disconnected fragment, but Angie felt glad to recall anything at all. A few years ago, she belonged to a women's group that tried to raise their consciousnesses. She had laughed at the phrase because the meaning seemed so vague. "Airy fairy," Luke called it, yet Angie became adept at dream recall. The experience turned out to be a happy one—sharing dreams, learning about herself, opening the mystical part of herself. Angie needed to start remembering again. Maybe she could connect with Ty in dreams somehow.

Though fatigued, she gave up trying to go back to sleep. With coffee and recorder, Angie turned all the lights on and roamed the house, listing items to be sold, given away, or kept. As executor, Samuel would have to send her a power of attorney.

Angie ran one hand over the high polish of the dining table, planning to sell her own to make room for it and the oak rocker. Surrounding herself with Ty's workmanship comforted her. Samuel should have one of his son's best pieces, the writing desk perhaps. She called Goodwill and arranged for a truck the next day, intending to send Ty's clothes in the first load. Their scent aroused too much need in her.

Exhausted by the end of the day, Angie lit a fire in the fireplace, opened a bottle of Chardonnay, and settled down to reminisce with Ty's high school yearbook, 1958, her junior year and his senior. She knew her own by heart, of course, as did her journalism students, but she had probably not seen this one since 1958.

Turning to the undergraduate pages, Angie laughed aloud as she remembered one embarrassing day. She had been angry because Barbara had made her wear a pink sweater with a wool plaid skirt. Angie had no collar to match the skirt, a fashion that her girlfriends honored fervently. The same day the school photographer came. Wouldn't you just know! Here was seventeen-year-old Angie immortalized—collarless—on the same page with four girls in stylish collars. To make it worse, she wore pearls at her mother's insistence.

"Yuck on pearls... they're for squares," Angie told her mother and pouted for at least a week.

Leafing through the pages she found a photo of herself and Ty walking across campus, his arm around her waist. The caption read "future plans?" The photographer had snapped Ty looking down at her with a melting smile, a shot worthy of an A anytime. She wondered if that long ago photographer had gotten a good grade.

Angie and Ty used to dance for hours together in the high school gym to *Rock Around the Clock* and *The Twelfth of Never.* They planned their wedding there one night—for the first time—then argued about how many babies to have. Ty had optimistically wanted five boys for a basketball team. Angie wondered what their kids would have looked like, definitely blue eyes and black hair like their mother and daddy.

Sweet times, but then Ty met the WAVE. How different their lives might have been had Angie been able to forgive him for his infidelity, but in those days she had not known how to rise above the blow to her ego. Her affair with Russell soon after had only one purpose—to hurt Ty, something she managed to accomplish very well.

Angie had felt so angry and betrayed that she thought nothing good could come of her life, but she had been wrong. Russell gave her very little in the way of a marriage, but he did father her precious Luke. The divorce made her grow up. She had much to thank irresponsible Russell for with regard to that.

When Angie and Ty finally found each other again, they had both gained the maturity to appreciate the powerful love they shared, one time had enhanced. As she stared into the dying fire, Angie wondered if Ty were thinking of her.

One softly glowing ember held her attention, entrancing her as consciousness of her body ebbed away.

Sighing, Angie glanced toward the hallway, not surprised to see a fragile shadow of light in the shape of a man.

"Hello, darling." A gentle voice, not unlike Ty's, came from the right of the fireplace.

Strangely calm, she turned to see Ty sitting in the high-backed rocker, smiling at her. She must be dreaming. Angie nodded to him, and he pointed toward the hallway. There stood her brother, Bobby, a small sorrel pony beside him. As a boy, Bobby had always wanted to own a pony.

Angie felt happy and at ease. It seemed she could reach out and touch the two men. Their skin looked luminous, burnished in firelight. The room itself took on intense color. Sharper, as if the F-stop were turned up to Cosmic Bright.

Angie must have nodded off because she awakened at the sound of a noise outside or inside, she could not discern which. It sounded like a door banging, a distant car backfire, or a gunshot. A shiver passed through her. Because the fire had burned out as she slept, she stumbled in the darkness and fell over the coffee table. Angie scrambled to the wall and turned on the overhead lights. The yearbook lay on the floor, and the wine bottle clattered across the floor.

Hurrying to the hall, she felt the tile cold to her bare feet. The front door stood ajar. Not remembering whether she had locked it, she snapped the dead bolt into place. Hands icy and trembling, she ran through the house, flipping on lights, checking to make certain the windows were shut, opening every closet and cupboard, and looking under the bed.

Satisfied that she was alone in the house, Angie returned to the living room to clean up the spilled wine. A glance out the front window chilled her. She saw a momentary light flare, like a cigarette being lit.

Flipping the lights off to better see outside, Angie identified a white Navy sedan parked down the block. A man sat inside, smoking as he faced the house.

Her stomach churned with alarm.

Seven

The Princess of Desire

Phoenix—a few days later

Luke sat in the quiet law office with its teal wool carpet and beige walls. Pulsing stars burst from the screen saver on the computer with hypnotic rhythm. For sure, he'd stuck too close to home lately, tending his mother. He was not doing either one of them a favor by worrying, though he owed her for that seizure episode a couple of months ago.

All he remembered was hearing music from an unidentified source. He awoke, seemingly the next second, lying on his side on the garage floor with Angie chafing his hands. Luke did not know how she had managed to wedge him safely between the car and tools scattered everywhere. He outweighed her by forty pounds and must have been thrashing around big time.

It touched him when she had offered to call off her wedding and the move to San Diego because it meant leaving him alone. Epilepsy or not, Luke could certainly take care of himself. He felt guilty for screwing up.

With several years since the last seizure, he thought he had outgrown the need for pills and entertained some idle thoughts about beating the disease on his own. Stupid macho pride. After that episode, he promised Angie that he would never go off the medication again. Both of them deserved to feel free and have a life separate from each other. Now she might never have a chance for happiness.

"Ready!" Ted leaned in the doorway, affecting the practiced swagger of a Top Gun pilot. He brushed a hand through well-groomed black hair, his eyes crinkling in spite of his efforts to keep them staring intensely. Someone must have flattered him once by saying he looked like Tom Cruise because cockiness seemed a permanent component of Ted's personality, too.

Luke glanced at the wall clock hanging beside his diplomas, clicked off the computer, and rolled back his chair. "Five forty. We're outta here."

They took off their jackets, loosened their ties, and rolled up their shirtsleeves. The two raced down the twelve flights of stairs. Luke needed to work out the kinks from computer posture and file-cabinet overhang.

A blast of heat hit them at the side door of the high rise. Donning sunglasses, they headed down Central Avenue on foot.

"Wait'll you see these chicks." Ted slung his light blue jacket over a shoulder. "Can't believe you've never been to Sullivan's. Hottest spot around. Everybody goes there."

"I've got a lot of catching up to do." Luke laughed. "Let's get started!"

Ted opened the door to Sullivan's, and Luke walked through, blinking in the gloom. A blast of air-conditioning blew the smell of cigarette smoke toward them. Metallic bars, neon art, and pop music filled the nightclub.

"Good. We're early. Over here." Going to a tall table, Ted leaned on his elbows, his back to the dance floor.

Straddling a tall stool, Luke smiled at a pretty waitress in a low-cut halter top. "Bud Lite, please."

"Same for me." Ted smiled as she wrote down the order. He watched the waitress with a hungry look. Her long ponytail bobbed above short shorts, "Mighty fine little ass. Yes, mighty fine." He pointed at three gals walking through the door. "Now, look. First National Bank stuff. See anything you like, I'll introduce you."

"Know all of them, do you?" Luke asked, amused by Ted's lecherous mind.

"Maybe not all, but some." Ted waved to them across the room.

"A lot of smart chicks come here." Luke shouted over the jukebox playing a Bon Jovi tune, *You Give Love a Bad Name*. "Glad I came."

"Hey, look." Ted nodded toward two gals who entered and turned in the opposite direction. Waving a dismissing hand, he said, "Who needs them? Marriage market. Just wait till the Pacific Savings and Loan gals get here. Now, that's a party. Good dancers, don't tease, if you get my meaning."

"Yeah?" Luke was surprised at Ted's crudeness, a quality he kept a bit more subdued at the office. Even with the strut, he was always proper and polite there, treating the secretaries and the senior partner, Ms. Pomeroy, with respect, at least to their faces. Luke decided that Ted might be okay for the bar scene but not for a double date.

"Where you been, Luke," Ted asked, eyes, crinkling, "under a rock?"

"Guess so." Luke whistled softly. "Whoa! What is that?"

The most elegant woman Luke had ever seen walked through the outside door. Momentarily silhouetted in bright sunlight, she looked longer legged than most Hispanic women, with olive skin and black hair cascading over her shoulders. She tilted her head regally, hinting of ancient Aztec ancestry. Two shorter women entered a step behind her, like handmaidens.

"Never saw her before," Ted said.

"She's drop-dead gorgeous." Glancing at his companion, Luke said with amazement, "You don't know her? Ted, you're a big disappointment to me."

"Me, too." Ted seemed genuinely sorry.

Dancers filled the floor. Luke watched the beauty sit down, order a drink, and laugh with her friends. When

Whitney Houston's *Greatest Love of All* came on the jukebox, he hurried to ask for a dance.

"I'd love to," the beauty said, offering a slender hand with immaculately painted nails.

Her touch warmed Luke. He felt instantly captivated. Her small waist fit perfectly in the curve of his arm. She was as tall as he and more striking up close, with high cheekbones, a dazzling smile, and almond-shaped eyes, black as onyx.

"My name's Melinda Chacon." She leaned toward him, the brush of her cheek tantalizing against his ear. "What's yours?"

Her question interrupted his staring, and Luke laughed aloud. Chacon—she'd told him her last name—not bar protocol. What could that mean? "Call me 'Obvious,' I guess." He realized his admiration showed. "Happy to meet you. I'm Lucus Brock, but call me 'Luke.'"

Melinda smiled and talked easily about herself. This was her first time at Sullivan's. She worked for a big accounting firm on Central, graduated from the University of Arizona, and rooted for the Phoenix Suns.

"I've said 'me, too,' so many times I must sound like the mechanical man," Luke said. "Tell me more. I need details."

"Details?" A look of confusion crossed her flawless face.

"For my imaginary news story." Luke hoped to charm her. "I create headlines in my head, to amuse myself."

"Really?"

"Uh-huh, How about this one." Luke waved a hand, spreading his fingers as if reading skywriting. "ASTOUNDINGLY GORGEOUS ACCOUNTANT WOWS LAWYER."

"You're funny." Although her laugh was small, it seemed authentic. "I like that in a man."

"I'm glad." Luke felt her move away. "Why'd you stop?"

"Music ended." Melinda dropped her head, as if suddenly embarrassed.

Thanking her, Luke walked with her back to her table then returned to his own. He could see Ted in animated conversation after the dance with a short, shapely blond. Luke stood by himself and finished the beer.

Unable to think of anything except Melinda, he watched her with her friends. When she talked, her hands danced in the air. Her hair flipped as she turned, smiling at everyone. She seemed very popular. He averted his eyes but glanced back again, wishing he could stop staring at her. When she turned toward him, he smiled, but she didn't notice.

A fast Tina Turner number played, and Luke decided to wait for a slower one although he wanted to ask Melinda to dance again. A jeans-clad Hispanic guy leaned over her, his face far too close to hers. Luke hoped she would refuse him, but she smiled and offered her delicate hand to the other guy in the same way.

When the two went out to the floor, Luke sighed, vowing to work on his self-confidence with fast dances. He looked around for Ted, who had staked out the blond. Luke ordered another drink.

A slow song came on, and Melinda danced with her new partner again. Luke decided to get to her as soon as possible. *Would that nervy guy ever leave her alone?* Luke could not blame him, though. Melinda was so fine. As he considered asking one of her friends to dance, just to get into the vicinity, the music stopped, and the competition walked away.

Crossing the floor as quickly as possible without running, Luke held out a hand to Melinda, "May I have this dance?"

"Oh, no, thanks," she said in a vague tone without focusing on his face. Had she even heard him?

"Okay." Luke decided she was probably tired. "Maybe later?" He hoped his disappointment didn't show.

At the same moment, Melinda said something to one of her girlfriends and turned her back to him. Luke returned to his table, wondering what went wrong. She obviously was not interested in getting to know him better. Reviewing their conversation word for word, he did not think he'd said anything foolish. Imagining he might be getting paranoid, he decided to wait a while longer.

A group of strangers stood around his table when Luke returned, probably because the waitress had taken his drink away. Neither Ted nor the blond was anywhere in sight. Giving the intruders a dirty look, Luke checked to make sure his tie remained in the pocket and threw the jacket over his arm. He strolled to the snack table, filled a plate with meatballs and chicken wings, and ate them while he watched the dancers. Melinda still talked with her companions and never looked his way.

Determined to have another chance with her, Luke went to the jukebox and selected three slow songs, then asked her to dance.

"No, thank you, I was just leaving," Melinda rose. "I've got a one-glass limit on workdays."

From the jukebox, Billy Ocean wailed, *There'll be sad songs...*

Surprised at how sorry he felt, Luke hoped logic would change her mind. "Today's Friday."

"I always go in on Saturdays if there's any work to do." Melinda carried a tone of finality in her soft voice.

"I'd like to see you again."

Bending down to pick up her purse, Melinda spoke in a low voice to her friends, who both got up quickly and headed for the door. Tremulously, she asked, "How about dinner tomorrow night?"

"What? Great. Where?"

"Blue Willow. Six o'clock."

A small smile played around her graceful mouth. Was that nervousness at being assertive or amusement at his surprise?

"I can pick you up," Luke said, delighted to make plans for a real date.

"I'd rather you didn't. Meet you there."

Melinda turned and walked toward the door, head high and firm, round hips swinging. The two handmaidens fell into step a beat behind her. One of the girls with Melinda glanced back at Luke and winked as if impressed with him.

Hallelujah. Tomorrow would be Luke's lucky day.

The next evening while shaving, Luke leaned toward the bathroom mirror to examine his appearance, imagining how Melinda might view him. Blond hair, bountiful and unruly, and eyes that came from no known place. His mother had black hair and blue eyes. He'd seen pictures of his father with brown eyes and hair. Luke arched his brows and gazed into his own eyes. Green and brown flecks floated between the pupils and black outer rings, giving his eyes a mottled and changing look, like craggy mountains at sundown. He twisted to examine his neck. Silky smooth. *The woman wouldn't be able to help herself!*

Luke found her full of surprises and wanted to know more about her. He already knew they had much in common.

Rinsing the razor out, Luke tapped it on the sink, wiped his face, and applied his favorite aftershave, pungent sandalwood. Why hadn't he and Melinda met before at the University? They probably weren't ready to know each other until now. Destiny makes its own time. *Whoops! That sounded like something Mom might say.* He had to watch out. Getting mystical over his exquisite Aztec maiden already.

Not *his* yet, Luke thought as he drove to the restaurant, but he had a very good feeling about tonight. Yet, he wondered why she had insisted on meeting him there instead of his picking her up at her house. He wanted to meet her family and have a real old-fashioned date. Next time, for sure.

When he arrived at exactly six, Melinda already sat in the busy lobby. She rose and greeted him with a warm smile. The waitress seated them in a secluded niche. Silk willow boughs wept down around them, creating the illusion of a wooded glen.

Luke sank into the moss green, curved booth beside her. "Good to see you."

A waitress in a flowing beige dress embroidered with leaves came to the table.

A tiny blush crossed Melinda's face as Luke asked, "White Zinfandel okay for you?"

"My favorite." Melinda crossed her legs beneath the table and brushed against him. "Excuse me."

"No need." Her touch excited him. "Tell me about yourself... what you like... what you want."

Without hesitation, Melinda said, "I love my work. It's the most important thing in my life."

"Really. Why?" Accounting was the most boring subject Luke had taken in college. He couldn't imagine doing it for a job. So cut and dried. At least law allowed room for opinion and flair.

The waitress brought the wine and left forest green leather menus with gold-tasseled bookmarks inside them. Luke liked the style of the restaurant.

"Accounting is my future." Melinda's features became more fluid with her enthusiasm, and her hair flowed with her movements like an advertisement for shampoo. "I intend to have my own firm someday." She squared her shoulders. "It will be the first all female, Hispanic firm in Phoenix."

"Hey, be careful, that's illegal," Luke teased.

Blushing, Melinda said, "Well, at least I'll be the first female, Hispanic owner, and I'll be able to give my sisters a chance."

"That sounds good!" Word games like he'd always played popped into Luke's mind. "You could call it *Chicanas Por La... Cuenta.*"

"Hispanic women for the bill?"

"Or," Luke sipped the sweet wine, "how about *Ledgers Latinas?*"

Melinda seemed confused by his jokes. Poor ones. He wished he'd not said anything. She might take offense where he didn't intend any. He loved playing with words in any language.

Relaxing, Melinda laughed, then sputtered, "How about *Bookkeepers Bonitas?*"

"Yeah. You got it." Luke felt glad she enjoyed his sense of humor. Touching her hand, he said, and really meant it, "I hope your dream comes true."

"Thanks." Melinda moved closer to him. "You speak Spanish?"

"A little. College minor." Luke felt content, happy to spend time with such an intelligent, charming woman. He ordered steak, and Melinda decided on some exotic pasta concoction. They dawdled over the food for a long time. He told her of his legal work and hopes of becoming a writer someday.

"What do you want to write?" Melinda asked, apparently as interested in him as he was in her.

"Oh, I don't know."

"Comedies, mysteries, detective stories? There's a big market in mysteries. I've got a client who publishes them."

"I'll probably write about ideas, maybe philosophy or ethics," Luke mused, cocking his head and gazing up without seeing anything. "Whatever I learn along the way."

"Interesting." Melinda described the elegant suburban home she wanted to live in, the Mercedes she would drive, the tennis club she would belong to, the investment portfolio she intended to build.

Luke daydreamed with her. They both wanted the good life, and he imagined her fitting easily into all of his plans. He could be a part of hers, too. "We've got so much in common. Why haven't we met before?"

Propping her chin in her palm, Melinda grinned. Her hair framed her face in a dark halo. "I'll tell you a secret."

"Okay."

"You don't know me, but I know you."

"How?" Luke enjoyed her jesting.

"At the University," Melinda raised her eyebrows and whispered," I watched you play soccer, but you never noticed me."

"Naw. I'd remember you." Luke felt flattered.

"You were the best player on the team—and the sexiest." Melinda said with her amazing ability to be innocent and childlike one moment then forward and suggestive the next. "The... uh... don't tell me... Dale Hall Diablos. Right?"

"I can't believe this!" It thrilled Luke to think she'd admired him from afar. Now, he understood why she'd given him her whole name at Sullivan's. She felt like she knew him.

"I always wanted to meet you," Melinda confessed with wide eyes.

Putting his arm around her shoulders, Luke drew her close and kissed her ear. "Why didn't you introduce yourself?"

Looking shy, she murmured, "I never thought you and I could... the differences... you know..."

The waitress brought the check. Luke gave her his credit card and turned back to Melinda, intending to ask her what she meant, but she was already standing.

"Excuse me. I'm going to the ladies' room. Would you meet me in the lobby?"

"Sure." Luke paid the bill, walked to the restroom entrances, and waited for her, anxious to ask what bothered her about the differences between them.

There seemed to be lots of possibilities. Different race, culture, sex, occupation, brain orientation, eye color, maybe religion. He wondered if she thought any of those held importance? Luke didn't. The similarities between them compelled far more notice. If she brought up the subject again, he would skip the jokes. The fact that she worried about such things must mean she liked him.

"Hi. Sorry I took so long." Her hand clung to his as they walked outside. Sundown had brought a brisk breeze that scattered pink blossoms off the feathery desert willow tress bordering the restaurant parking lot. "I've had a lovely time, Luke. Thank you for dinner."

"Thanks for asking me," Luke grinned. "How about a movie?"

"Really, I've got to go." Melinda hesitated as if reconsidering. "Thank you again." She hurried to an early Eighties model Honda. Climbing inside quickly, she started the engine and pulled out of the stall. "Good night," Melinda called and waved.

"Melinda," he shouted. "I don't have your phone number." Luke ran toward her car, white like a million others in the Valley. She drove onto the street and merged with the traffic.

Catching up to her now would be out of the question. He knew he had to find her again, but how? Discouraged, Luke trudged back to his own car and banged his fist on the hood.

Eight

Dreams of War and Bliss

On impulse, Angie hired a realtor over the phone, feeling immediate confidence in the young woman.

Later in the day, the realtor came to inspect. Dressed in a crisp linen suit, the tiny Asian woman walked through the house, making notes, her manner professional and reassuring. "Floors well done... window treatments good... appliances could be newer... but overall, looks marketable, Mrs. Brock."

Angie followed her with mixed feelings, needing to sell, yet reluctant to let go of this tangible link to Ty. "I thought I'd have the walls repainted before we list it."

"Not necessary. It's charming." The realtor ran a graceful hand across the sofa back. "Are you going to sell it furnished?"

Angie could live here permanently, but that would leave her and Luke with two households to support, something they really could not afford since she had quit teaching. Ty's life insurance would sustain her for a while, but eventually Angie would have to find another job. "No, I'm having the furniture shipped to Phoenix, but I could delay if it would be an advantage for selling."

"Good." The realtor smiled with pencil-perfect lips. "It's going to show nicely. How much?"

Angie sighed. "That's your department. What do you think?"

"A hundred and eighty-nine thousand. You'll probably get one seventy-five. Is there a mortgage?"

"No, he owns it free and clear." Talking price made everything seem so final. With Ty gone, Angie had no reason to stay in San Diego. Besides, on the phone Tearlee and Samuel expressed eagerness to have things settled.

Over coffee, they signed the listing papers, and the realtor slipped them into her briefcase. At the door, she flicked the dead bolt. "These will help the sale. Been some break-ins in the area."

"I didn't know." Angie remembered finding the unlocked front door a few nights ago. Although she had convinced herself she forgot to close the door, something about the incident still bothered her.

"Nothing reported on the news except some stolen jewelry and computers." Smiling, the realtor opened the door. "But, you never know for sure what's going on. Last year there was a series of robberies in North County. Later it came out some women had been raped. Sometimes they don't tell the police."

"Yes, I know." Angie doubted she would report such an embarrassing and shameful occurrence.

"You here by yourself, Mrs. Brock?"

Shuddering at how alone she felt, Angie said, "Yes."

"Be careful." The realtor shook Angie's hand. "Thank you for your trust. I'll have this house sold in no time."

That night, Angie remembered the realtor's admonishment. Shrubs shielded the bedroom windows. From the street, no one would be able to see a robbery or any worse crime. Her hand shook as she checked the dead bolt on the front door. The shady side street did not get much traffic. Needing to make certain no one lurked around, Angie peeked out on the quiet view.

Only the Navy car, with its perennially smoking occupant, sat parked down the block. Angie shivered. Did he represent threat or protection?

The day before, when she had marched outside and confronted the man, he claimed "orders from Jamison," as she suspected. Her effort to contact Admiral Mahoney had resulted only in a vague secretarial assurance that he would call when he returned from out of town.

After checking the dead bolt on the back door, Angie went to bed, lying still and alert. Her fingers clutched the blanket. She felt foolish and hummed like a child who had heard too many ghost stories. She told herself to calm down. No one could get in from outside. No one lay in wait inside to harm her. Finally, she relaxed.

Jerked awake in the black quiet, Angie sat up. Certain no one could get into the house, she wondered if her desire to contact Ty had manifested in his coming to her in spirit. She fancied smelled cherry blossoms and whispered, "Ty, is that you?"

Angie glanced around the shadowed corners of the room but could detect no sounds, not even her own breathing. She had a sense of something like a presence, maybe the shape of a man, standing by the dresser. "Ty, if you're here, answer me. Please talk to me, darling."

When no answer came, sweat erupted on her arms and legs. Her stomach knotted. Her breath came in shallow gasps. Paralyzed, she sat unmoving until the pale dawn light seeped into the room and she could see that she was alone.

Exhausted, Angie slept until noon then recorded a late morning dream in her journal:

...dreamed I swam along the bottom of a crystal clear pool. Ty took my hand, and we skimmed through the water, arms out to our sides, like flying. Suddenly, I was in my classroom, trying to get my students to settle down. They were all running around the room ignoring me. I felt frustrated.

Glad to dream of Ty again, even with frustration, Angie wondered if the flying sensation might mean more than she understood. Had she flown before?

Some experts she had studied indicated flying dreams often preceded the onset of lucid dreaming, the ability to realize one is dreaming without awakening and to control the dream content. It would be a kick to take her waking mind into the dream, to steer it, and to make it do what she wanted. If she could become lucid, she would dream of meeting Ty. They might talk or even make love. The prospect excited her.

When the Goodwill truck arrived later that day, Angie set out boxes full of dishes, linens, garden tools, and Ty's clothes. Forcing herself into action to avoid tears, she phoned the man who'd bought the boat and arranged to send the keys and papers to him. She ran an ad to sell the Mustang then, considering she'd done all she could for the day, she wandered into the study.

Only Ty's Navy texts remained unpacked, intended for the base library. Angie went to the kitchen, opened the refrigerator door, and gazed inside. Though she was low on groceries, standing in the checkout line seemed too much of a challenge. She grabbed a half-empty wine bottle and a glass then sat down on the couch. Could be she had been drinking too much... or not enough.

Not caring, Angie selected a log of daily activities written in Ty's scrawling hand. She sipped wine and leafed through the pages while a cool breeze blew through the open window.

As a flyer in Vietnam in the Sixties, Ty had conscientiously documented orders, given and received, miles traveled, and targets spotted. Details of flights and the devastation on the poor country saddened Angie, both for the Vietnamese people and for Ty because he had to fight in a war. From time to time, Ty had noted in the diary how difficult those days had been for everyone but never dwelt on the subject. He mentioned the children's suffering, especially, but characteristically put the events behind him as unpreventable.

One passage stood out from the rest:

> April 17: Took a hit in the left wing and parachuted into the jungle. Felt confident rescue helicopter would spot me in short order and began hacking foliage to help with visibility. Hiding in jungle, Cong taunted with clavet sticks, cowardly as always. The wooden instrument's clacking sound is unsettling when accompanied by whispering. That's what the guerillas intend, of course. Monkeys swinging everywhere, sticky hot, too muggy to breathe, took great effort to swing machete.
>
> Got confused somehow. Weapon looked like a sword, trousers too tight, boots different. Strangest part was I could see fires, sickening stench like human flesh burning, pine trees all around, and clothes smelled like sheep shit. When the 'copter spotted me and started its descent, I didn't recognize it for a minute and imagined a monster about to attack me.
>
> A strange experience, almost like I'd dropped down into another time and place, fighting another soldier's war. Must have been more afraid than I thought or I'm losing my mind.

Ty had been shot down and had never told her. Why? Angie wondered if he dreaded to distress her. Maybe he thought her too weak to handle such a raw, life-threatening experience.

While settling into bed that night, Angie suggested to her dreaming mind to work on an answer. Her dream life had become more interesting than her waking life. Other people might think her crazy. The old fears from the orphanage came up in her throat—that she was as unstable as her mother, that her visions were a sign of insanity. Even Barbara said so.

Sighing, Angie guessed she should find a counselor to help sort things out. One had helped when she first moved to Arizona, suffering from stress then, too. Maybe she would consult one later after the house sold. Tired, she did not want to quit trying to contact Ty.

Chanting in her mind, "I am awake and aware in my dream," Angie dozed but awakened with a start. She sensed someone, a man at the back of the house. "Ty, is that you?" If it were Ty, he would answer to let her know somehow and not scare her half to death. An intruder might be trying to get in through the utility room. Knowing she had not gone out there since checking the dead bolt the night before, she felt afraid. "Who's there?"

Swaying shadows fell across the dark carpet. Cold chills ran down Angie's shoulders and arms. Propped on one elbow, she waited, gaze fixed on the open doorway. She heard a faint sound, like soft-soled shoes on tile.

Someone was in the house.

Shaking, Angie dialed 911 and whispered her address into the phone. She silently sped to the door and waited on the front porch, shivering in the nighttime sea air. A part of her hoped her fear turned out to be silly. Then, she could dare to believe Ty awaited her inside the house. Before making such a logical leap, she needed the confidence of a policeman's presence to keep reality sorted.

An officer arrived within minutes of her call, so quickly she imagined he had already been patrolling in the neighborhood.

After checking the house and the backyard, he strode to her in the front hall. "No one here, ma'am. You're safe now."

"But I know I heard someone."

"May have." Pistol glistening on his hip, the policeman moved toward the front door. "But no one's there now."

"Are you sure?" Angie hoped she did not sound hysterical. If there were no intruder, she could come to only one logical conclusion.

After the officer left, Angie huddled in bed, wide-eyed and amazed at how much courage it took to accept the idea that her loving, vibrant Ty could be a ghost. A part of her finally gave up the notion that he might reappear as a living being.

The business in Vietnam made sense. Ty may have had some kind of psychic experience himself, perhaps connecting with a former lifetime. Angie wished she could remember one. Other people had written books about it, so remembering was possible.

Ty's fear of the experience might have contributed to his unwillingness to believe her prediction that his plane would crash. Maybe he rejected her warnings in an effort to prove his physical reality as the only truth. If so, he had paid an awful price for his denial.

Settling against the pillow, Angie looked forward to her dreams with a new willingness to accept them as an alternate reality. She remembered an unrecorded scrap of what she took to be a dream of Ty and Bobby appearing in her living room. Perhaps instead the two had visited her in their spirit bodies, but she had failed to grasp the fact.

Grandma definitely believed spirits of the dead came to the living. From now on, Angie would, too.

"I am awake and aware," Angie chanted in her mind and soon seemed to float into a dream place.

She looked down and saw a woman's face. The woman looked familiar, then Angie realized she saw her own face. Surprised because she had never seen herself with her eyes closed before, she looked around and could see on all sides at the same time. Pink tree limbs, boughs heavy with cherries, swayed in bright air.

Angie mused that Ty would enjoy standing in the air. Then, he stood before her, glistening in bright green and blue lights. How beautiful he looks, she thought.

When Ty smiled, yellow sparks radiated out from him. "Handsome, maybe. Beautiful is a word for ladies like you, my darling."

Although she heard him, his lips did not move. Angie felt awed and amazed that he "thought" his meaning to her. Delighted that they could communicate, she laughed and said, "Thank you."

"Come to me." Ty held out his arms.

Feeling incredible desire, Angie reached for him. Purple and pink waves of love pulsed from her fingers. She merged into his body... into his mind. As if they stood together in the center of the cosmos, he was all around her and inside her at the same time. Rainbow lights flashed and whirled around and through them.

Their joining felt wonderful. Better than wonderful. She felt ecstasy, like having an orgasm all over her body—arms and legs, brain, breasts, everywhere. Angie knew Ty felt the same bliss. They shimmered as they held each other and exploded together.

Golden firelight fanned up all around them.

Nine

I Think I Love You

Luke awakened Sunday morning with the idea of walking up and down Central Avenue until he found the office where Melinda worked. The phone book would be even quicker, he decided, because he had to find that woman. His waterbed sloshed when he swung his legs over the side.

Bounding down the stairway, he made coffee and cleared a space among the stacks of newspapers, articles, and books on the large maple trestle table. From the *Yellow Pages*, he made a list of the accounting firms on Central Avenue. He propped his legs up on the table and relaxed. The coffee tasted rich with hazelnut.

With only eight possible places, it would not take long to find her. Luke would call the next morning, first thing. When he found her, he would go there on his lunch hour. *Yes, this is an excellent plan.*

"A plan. Gotta have one. Ta-dum." Luke's voice energized the empty room as he strummed a beat on the tabletop. How would Melinda react when she saw him? Maybe surprise, hopefully delight, surely not anger. With any luck, she wanted to see him as much as he wanted to see her.

The vague memory of a dream passed through his mind, something about a machine, maybe a calculator or a telephone. Those images had probably given him the idea of how to look for Melinda.

His mother described dreams that gave her ideas or helped to solve problems, but she agonized a lot about whether to trust her own mind. She worried way too much. If it worked, it worked, like when he got a fever and vomited at camp as a fourteen-year-old. Before the counselor even got organized well enough to phone Angie, she had shown up to take Luke home. Hers had turned out to be a very handy ability.

For the hundredth time, Luke's thoughts returned to the night before and Melinda's sweet face. How he had wanted to kiss her and press her gorgeous body against his. When she stepped in her car, she had looked so defenseless. Why? And that mention of differences? What was she thinking? They would have a lot to talk about when he found her.

The cluttered tabletop reminded him to tidy up the house and do some laundry. Angie would definitely take a dim view of his housekeeping. Not that he did not know how to keep the house looking topnotch, but, when she left, he always descended into his own lax comfort level.

Luke sensed more going on inside him than mere impatience with housekeeping details. Because of religiously taking his medication, he had experienced no sign of a seizure since that miserable day in the garage. He wanted to be on his own in every way and have a family of his own. Maybe Melinda would be the woman to share that dream. Maybe not. Probably too early to tell.

Other guys he knew rarely saw their parents. Had being an only child created a greater dependency in him than normal? Certainly the epilepsy threw a clinker in the works. Having only one parent complicated things, too. He felt responsible for his mother.

Since Ty's death, she'd been needy—crying a lot, skipping meals, staring out the window. She hardly talked to anyone except Luke. Only rarely had she invited Jillian to the house. Before, the two women had gone lots of places together. Those first few days after the funeral, Luke feared he'd awaken some morning and find Angie dead. At least she seemed willing to live now. He hoped the time in San Diego would bring back her old vitality.

Luke decided the cleaning could wait and headed to the gym to play basketball. He needed to vent some of the agitation such thinking stirred up.

Just as Luke walked up to the receptionist's desk at Dickinson Brothers, he saw Melinda sitting not far away, watching him through a glass cubicle. She looked surprised but got up and came toward him. In an emerald silk blouse and slim black skirt that revealed long legs, she looked very classy.

Smiling, Melinda touched his arm. Her fresh scent enveloped him, like a pine forest on a crisp autumn day. "How did you find me?"

"Talent." Luke rubbed his fingernails across his jacket lapel.

Melinda tugged on his arm and led him away. "I can't have visitors."

Luke chuckled. "Hey, I'm glad I found you, too."

"My boss is very strict." Melinda looked at her watch. "If he comes back from lunch and finds you here, he'll—"

"What? Fire you?" For a moment Luke regretted his pushy behavior.

"Well, no, but he might give me a bad rating." Squeezing Luke's arm, Melinda gave a nervous laugh. "I'm up for a promotion."

"I'd give it to you, if I was your boss." *That's not all he'd give her, if he got the chance.*

"Wish you were." Her almond-shaped eyes narrowed, and Melinda guided him toward the chrome elevator doors.

Maybe a little tease would help. "Run away with me."

Melinda's hearty laugh hinted at an ability to abandon herself to pleasure. Maybe Luke could give her the opportunity.

She pressed the elevator button. "You've really got to go."

Her dark loveliness troubled Luke, and he wondered if he felt love or an urge to conquest. "Too soon, huh? I'd settle for dinner tonight." When she nodded agreement, a look of surrender added to her allure. Before she could change her mind, Luke said quickly, "Pick you up at seven-thirty. What's your address?"

The elevator door opened, and Melinda nudged him. "Meet you there."

Luke saw no profit in resisting. "Where?"

"Same place." Melinda's answer dissolved in the closing doors.

Luke congratulated himself. That encounter hadn't been so tough. The woman had obviously been glad he came looking for her. Why did she still refuse to tell him where she lived? He needed to slow down. He didn't have to know every single thing about her right away.

At dinner they talked about the coming election, agreeing George Bush was a shoo-in over Dukakis, though they both hoped the Democrats could field a better candidate. They quickly dispensed with religion by naming the faith they'd grown up with, she Catholic, he Religious Science, neither an important part of their lives.

Over a month passed. They fell into a routine of meeting for dinner, seeing a movie, walking in Encanto Park, or dancing at Sullivan's.

Luke felt encouraged when Melinda let him hold her hand but discouraged when he'd try to kiss her. She would duck her head and make a little joke about needing to be good. She still hadn't told him her home phone number. Except for the fact that she turned south after their dates, Luke had no idea where she lived and considered following her home to find out. He decided cheap tricks were no good. He wanted an honest relationship.

Over the weeks, Melinda had become Luke's only topic for journal writing. He knew he was falling in love but didn't understand her feelings. He could not overcome her reserve. Compared with the way Angie and Ty had revealed themselves to each other when they talked, Luke and Melinda had a long way to go.

One night they danced late and walked to the Civic Plaza to cool off. They took off their shoes and dangled their feet in the fountain. Melinda entertained Luke with stories about the computer nerd in her unit at work. "He always gets embarrassed and stumbles over his words."

"Maybe you make him nervous."

Melinda seemed dismayed. "I don't know why I would. I like him."

As Luke moved closer, their legs touched. He'd hardly even kissed her. Hugs and pecks didn't count. He wanted more. "Do you like me?"

"Well, of course, I like you." Melinda's trust filled him with hope. Even when she avoided his advances, there was something comfortable and familiar about her.

Luke took her hand and caressed the long tawny fingers. "Melinda, I think I love you."

The fountain's slim tubes forced water out with a rhythmic swoosh. A cooling mist filled the air. The engines of passing cars hummed the downtown symphony, their symphony. Did she hear it, too? Luke gazed at her.

"I don't know what to say."

Although fearing rejection, Luke needed to hear the truth. "Say what you feel."

"Don't put me in this position, Luke." She sounded more sorrowful than angry. "I didn't intend to hurt you. I'm sorry."

"No, don't be sorry. It's just that... I..."

Luke tried to read her expression in the flickering fountain lights. He thought he saw yearning and openness, the opposite of her measured words. Maybe his heart played tricks on his eyes. "Melinda. Tell me *something!*"

Throwing her arms around his neck, she hugged him then pulled back and grinned wickedly as if delighted to be naughty. Her full lips parted, and she leaned toward him, dark eyes craving his mouth. Her kiss was hungry, her tongue searching.

Enraptured, Luke did not care whether she said she loved him or not, as long as she acted like this. He enfolded her and kissed her, releasing the ardor he had known her mouth would provoke.

Melinda broke away and stepped out of the fountain. "We can't do this."

"Just did." Luke grinned and jumped out behind her.

"I don't want to care for you. Not for anybody. A man isn't in my plans. Maybe I should say "wasn't" in my plans. Now, I..." Melinda wiped off her feet with a tissue and stepped into her heels. "I've been pretending to myself that we are just friends, but we aren't. We're more."

"That's okay by me." Luke picked up his shoes and socks and put his arm around her waist.

Regret filled her face and her voice. "I can't have a relationship with any man."

"Why not? And this better be good." Luke kept his voice jaunty despite his anxiety.

When Melinda fell silent, Luke knew she was analyzing what she wanted to say in her left-brained way, methodically considering each point in order. He hoped she would end up wanting him, in spite of what he supposed would be a list of objections.

Tapping her left index finger with her right, Melinda said, "First, I have to devote my time and energy to my career. A lot of people are depending on me to be successful. I wouldn't feel good about myself if I let them down." She tapped the middle finger. "Second, my goal is to build my own accounting firm and hire Hispanic women. If I can do that, I'll feel like I've made a real contribution. I'm proud to be a Mexican-American." She headed across the plaza toward the intersection.

"I know," Luke followed her, willing to agree with most any of her ideas. Not understanding why, he responded to some primal directive to make her his wife.

"It's important to me to make life better for my people." Melinda touched her ring finger several times, hesitating as if the most important reason were about to come. "Third, there's too much risk, especially with you. I don't want to have children, at least not for a long time, and I know you do."

"We can prevent that. Don't you take the pill?"

From around the corner, several teens drove past with the top down on an old, converted Chevy pickup. They shouted and laughed as they passed the Hyatt Regency. Luke steered Melinda away from the revelers to a park bench beneath a lacy mesquite tree.

As they sat down, Melinda looked despondent. "We've got a lot in common, but the two things we disagree on are critical."

Luke felt happy about this first foray into real communication. If she were embarrassed to talk about sex, they could get back to that later. "Okay. Our timing could be off about kids. What else is a problem?"

"Race."

Finally she'd said it. Luke felt relieved. He'd feared she'd present a problem he didn't know how to field. "Melinda, race isn't even a—"

"I know it doesn't mean anything to you, but it means a great deal to me. Haven't you wondered why I always meet you in public places?" When he nodded, she wrenched the words from her throat. "Because I don't want you to see the house I live in. It's not dirty or anything. Just... well... there are ten of us, and my family is poor." She looked close to tears. "I'm ashamed."

"You don't have to be." Luke drew her to him. "I want to meet your folks, get to know your brothers and sisters. What's it like to live with nine other people in the house?"

"Believe me, you'd hate it. Little stuff drives me nuts, like worrying every morning whether I'll get my turn in the bathroom early enough to get to work on time. But the worst of it is the lack of privacy. Never a minute or a place to be alone. Everybody knows your business." With a wry smile, she pressed his cheeks with her graceful hands. "Know something, Luke, you're the first secret I've ever been able to keep from them."

"They don't know you see me?" Luke didn't know how to feel about being a best-kept secret.

Seeming proud, she straightened and shook her head vigorously. "My dad yells all the time." Melinda's hand fluttered out, then fell into her lap. "And my mom appeases him. She's like a sponge, soaking up his anger. I love them, I guess. Sometimes it doesn't feel like love, though."

Melinda looked so gloomy he wanted to fix her problem. "You're making good money. Why don't you move out?"

"My family needs the rent I pay, just to get by, though my dad's too proud to admit that. Besides, I can't..." A flush rose along her neck and cheeks then died away.

"Why not?" Luke waited but no response came. "Melinda, tell me."

She gazed across the courtyard toward the fountain. "No."

"This is hopeless." Luke quickly put on his shoes and socks. "We were doing so well opening up to each other, but if you can't speak freely, we might as well go home."

When Melinda turned back to Luke, tears welled in her eyes. "Because I'm not what you think I am."

"What do I think you are?" Luke felt annoyed at answers that sounded like evasion.

"My dad won't let me." Melinda looked down at her fingers, twisting her purse strap and said, "Daddy says it's not proper for a..."

Her relationships with her parents seemed a bit immature, but Luke decided to reserve judgment, since he'd only yesterday been dreading the separation from his own mother that he knew he should make. "What? Tell me, Melinda. What's not proper?"

"I can't move out." She took a deep breath and whispered, "I'm still a virgin."

We can fix that, he wanted to say, but he was moved that she told him. The intensity in her face showed the importance of her admission, almost a confession. She was a college graduate making a successful entry into the business world, but deep inside she honored her parents' conventions.

Melinda stirred his heart. Luke wanted to help her feel free to make her own decisions. He took her shoulders in his hands. Her lip quivered, and she looked so tentative he was afraid to kiss her.

"Don't you see?" Melinda asked. "I don't have any choice. I have to stay where I am and help support them, at least until my younger sisters graduate. My dad can't work because of his bad leg, and I've got a lot of ability. I've been blessed with brains and decent looks."

"You're beautiful." Luke wiped tears from her cheeks, dazzled that she could elicit so many emotions from him—desire, compassion, anger, protection.

"I've got the obligation to be successful. For my people."

Luke wished he could relieve her of her burden, self-imposed though it might be. "You can't accept responsibility for a whole race. You're a person in your own right, entitled to live your life."

"But I have to do my part. If I just ran away from my duty to be a role model for my sisters, I could never lift my head up again. I have to be successful for my family and for my race. No matter what the sacrifice. Do you understand?" Melinda looked desperate for his approval.

"Yes, I think I do. Come on, let's go." His arm around her waist, they walked in silence across the concrete plaza, through the intersection, and into the parking lot. Luke held open the door of his Trans-Am, and she sat down. He hurried around the front of the car, proud of the risk she'd taken in telling him about herself. All doubt about his feelings toward her had dissolved.

Sliding in under the wheel, he took a deep breath. "I know how important your career is to you. I love that about you." He caressed her silky hair, which covered her bent head so that he couldn't see her features. "What I need to know is how you feel about me. If you care for me, we can work things out."

After an interminable moment, Melinda shivered and turned toward him, squaring her shoulders. Her onyx eyes glittered in the amber parking lot lights. A small voice belied her intense gaze. "I love you. I didn't want to, but I do."

Luke pulled her to him and held her close. Her hair smelled like Christmas trees. He inhaled the cozy fragrance. "Don't worry. Everything's gonna be okay."

Tilting her head back, he kissed her delicious mouth, sealing his passion with commitment.

Ten

Return of the Soul Traveler

A soft August breeze rustled the palm fronds, which brushed the tiled roof of Ty's bungalow. Broad sun shone through the open bedroom window. Stacks of taped boxes towered on each side of the dresser. In a sheer white gown, Ty's favorite, Angie lay on dusty rose sheets and awakened with no lapse in awareness. Carrying her conscious mind out of the magnificent dream, she rolled toward her dream journal and wrote notes.

Satisfied at capturing the essence of another passion-filled dream, she lay back and stretched, long and lazily. Her body felt rich, sated, like right after sex. She glanced toward Ty's side of the bed, expecting to see him lying asleep beside her, but the pillow lay unhollowed by his head.

With eyes closed, Angie let the images flash through her mind again—the rich texture of the trees, the luminous ambiance of the locale, the consuming sensation of merging with Ty. They had both always believed they had a good sex life, but nothing compared to these exquisite experiences, more fulfilling than any physical lovemaking.

No one could dream such incredible joining. Angie believed Ty had somehow managed to help her enter his world. She thanked God for letting her keep her promise and laughed aloud. Most of the credit should probably go to the Goddess, if there were one.

Suddenly ravenous, Angie hurried to the kitchen, popped a potato in the microwave, and munched cheese and crackers while she cut up salad greens. Breakfast a thing of the past, she lived on a night-shift worker's schedule— active in the dark, sleeping during the day. *Part of the territory with an astral lover,* she mused.

The phone rang. Hooking the receiver under her chin, Angie diced a tomato as she answered.

"Hello, Admiral Mahoney here. How're you?" His usually friendly voice sounded formal and distant.

Over two months had passed since Angie had talked to him. He had never returned her calls about the investigation. Angrily, she refused to tell him anything important. "Okay, and you?"

"Fine, glad to hear it. Mrs. Mahoney and I were wondering if you could come over for dinner Friday evening."

Taken aback, Angie laid the knife on the counter and sat at the small table. "Well, uh, thanks, but I don't think so." Dressing and going out would take a lot of energy. She did not need people for company. "I've got plans." She had not actually told a lie because she wanted to be alone to think of being with Ty and relish her dream life. That seemed like a plan. Gotta have one.

"Well, maybe some other time." The admiral sounded surprised.

"Wait, don't hang up." Angie doubted she could believe much he said now. "What happened about the investigation of the plane crash?"

"Funny you should ask." Admiral Mahoney, Ty's so-called best friend, cleared his throat. "I just got a memo about it. Seems the original manufacturer of the fuel tanks developed some problems with this particular model. They've since gone out of business."

Shocked, Angie shouted, "You mean to tell me Ty died because of a mistake?"

"We'll take all the others out of service, of course." No doubt, the admiral knew his words fell far short of consolation, but what could he say? What could anyone say?

Anguish about Ty's death felt suddenly fresh again, energized by anger. "I was right, after all." It felt good to vent on the appropriate person, to have an object for her frustration. "I told that damned Jamison the truth, and he treated me like a criminal."

"Sorry, Angie." The admiral's words sounded genuine for the first time. "I warned him to leave you alone after that trip he made to Phoenix."

"But he hasn't. His flunky is still parked in front of my house. What are you going to do about that?"

With an apology and a promise to handle Jamison, the admiral said good-bye.

Dissatisfied, Angie wondered exactly what role the admiral had played in the investigation. Perhaps she would never know. The idea that Ty's death resulted from some mechanic's mistake appalled her. Laying her head down on the breakfast table, Angie sobbed, her lunch forgotten.

In the next few days, she cared less and less what became of Ty's possessions. She came to love the sound of soft footfalls as she lay in bed, half asleep. Her earlier fear of an intruder seemed laughable now. Angie felt safe in the house and in her dreams.

One morning she wrote in her dream journal:

> *Ty came to me and held me for a long time. Then we flew up into the sky. There were stars all around us. It was pitch dark, but I wasn't afraid. I knew Ty would be with me. This was my world, too. I felt safe. I took off fast and he flew after me. We were laughing and thinking enchanting thoughts to each other about exploring.*

The phone rang as she finished writing. She hesitated to answer, not wanting to talk to Mahoney again. Yet, someone might be calling about buying the Mustang, so she took a chance and picked up the receiver.

"Hi, Mom." Luke's clear, loveable voice came over the line. "What's goin' on?"

"I just woke up." Sitting up, Angie pulled the sheet up to her throat, abashed at talking to her son while lying naked in bed.

"At eleven o'clock? Hmmm. Ask me what's new in my life."

Relieved that he had not asked her to justify sleeping late, she played his game. "Okay, what's new in your life?"

"A woman... a gorgeous new woman. I'm in love."

Angie laughed at his enthusiasm. How much she missed her son.

He went merrily on, "This is it, Mom. She's great. Her name's Melinda. You're gonna love her."

"I'm sure I will." Actually, Angie had not had much opportunity to get to know his girlfriends. They never lasted very long. "How're you doing? Taking your medicine?"

"Don't worry." Luke's voice had a don't-nag-me tone.

"Not one slip-up?"

"Never again. When you comin' home? I want you to meet Melinda."

"Uh... not sure." Would the nighttime visits cease if Angie returned to Phoenix?

Ever insightful, Luke asked, "What's keepin' you there?"

"Plenty of people looking at the house, but no offers yet," Angie stalled.

"That's what you've got a realtor for." His grownup logic turned into boyish pleading. "Come on home."

Luke was right. The situation no longer required her presence in San Diego. Angie hung up with a promise to call when she had a departure date.

The phone rang again immediately. She chuckled, thinking real happiness lay in cutting off the phone service. The realtor wanted to show the house that afternoon.

Donning shorts and tank top, Angie went for a walk along the bay. On the warm, calm afternoon, the water glistened in shades of blue. Gentle waves lapped the rocky shoreline, and pelicans picked up "tourist droppings," as Ty called food scraps. Many people picnicked along the water, and a few boaters struggled to keep wind in their sails.

A day for "clean and repair," Ty used to say. Angie remembered teasing him about his compulsion for keeping the *Destiny* in perfect trim. Funny how that thought did not make her sad any more with the new turn their lives had taken. Their flight together last night felt joyous. Their love sustained her, their lovemaking more real than these boats out here in the bay.

Angie hated to withhold her newfound ability to astral travel from Luke. They'd always been honest and open with each other, but she did not want to tell anyone and risk ridicule that she might not have the strength to counter. She could not justify or explain what happened in a believable way. If someone else had told Angie of such a visitation from the dead, she might have doubted, calling it lucid-dreaming at best or self-delusion at worst.

These experiences, she hesitated to call them dreams, seemed unlike any others before, even the vision of the plane crash. Ty seemed actually present with her, his mind and heart intact, the same as in the hospital, only more completely. Angie refused to let other people's inevitable doubts, even her own son's, diminish her belief. She intended to keep this contact with Ty pure and preserve its sacredness.

Much she did not understand. There were moments when a timeless quality entered in, snapshots of the past and the future. Once Ty came to her in a tunic, carrying some kind of musical instrument like a guitar. He had laughed and asked if she recognized him. Another time he looked a bit like a soldier from the American Revolution. Angie even had flashes of herself wearing long dresses, cooking at a fireplace, or praying in the open air.

Wondering whether Ty knew more answers now than she had questions to ask, Angie felt curious about his days. Did he walk with her now, even without her awareness, or did he go off, doing other things?

That night, she fell asleep, repeating her nightly litany: "I am awake and aware. I am one with Ty."

The next morning, she wrote in her dream journal:

I blinked and turned, forgetting that I could see all the way around me. I passed through tall doors into a foyer with a golden floor. An archway opened onto a wide staircase.

Ty floated toward me, the light around him dim, his colors dusky. He held out his arms. I went to him, expecting to merge in the sparkling spray of light. Seeming morose, he held me to him.

"I love you, my darling." His meaning came into my mind.

Enchanted anew that we could read each other's thoughts, I relayed to him, "I love you, too, and am so glad we can be together like this."

Ty's melancholy smile told me he understood. "I must say good-bye to you for a while."

"Oh, no! Oh, why?"

"I have to go to a place you can't follow."

"Please, don't go." I clung to him.

"I must. It's part of my learning. And part of yours." Ty's thought seemed gentle but carried finality.

"I don't understand." I stalled to keep from hearing another good-bye.

"It's more difficult to come to you each night. It takes all my energy. I have to let go for a while. I'm sorry."

"I'm afraid I'll never see you again," I pleaded, feeling hopeless.

For a moment, Ty looked completely colorless, as if he were dissolving. Then he thought to me with great sadness. "I promise, my darling, we'll find each other again."

"Tell me how." I felt compelled to understand. I had a sense that the responsibility for our next meeting would rest on me.

"I wish I knew." Ty seemed fragmented as if his energy had weakened even more. "Have to go. So sorry."

We clung together in shimmering soft lights for a long moment, then he turned toward the stairs and floated away—a muted cobalt light, fading.

The next day the realtor called to say a couple had made an offer of the asking price on the house, something Angie should not turn down. They wanted to take possession as soon as the title company could close escrow, hopefully within the next two weeks. As Angie hung up the phone, she felt jarred by the intruding reality of the house sale, too much to absorb.

Lying back in the bed, she closed her eyes, remembering the dream meeting with Ty. The intensity of saying good-bye to him had sapped her energy. Why was this happening, just when she had found him again? She did not want to go on living in this world while he went on in the next. Their life together had been one long series of good-byes.

Only one lesson could Angie salvage. Death was not the barrier she once believed it to be. They'd breached it, though she could not define the reality—dreams, visitation from the dead, or living on the astral plane. They were together in some kind of bodies in a place she could not name, but that did not mean it did not have one.

"I'll bet I'm not the only person to ever have such experiences," Angie said aloud. "I'll find someone who knows about them. I can figure out how to get back to you if I have some help, Ty. You said it was possible. What were your words? 'I promise we'll find each other again.' Well, I believe you. I'll find another way."

Eleven

A Palpable Sorrow

The first few days after Ty's house sold, Angie fooled herself into thinking that her nightly rendezvous with his spirit would go on. Ty did not come into her dreams again. Unwilling to settle for memories, she intended to find some way to make him a part of this life though so far at a loss to know how. Realistically, Angie had to put some of the grief behind her to go on living, to strike some kind of balance between searching for Ty and playing a part in her son's future.

Angie needed to go home. Because Luke usually played golf on Saturdays, then went out with his friends or on a date, he probably would not be home before midnight. Angie decided not to call so she could surprise him.

By two o'clock that afternoon, hot and tired, she parked the car in her driveway in Phoenix, turned off the ignition, and sighed with relief. Never again did she intend to drive nonstop from San Diego in one hundred fifteen degree weather, even though she rivaled Luke's lead foot in making a record time of five hours.

Angie realized how much she had missed her son and their little home. The house looked the same, the yard bare. Luke had trimmed the palo verde tree, leaving dried and wilted rosebushes and a meager few petunias that had been scorched by the sun. The shutters were closed, probably to keep the house cool.

Although she had just turned off the engine, it took only minutes for the air-conditioned interior to become sweltering. Angie hurried out of the car, popped open the trunk, and grabbed two suitcases, leaving the rest until after a tall iced tea.

When she unlocked the front door, she heard a rustling noise that she could not identify in the darkened interior of the living room. "Luke, is that you?"

"Mom? Hi." Sunlight streamed through the open doorway. Luke and a young woman scrambled up from the couch, he pulling his shirt down, she adjusting her long hair with an embarrassed giggle. "I didn't know you were coming home today." With a foolish smile, Luke moved toward Angie. "It's good to see you."

As mother and son hugged, the beautiful stranger stepped toward Luke and put her hand on his shoulder with an air of ownership. "Luke?" Her perfectly shaped black eyebrow lifted, demanding an introduction.

Luke squeezed the young woman's waist. When he grinned, his face looked brighter and more mature than Angie had ever seen it. "Mom, I'd like you to meet Melinda Chacon. Melinda, my mother." The pride and love in his voice gave evidence of a strong bond. How could that have happened in only two months?

A radiant smile spread across Melinda's face as she took Angie's hand in both of hers and held it tightly. "Mrs. Brock, I'm happy to meet you."

Melinda's warm touch magnetized Angie, as though pulling her into a vortex. Gazing into the younger woman's eyes, Angie became hypnotized by their inky depth.

As if entering a dream, Angie lost awareness of the people and the room around her. She focused her inner eyes on a sepia-toned scene, its colors muted brown, and saw a vision.

Melinda ran down a silent street where fog floated, damp and ominous. Hair streamed out behind her. She wore a bronze raincoat and carried a fawn-colored bundle, so large she clutched it in both arms. Burnished gold hair clung to Luke's face. He stood before an empty house. His shoulders sagged as if he despaired to see Melinda go.

Like a lost child, the crying wind swirled the fog mournfully about his legs.

A palpable sorrow wrenched Angie's heart, and she sobbed aloud.

"Mom, what's the matter?"

"Mrs. Brock, are you all right?"

Angie tore her attention away from the alarming scene in her mind and freed her hand from the young woman's grip. "So sorry. Don't know what came over me." She hesitated to tell them she had witnessed some kind of psychic event, just what remained a mystery. Ridding herself of the sadness it provoked would require time alone. "It's very nice to meet you. Please excuse me." Angie grabbed the suitcases and headed toward the stairs.

"Mom, don't go."

"Sorry, honey," Angie muttered as she passed through the dining room.

"Let me carry these." Luke took the suitcases and followed her upstairs to her room where he set them on the bed. Concern in his voice, he asked, "Are you okay? What happened?"

"Yes, I'm fine." The last thing Angie needed was to have to talk to him with his new girlfriend waiting downstairs, no doubt considerably confused. "Go on back to your friend. I'll be down in a little bit."

"You're sure?"

"Positive. Go on. We'll talk later, okay?" Angie squeezed his hand then closed the door after him.

Shedding her clothes as quickly as possible, she stood in the shower, letting cold water blast her skin. The psychic impressions had caught her off guard and assaulted her with a grief not her own. She felt certain the emotions belonged to her son. Whether his from the past or in the future Angie could not determine because of the unrealistic quality of the vision, almost a metaphor.

Wrapping herself in a chenille robe, Angie sat in the wooden rocker. The chair's motion and familiar creak calmed her. Perhaps the relationship between Luke and Melinda would end badly. Or, Melinda might plan to steal something from him. The muted colors suggested foreboding.

When would the girl go home so Angie and Luke could talk? Angie had looked forward to spending time with him, like they used to, and resented having to share his attention immediately. She reminded herself to watch the little jealousy pup nipping at her heart. Everything in her world and her son's had changed recently and would take some getting used to.

The adoration on Luke's face when he introduced Melinda reminded Angie of the way Ty had looked at her. As a mother, she hoped that Luke would feel the same joy in a relationship. Because she did not know what the melancholy vision meant, Angie felt alarmed and decided not to say anything until she understood better. Had she embarrassed him? Melinda probably thought her a total kook. Something about the young woman, a hint of antagonism and vengefulness, seemed most distasteful. Aware of more neediness in herself since Ty's death, Angie hoped her own jealousy had not provoked the vision.

In fresh shorts and blouse, Angie went downstairs to find Luke and Melinda sitting close together at the dining room table, heads touching over the newspaper. He read the comics to her, just as Angie had entertained him as a child until he learned to read and took over the task. Melinda laughed and seemed to enjoy his cartoon voices.

"Sorry I zoned out on you two," Angie said. "Guess I let myself get too tired from the trip."

"Go to the Bahamas, did you, Mom?" Luke kissed her cheek.

"Are you feeling better, Mrs. Brock?"

"Please call me 'Angie.' Yes, much. Thanks." Angie moved a stack of books from a dining room chair and sat down at the table, observing with chagrin the piles of newspapers, notepads, and books on the tabletop. Luke considered drawers enemies of the state. Attempting to deflect her feelings of disapproval, Angie glanced around the room and noticed her favorite Gauguin print had been replaced with a new Jazz on the Rocks poster. "Been to Sedona, have you?"

"What?" Luke cast the newspaper on the top of a stack.

Angie nodded at the poster. "To the Jazz Festival?"

"Yeah. Melinda'd never been there before."

"Really?" Poignant memories came to Angie of many warm evenings sitting on a hillside surrounded by the awesome red rocks, listening to jazz in the open air. The concert had been the highlight of many summers for Angie and Luke. Then, she had treated Ty to the event. Now Luke had taken Melinda. "How'd you like it?" Angie asked.

"Very much, thank you." Melinda said, rubbing his hand. "Thoughtful of Luke to take me."

"It was Melinda's idea to put the print on the wall, kind of a memento of a wonderful evening, huh, babe?" Luke kissed her cheek, just as he had Angie's.

His term of endearment was a poignant reminder of Ty's for Angie.

Parting perfectly formed lips, Melinda smiled at Luke, probably acknowledging some private moment. She said to Angie, "Hope you don't mind. We can put your print back up, if you prefer."

"Not at all. This looks good." Angie thought it might be well to guard against other surprises this new girlfriend might present. Angie walked into the kitchen, stretching her back. "Could I interest the two of you in some dinner?"

She opened the refrigerator door and surveyed the sparse contents, two beers and a doughnut box, not even any iced tea. "On second thought, how about ordering pizza?"

Luke said, "Fine by—"

"Thanks, anyway, we have to be going." Melinda spoke quickly.

Surprise crossed Luke's face.

Melinda must have noticed it, too, because she stood and leaned over him. Her breasts lay against his shoulders as she whispered in his ear.

"Oh, I forgot," Luke said. "Let's call and cancel, now that Mom's home. Furrowing her dark brow, Melinda shook her head in a manner that indicated the importance of their plans. Luke looked apologetically at Angie. "Guess we'll be taking off. We've got dinner reservations and we're meeting some friends afterward."

"That's a shame." Angie felt put off. Melinda seemed to have some strong ideas, but it would be good to try to avoid judgment. "I was hoping to get to know Melinda."

"Some other time." A bit too abruptly, the young woman flipped her hair and walked toward the door.

Giving Angie a quick hug, Luke said, "It's great to have you back. Don't wait up."

Stifling a yawn, Melinda held the door open while he passed through it. She flashed her brilliant smile, walked to Angie, and shook her hand formally but politely. "Very nice to meet you, Mrs. Brock."

Angie could not resist looking into Melinda's eyes again to see if another vision came, but she could not make eye contact. All the windows were closed and the blinds carefully drawn inside the young woman's mind. Whatever had passed between them, Melinda had sensed it, too.

Early the next morning, Angie found her clippers and went outside. Hopefully, the cool breeze would continue until seven or eight, the best time to do yard work. Because he arrived home late the night before, Luke was sleeping in, and she wanted him to have a quiet house.

Her rosebushes always suffered from the late summer heat but were more pitifully bedraggled because she had neglected them this year. Luke did not have her green thumb. His taste ran more to cacti and ironwood trees, plants that could survive on their own in the desert.

As she trimmed off the dead pink and yellow blossoms, Angie wondered how committed her son actually felt to Melinda. What had she thought of Angie? Undoubtedly the young woman had noticed something awry. Perhaps that explained her eagerness to leave so suddenly.

The crackle of the opening garage door startled Angie. Luke backed his Trans-Am into the driveway. Leaping out clad in a swimsuit, he hosed down both his car and Angie's.

"It's fun to be doing Sunday chores with you." Angie went into the garage and moved clay pots, searching for rose food and the hand shovel.

"Oh, you just say that because I'm such a fascinating guy." Luke flashed the hose spray on her, laughing when she sputtered.

Enjoying the cool water on her warm skin, Angie noticed that he teased her in the same old way, but she sensed a new maturity about him, a sureness he had lacked before she left for San Diego that awful weekend. She remembered his seizure and his immature attitude about going off his medication. At the time, she had believed he could not cope alone. So much had changed she found it difficult to believe only three months had passed.

"I want you and Melinda to get to know each other." Luke looked happy, like he was in love.

"Me too, I'll cook dinner for her sometime."

"Tonight too soon?" Luke's tousled blond hair fell over his brow charmingly.

"That'll be fine. I'll go to the grocery right away."

Luke shut off the hose, came to her, and draped his arm around her shoulders. "Sit down here a minute and talk to me." They sat on the soft grass. "What happened when you met Melinda?"

"Just tired from my trip," Angie said, feeling uncomfortable. "I told you."

"Mom, you think I was born yesterday?" His broad, tanned chest had already begun to gleam with perspiration. "You saw something, felt something. However you say it, you blanked out. Tell me what happened."

Angie picked dirt off the shovel. "I don't really know." His intense gaze made her regret that she had worried him, but she did not know how to avoid doing so. "You're right I saw something, but I don't know how to interpret it."

"What do you mean?"

"The images were muted. You and Melinda, maybe a long time ago."

"How can that be? I've just known her a few weeks."

"I know you've never had much of an interest in this," Angie said, "but maybe you knew her in a past life."

With a quick, uncomfortable laugh, Luke dropped his arm from her shoulder.

"Let's forget about it, if you're going to be that closed-minded." Angie felt annoyed with herself for taking offense so quickly. She walked to her car, picked up a spray bottle and roll of paper towels, and scrubbed bug juice off the windows.

Luke took the bottle of cleaner out of her hand. "For God's sake, Mom."

When in doubt, say the truth. That rule had worked for her many times in her life. Setting the roll of towels on the roof of her car, Angie wiped her forehead. The warming day and her agitation made her feel sticky. "I saw Melinda running away from you, carrying something. Maybe stealing something."

"Naw."

"See, I don't know how to interpret it. If I did, I'd tell you. It was different from seeing Ty's plane." Angie shuddered, her eyes misting at the memory. "That was clear, precise, exactly like it really happened. What I saw in Melinda's eyes confused me."

Folding his arms, Luke shook his head. "She sure called this one right."

"What'd she say?" Angie did not like the scowl forming on her son's face.

"Lots of her relatives see spirits and have visitations and such." Luke waved a dismissing arm and leaned against his car. "One of her aunts even claimed to see the Virgin Mary in the backyard."

"Then she understands?"

"Melinda wants to get away from psychic stuff. She says it holds people back." Luke seemed clearly more concerned about Melinda's negative opinion than about the truth or falsity of the vision.

"Holds them back from what?" Angie asked. When he did not answer, she went on. "Tell me what you think the vision meant."

"Mom, don't talk about this tonight, okay?"

Angie sensed he had given his loyalty to Melinda and felt shut out. "I didn't want to talk about it at all. You dragged this much out of me."

"Sorry, I did." Voice sharp, Luke stared at her. "Sometimes I wish you were a normal mother. Why does everything with you have to be some big dramatic event— visions and prophecies of the future and airplane crashes? It's all so complicated. Makes people nervous. Melinda's no different."

What had become of the son who so zealously tried to protect her from Jamison and the Air Force investigation? Frustrated, Angie shot back, "You should be used to me."

"Oh, I am." Luke's hearty laugh dissolved some of the hurt in his words. "It's just tough to deal with sometimes.

People think you're spooky. Makes me feel like we're not normal. Other times I'm proud of you for being true to yourself." He sighed. "Guess the real problem is I'm undecided about what I believe."

"I know how you feel." Angie relaxed against the side of the car. Maybe they could talk about this situation after all. "I don't understand the process. All I know for sure is information comes to me. I worry about whether to tell people. Ty ignored me, and I begged him not to get on that plane. Now, I don't know what to tell you—stay away from Melinda, she's bad for you?"

Luke's chin went up. "You're out of line there, Mom."

Patting his arm, Angie wanted to take his tension away. "No, honey, I didn't mean you should. I don't even know if what I saw was a warning. Maybe I just saw pictures of the future or the past without being able to change them. Hope I get some answers from... uh... the new experiences I've been having."

"What experiences? Tell me about 'em."

"You sure you want to know?" Angie thought he winced, but he nodded. Nervous, she almost wished he had said no. Why had she brought up the subject anyway? Wishing she had time to plan her words more carefully, she sat on the lawn and wrapped her arms around her knees. "Something happened in San Diego, more than dreams." She told him about the episode where her brother and Ty seemed vivid, then the noises in the house, calling the police, her belief that Ty was physically present and that she had communicated with him.

Sitting beside her, Luke idly triggered the spray bottle. He listened without interrupting, but his face grew more and more grim. When she finished, he got up, grabbed the paper towels, and briskly cleaned his windshield. "That's a lot to swallow. You must've had the experiences because you wouldn't lie to me. I just don't know what to think."

"It's okay, honey." Her son was slipping away, just when she needed his belief and support.

"Dreams I can accept because I've had some myself. In fact, I had one that solved an important problem for me while you were gone."

"Really? Tell me about it." Angie followed him around the Trans-Am.

"Some other time." Luke industriously cleaned the rear window then turned to Angie with determination on his face. "Visions are stretching it for me, though I know you've always had them. But this? Dead people actually showing up in your house? That's overboard... you can't really believe Ty was there in the flesh."

"I'm positive. We were together somehow, maybe not physically, but I could touch him, talk to him. I intend to have that again. Whatever it takes. He said it was possible."

With a sarcastic grin, Luke tossed the soggy paper towels in the dumpster. "Mom?"

Even though the conversation had taken a bad turn, Angie believed she might as well get everything out. What more could she lose? "I'm going to look for Ty. I'll find him. I just don't know how to accomplish it right now."

"How can you look for him?" Luke's voice rose angrily. "He's dead. Admit it."

Heedless of neighbors who might overhear, Angie shouted, "I'll find a medium. Or somebody."

"This is crazy." Luke slammed the paper towel roll and plastic bottle on the worktable in the garage.

"Don't say that. I'm not crazy." Grabbing her tools, Angie stomped into the garage and slammed them against the wall so hard two rakes fell down. "Shit." She knelt to retrieve them.

As Luke hung the rakes back on their nails, he asked in a more reasonable tone, "Have you thought about going back to work? Maybe you could get your old job back at the high school. Might be good for you."

"I'm fine." Having lost all patience, Angie put her hands on her hips. "There'll be money from Ty's estate when it's settled, enough to support me for a while."

"What'll you do all day? You can't sit around the house by yourself."

Angie glared into his mottled eyes, and he looked straight back into hers. She felt no wavering in herself and saw none in him. "I'm going to contact Ty. Somehow."

"You know I really don't get this change in you." Luke folded his arms. "Always before you worried about what people would think and distrusted your visions. Where did this flip-flop come from?"

The same idea had bothered Angie. Her perceptions of herself changed daily. Grief dug into her soul in ways she had yet to understand. "I can't deny my reality anymore, son. This is who I am."

A note of pleading crept into Luke's voice. "People are gonna think you're nuts."

"You mean Melinda will?" Angie spoke with steely annoyance at the intrusion of this new girlfriend. "Or you?"

"Give it up, Mom. Please."

Kicking open the back gate, Angie plunged into the pool. She heard Luke's car start and drive away. Head down, she swam back and forth, churning the water until her arms ached.

Twelve

Meeting the Enemy

Angie set the scarlet ceramic salad bowl in the center of the dining room table, adjusted a rosette-folded napkin, and stepped back to take a long view of the dishes—turquoise for Melinda, orange for Luke, and yellow for her. Bright, maybe even a bit gaudy, but Grandma's Fiestaware gave just the right blend of family tradition and modern styling and would look even better on Ty's oak table when it arrived. Angie wished he were here to meet Melinda. Thinking of setting his place at the table caused her to miss him anew.

Upstairs, Luke whistled while he showered and changed clothes for dinner. Even if he had disappointed Angie earlier by not accepting her explanation of Ty's nighttime visits, it pleased her that Luke questioned things. That made him a good student of life and less gullible than the average person. If he believed in the possibility of finding Ty, her search would be easier, but she did not have to have her son's support or anyone else's. Nothing could stop her.

Back in the kitchen, Angie picked up the pan lid and stirred the simmering pasta sauce, breathing in the spicy fragrance of tomatoes mixed with bay and oregano. Luke came up behind her and put his arms around her waist, hooking his chin on her shoulder.

Angie turned to him, leaving the lid ajar. "Didn't know you were there."

"Sorry I was a shit this morning," Luke said, hugging her. "Forgive me?"

"Oh, all right." Angie gave him a squeeze then held him at arm's length and looked into his clear eyes. "But I've not changed my mind. I intend to find Ty, and I'd like your understanding, at least."

"I know. The whole idea makes me nervous, but I promise not to interfere. Will you settle for that?"

"Guess I'll have to."

"Okay." Releasing her, Luke walked to the front window and peered out. "Wait'll you get to know Melinda. You're really gonna like her."

"I'm sure I will." Angie wished she felt more certain.

Opening the front door, Luke leaned against it, smiling. "Here she comes."

When a car door slammed, Angie turned off the burner under the marinara sauce. Luke and Melinda's voices rose together in a greeting. The young woman's high heels clicked across the parquet floor of the living room. *Here goes,* Angie thought, as she went to meet them.

Striking in a crimson sundress, Melinda grasped Angie's hand firmly, shook it, and withdrew her own quickly. "Nice to see you again, Mrs. Brock. Thank you for inviting me." Her smile was wide, but her presence controlled. No more psychic impressions from her. She had shut Angie out.

"I'm glad you could come." Angie turned back to the kitchen.

"Need any help, Mom?"

"Why don't you serve drinks?"

Luke stirred margaritas while Angie brought chilled glasses from the kitchen. They all sat down in the living room, Luke on the couch with Melinda beside him, Angie perched on the edge of a wingback chair while Luke poured the drinks. Everyone sat silently, looking at the antipasto on the coffee table. After a moment, Luke told Melinda about his golf game that afternoon.

Nibbling a cheese cube, Melinda asked, "Do you play golf, Mrs. Brock?"

"Call me 'Angie,' please. No, I tried but wasn't very good at it. Do you?"

"Yes, a bit." Melinda smiled shyly. "My company holds a tournament every year."

"She came in second in her first competition," Luke bragged.

Laughing, Melinda tapped his arm affectionately. "Luke is such a good PR man. If he worked for my company, he'd be a vice president already."

"Don't let her fool you, Mom, she's good." Luke's face beamed his pride.

So far the evening was going well. "What kind of work do you do?" Angie asked as she picked up a rye cracker.

"Accounting." Again, Melinda seemed shy, even though glad to talk about herself. "Get my CPA in another year."

"Congratulations," Angie said, "that's quite an accomplishment."

"What'd you expect from a U of A grad?" Luke leaned back against the flowered cushion, pulling Melinda with him, and sipped his drink. She flushed.

"Did you know each other at the U?" Angie turned the uneaten cracker over in her hand. She felt just anxious enough about the evening's outcome to lose her appetite.

"No," Luke said, "sorry to say we didn't."

Melinda grinned. "Well, sort of. From afar, let's say."

Although Luke blushed, another knowing look passed between them, more shared memories. They were attuned enough to make the color rise in each other's faces. Angie remembered in high school she blushed every time Ty said her name.

"Excuse me. I'd better check the dinner." Angie glanced at her untasted margarita and headed toward the kitchen. When she turned to ask if they'd like their drinks freshened, Luke held Melinda's chin and touched his lips to hers.

Angie looked away quickly, feeling like a spy. He looked so manly, her boy gone forever. A little afraid of being left out of his heart, she reminded herself to get used to second place and wondered if he had felt the same way about Ty.

After mixing the pasta and sauce, she set the bowl on the table with a platter of tangy garlic bread then called Melinda and Luke into the dining room. Sitting, Angie stared at her yellow plate, hoping she could come up with some dinner table topics.

"Smells great, Mom." Luke pulled a chair out for Melinda.

"Why, thank you, good sir," Melinda said and sat down.

Over salad, Luke regaled them with stories of his infamous coworker, Ted, who had recently become crude and uncouth on the job. At least five women, both secretaries and lawyers, had grounds for sexual harassment suits against Ted, one maybe even a paternity suit. In any case, he definitely created a lot of work for a good lawyer, but Luke was not willing to lower himself to take Ted's case.

Enjoying his exaggerations, Angie laughed and turned to Melinda. "Since kindergarten, he's been entertaining me with tales of the no-good-niks in his classes. Now that he's grown up, he has to work with them, too?"

"What can you do?" Luke shrugged. "They're everywhere. You had a bunch of them at your school."

"Luke told me you're a high school teacher," Melinda said. "Are you intending to teach this year?"

Envisioning all the class preparation, meetings, and unruly students seemed overwhelming to Angie. "No, I don't think so."

Black eyes clear, Melinda held her gaze. "Not enough time gone by?"

Surprised at such a casual mention of Ty's death, Angie wondered how much Luke had told her and mumbled, "Maybe next year."

"You're' doing great." Luke patted Angie on the shoulder. "I'm proud of you." He turned to Melinda. "I forgot to tell you, Ty's house sold."

"Bet you're glad of that. Sorry about your... bereavement." Melinda's tone seemed far more casual than her words. She also knew a great deal about Angie's business, so Luke obviously trusted her.

"Thanks." Angie felt guarded, not understanding Melinda well at all but willing to give her the benefit of the doubt for Luke's sake.

"Dinner's great, Mom." Luke twirled pasta in his spoon.

"Thanks. More garlic bread?" Angie offered the platter.

Shaking her head so that the dark waves of her hair flipped, Melinda laid down her fork and leaned toward Angie, resting her chin on her palm, as if fascinated by Angie's ideas. "Do you think it's easier to deal with death or divorce, Mrs. Brock?"

Angie had almost said "call me 'Angie'" again but did not particularly want such familiarity. Remaining formal seemed safer.

Had Melinda purposely tried to be hurtful? Her face, flawless as a makeup ad, betrayed no clue about her intention in asking such a question.

"I mean at the end of a relationship?" Melinda continued casually, as if discussing split ends. "My mother always says divorce is the worst thing that could happen. Since you've had both... I just wondered how you'd compare them."

What the hell was going on here? Angie felt as if she were being grilled by a student testing her to find out the limits of her classroom control. A glance at Luke gave no hint of his perception of this type of questioning. He appeared intent on refilling his plate with pasta.

Melinda averted her eyes and shrugged. "If you don't ask, you can't find out."

"Well." Angie coughed to stall for time. She did not want to act rude or embarrass Luke but could not let Melinda get away with such effrontery. "I guess that would depend on the person. Dealing with the guilt and embarrassment of a divorce is a far different experience from grieving over the death of someone you love, at least in my mind. Have you ever had a loss, Miss Chacon?"

"No, can't say I have." Melinda smiled at Luke as he gave her another approving glance and patted her hand.

"If you had," Angie said, trying to keep an angry edge out of her voice, "perhaps you'd have an awareness of how vulnerable we all really are."

"Maybe." Melinda cocked her eyebrow.

The young woman might be what she presented herself as, a naive gatherer of information, not unkind, just insensitive. Angie opted for that conclusion. "It's not what happens to you that's important, it's how you deal with it that makes the difference."

"That's good." Luke grinned as if Angie's words carried more meaning than armchair philosophy.

"How'd you deal with the divorce, Luke?" Melinda asked. "Was it a problem for you?"

"I was only three. Can't remember."

"Did you know your dad at all?" Melinda had a knack for hitting nerves in the guise of interest.

"Huh-uh." Luke glanced down. That old hurt would probably always stay with him.

Luke's father had been too cowardly to face the demands of the boy's epilepsy. Remembering her own outrage when her husband deserted them, Angie felt stung anew by the lack of support from her family. Bobby ignored the situation, and Barbara preferred to disapprove of Angie's decision to divorce, afraid of what the neighbors would think, as usual. Nice Indiana girls did not get

121

divorces, according to her mother, but Angie refused to play the long-suffering martyr.

In those days she had believed she would never see Ty again though longed for him. Starting over seemed her most appealing option, so Angie sent out applications and had offers for three jobs, all in Arizona. How afraid she had been of leaving her home and driving across the continent with her frail son to face life alone in a new place! Even now, she felt pride in herself for making the right decisions, both for herself and for Luke. He had thrived in the western desert, and she had finally felt free to be her own person. There was no way to make Melinda understand all of that.

"We both dealt with the divorce well," Angie said. "It was the smartest thing I've ever done." She wondered what motivated the girl to ask.

As if in answer to his mother's thought, Luke said, "Inquisitive, isn't she?"

More like insolent, Angie thought, then noticed Luke's confused frown and guessed she had not hidden her irritation. She offered a smile in the hope of convincing him of a sincerity she did not feel.

Luke kissed Melinda's cheek, then Angie's. "My two favorite gals."

Why had Luke fallen in love with a young woman so different from the others he had dated? Perhaps Melinda's unusual qualities blinded him to her brashness because he was usually much more insightful. Now, Angie must swallow her need for him and encourage his freedom to make choices, even if she disapproved of them. She refused to be like Barbara and would support Luke, no matter what.

While Angie served cheesecake dripped with cherry sauce, Luke told a story about his soccer team. After the tasty dessert, they cleared the table. Luke and Melinda decided to see a movie and invited Angie along, but she declined, saying she had not recovered from the drive from

San Diego, an excuse only partially true. Tense from the ordeal of meeting Melinda, Angie needed time to absorb so many new thoughts and emotions.

Melinda flashed her glorious smile, and the two young people left with profuse thanks for the dinner.

Confident of Melinda's response, Luke closed the passenger-side car door and leaned in the window. "Well, what'd you think of her? Neat, isn't she?"

"Your mother's very nice." Melinda smiled sweetly.

"Yes. One down." Luke thumped the hood of the car as he jogged around to the driver's side. Dinner went fine, maybe a bit stiff and formal, but Melinda probably felt a little nervous, and Angie certainly was not herself. In time, his two gals would get along just great.

Luke wanted to make the evening romantic. He put the car in gear and headed toward downtown.

"Thought we were going to Metro Center to a movie." Melinda looked ravishing in her red dress. Her eyes shimmered enticingly in the headlights of oncoming traffic.

"Got a better plan. Do you mind?" Luke doubted she would, since Melinda always seemed to respond to his ideas.

"No. What is it?"

"You'll find out." Turning on the radio, he beat the dashboard in time with the music and sneaked a peek at Melinda, who looked at him questioningly. Luke enjoyed keeping her in suspense and thought she liked it, too.

Arriving at the fountain at the Civic Plaza, they dangled their feet in the water. Luke kissed her, enjoying the touch of her warm lips and bare shoulders. Melinda did not resist him anymore but responded passionately and trustingly. He would not be able to keep his hands off her much longer.

Pulling back from their embrace, he fondled her perfect, red nails. "I want to meet your folks, babe."

"Aw, why?" Melinda looked cute when she pouted, like she must have as a child. She probably only hesitated out of fear that he would disapprove of her folks. But, if she loved them, he would, too.

"Turnabout's fair play. Besides, I've got something to ask them."

Eyeing him with mock distrust, Melinda asked, "What?" Smart as she was, she had probably already guessed what he intended to ask.

"If they'll let you marry me." Luke found this proposing heady stuff. "Think they will?"

With an expression of surprise, Melinda moved across the fountain's stone bench. "I can't get married. My career." Her old resistance had faded as her love for him had grown. Her teasing tone of voice gave her away.

Luke plunged ahead with conviction. "You said you couldn't have a relationship, but you sure as hell have one with me." Trying to look serious in spite of a growing sense of delight, he took her hand. "I not only think we can get married, I think we should."

"You do? Why?" Her broad smile left no doubt that she wanted to marry him.

"Actually, for three reasons." Imitating her characteristic mannerism, Luke held up one finger and said, "First, we could cut down on the number of cold showers we both have to take," then another finger, "Second, you could get away from home and live with someone who understands you."

"And?" Melinda's face glowed with fond indulgence.

"And, three, Miss Career Accountant, we love each other." Luke took her in his arms and kissed her gently. She melted into him as she never before had. His hands suddenly trembled as he whispered in her ear, "So what do you say, babe? Is it a go?"

"Wednesday night," Melinda murmured, her hair soft against his face.

"So soon?" Luke tried to stay calm.

"Meet my folks Wednesday night. Ask my dad. If he says yes, I will, too." Melinda's excited whisper made her sound like a conspirator. "You can make him say yes, if anybody can."

Luke feared his chest would break from the surging love in his heart.

Meanwhile, relieved that Luke and Melinda had gone, Angie lay on the couch with a magazine across her lap and closed her eyes, listening to the dishwasher hum in the quiet house.

Strange young woman Luke had found. Angie could not get a fix on her. Polite, but cold, almost cruel. Why did she ask such personal questions? She reminded Angie of some students, ones from dysfunctional homes, who failed to develop any tact. Melinda might not realize her questions were offensive. Maybe she had not had enough social experience.

On the other hand, being involved with the only son of a single mother might scare her. Possibly, she saw Angie as the enemy, even more so because of that episode with the vision. Melinda may have felt something, maybe just the gut feeling that the situation had gotten out of her control. Clearly, Melinda liked being in control. Her glassy smile showed that.

At least Luke seemed pleased with the evening. Angie wondered what he saw in Melinda. No girl would ever be good enough for Luke. Angie might as well accept the one he chose. Inevitably, he would someday marry, and Angie would have to go on alone, tougher now with Ty gone. No, not gone, their relationship had just taken a different turn, Angie reminded herself, hungry to again feel his arms around her.

Picking up a news magazine, she flipped through the pages and threw it down with disgust. Bored and restless,

Angie went to the car and retrieved Ty's arrangement of dried sunflowers. Deeming it too tall for the table, she set the vase in a corner of the living room and stood back to evaluate the effect.

The phone rang. Her friend, Jillian, had called for a most welcome chat.

The two women had taught together for several years. They were both hands-on, experiential teachers and matched each other's adventurous spirits, sharing thoughts and feelings freely and unselfconsciously. Angie had helped Jillian through some bumpy places after a divorce and encouraged her to take a masters degree.

Conversations with Jillian usually went on for hours, ranging from students' misdeeds to men to teaching methods to metaphysics, dresses, or politics. Angie loved her talkative friend and relaxed, telling her of the house sale and her reservations about Luke's new girlfriend. Before Angie knew it, she was doing all of the talking herself, pouring out the story of Ty's visitations and her need for someone to believe in her search for him.

"You can count on me." Jillian's voice sounded warm.

"Great. You know any mediums?"

"Yeah, I've heard of one. Aunt Gildy went to him for a reading. Hold on a minute." The phone clattered. The rustle of turned pages came through the line. "Huh-uh," Jillian mumbled. "Nothing under Mediums. Clairvoyants? Uh.... maybe Fortune-tellers."

"I doubt there's a listing for fortune-tellers in the yellow pages, Jillian." Amused, Angie lay back on the blue-flowered couch, wondering where to find a good psychic. "Besides I don't want just anybody. There are a lot of quacks out there. I need someone I can trust."

"You never know. This guy may be good. Aunt Gildy swears by him. What's to lose? If you don't like him, we'll go somewhere else," Jillian rattled on as she flipped more pages, then sounded excited. "Here it is under Churches—

Spiritualist. Rev. Hank Wilson. Gifts of the Spirit, six-thirty, Sunday."

"Guess it's worth a try." Angie looked at her watch but felt disappointed at reading eight o'clock. "Too late."

"...and Wednesday." Jillian breathed into the phone. "I feel really good about this."

"Six-thirty, Wednesday? It's a date!" A thrill passed through Angie, and she silently prayed Ty's spirit had heard.

Thirteen

Don't Do That

Angie had expected a church building of some sort, not a space in a strip mall with no music, crystal balls, or other exotic paraphernalia available for evoking spirits. This church looked like any public meeting hall, unadorned and brightly lit from overhead fluorescents.

A few people waited on folding metal chairs around the almost-empty room. An old man and a chubby girl sat quietly down front. Two middle-aged women whispered to each other on the right side of the aisle. An elderly woman prayed alone while another sat in the corner, dabbing her eyes with a handkerchief.

When Jillian and Angie sat down, their chairs scraped against the tile floor with a hollow screech. Jillian patted her short blond curls then ran her fingers along the folds of a purple skirt. Her blue-eyed smile revealed how exciting she found their adventure.

Since Sunday Angie had felt tense about entering this unknown environment even though Jillian's Aunt Gildy assured her that the medium had an excellent reputation. Angie liked making her own judgments but had never attended a séance or visited a medium. Her knowledge of other people's psychic experiences remained limited to books. She doubted Ty would show up at a séance, under any circumstance. Still, he must know she needed to make contact with him. The plainness of the room encouraged Angie. Ty might feel comfortable coming here.

The two whispering women across the aisle fell silent, and the old man pointed his cane toward the back of the room as a mood of anticipation fell over the audience.

Reverend Hank Wilson, a tall, slender man, walked down the aisle. In an open-necked sport shirt and slacks, shined shoes, his reddish-brown hair stylishly combed, he looked more like a golf pro than a medium. Arriving at the podium, he turned and gazed at each member of the tiny congregation, his face calm, composed, and quietly beatific, the kind that could be in touch with spirits, Angie thought with relief.

When Jillian saw Reverend Wilson, she held one hand over her mouth and said, "This is great!" Her pretty face twinkled merrily.

"I'm glad you came." Angie's words sounded too weak for the enormous gratitude she felt toward her friend.

"Welcome, all, to the gifts of the spirit. Please take a moment to center yourself." Reverend Wilson spoke softly and closed his eyes. "Let the peace of the Universal Spirit fill your heart and mind. Be one with the flow of energy."

The audience tilted back their heads and shrugged their shoulders. Someone coughed. Still grinning, Jillian closed her eyes. A relaxed smile crossed her face. Wide-eyed, Angie watched.

Reverend Wilson stepped away from the podium, hesitated for a moment, looking into the air over their heads, then walked to the elderly man sitting in the front row. "May I come to you?"

"Thank you," said the old man, who struggled to a standing position, supporting himself with a cane.

Gazing at the man's shoulder, the reverend said, "I see good fortune for you. Travel, perhaps to another state, but soon."

"Thank you," the old man said.

"Someone wishes to give you a message. I get the name Eliza. Standing behind you."

The old man bobbed his head as if this were great news. "That was my mother's name."

"Yes. She says, 'take your medicine, especially vitamins.' Have you been taking your medicine?"

"I will," the old man vowed.

"Thank you. That is all." Smiling, the reverend stepped away as the old man sat down, thumping his cane.

"Sounds pretty general," Jillian whispered. "I could do that well."

"You don't want to be a medium," Angie teased, unable to imagine her friend serious long enough to even meditate. Angie's trust of the reverend grew. "General? Right. Like everybody's mother's named Eliza."

"Lucky hit?" Jillian shrugged. "Maybe they know each other?"

"Be serious." Angie tried to avoid letting Jillian's playfulness infect her.

"May I come to you?"

Angie whirled at the sound of Reverend Wilson's voice before her and scrambled out of her chair. "Yes, of course."

His pale hazel eyes looked directly at her, but his gaze seemed vacant. "I sense much sorrow around you. Tears. A grief that knows no bounds."

Catching her breath, Angie looked down. That described how she felt very well.

"A move from another state," Reverend Wilson continued, and she nodded, thinking of the aborted move to California. "A wedding close to you."

"Not anymore." Angie wanted to explain that there would be no wedding because her fiancé died but cautioned herself to avoid giving too much information. If Ty really sent this message, she wanted clarity, to leave no doubt.

Standing so close she could smell tangy aftershave, the reverend seemed remote, more in contact with the spirit world than with hers. "I think yes."

Confused, Angie asked, "What do you mean?"

"Yes, a wedding around you." Reverend Wilson gazed in an unfocused way over her shoulder, as if watching something far away. "I see a flower. Long stem, yellow petals. Someone is sending you a gift from the other side."

"Who is it?" Angie murmured, trying to keep her mind open, yet longing for a clear clue of Ty's presence.

"Sorry. That's all I get." The reverend walked toward a woman across the aisle.

"Thank you." Sitting abruptly, Angie imagined that Ty had attempted to send her a message. Perhaps he found working through a medium difficult. Although she felt no personal awareness of his presence, Ty had loved the big yellow flowers that the reverend's description invoked.

Almost taking the words out of Angie's mouth, Jillian leaned over and whispered, "California sunflowers?"

"Oh, God, Jillian. I think it's Ty."

"Don't you need a little more proof than this?"

"I've got to get a private appointment." Angie's conviction grew as she spoke. "Ty's trying to get a message to me."

The woman in front of them turned around, finger across lips. "Shhhhhh," she whispered fiercely.

Angie waited restlessly while Reverend Wilson gave more messages, said a short prayer, and dismissed the audience. At the doorway, she found his card. "I'll call him in the morning. I have to see him again." Driving home she told Jillian, "I feel really good about this. He's going to help me find Ty."

Jillian sounded more cautious than previously. "Don't forget, he talked about travel in your message and the old man's. There was also a ghost over the shoulder for both of you."

"Don't call Ty a ghost."

"I'm just saying go slowly. It's easy to sense your grief." Reaching across the car seat, Jillian flecked the corner of Angie's eye. "Drawn eyes, you know, darling, tiny crows' feet give you away. Hank Wilson could have been guessing about everything."

"Why would he do that?" Angie did not want to hear skepticism, even though she recognized such thoughts as prudent.

"I don't know, Angie. Maybe he's not. I'm sure he believes in what he's doing." Jillian's voice carried friendly concern." Just be careful, okay?" Grinning, she stopped the car at Angie's front door and said, "But, he could come to me anytime. What a foxy man!"

"You're incorrigible." Angie laughed, stepped out of the car, and closed the door.

"You know how hard good men are to find!" Jillian shrugged and drove out of the driveway.

Angie yelled thanks, not caring whether she disturbed the neighbors. She could not wait to tell Luke what the medium said and dashed in the house. "Luke?"

"Yo, Mother Dearest," Luke ran down the stairs. "Have I got news for you!"

Laughing, she closed the front door and threw her purse on the couch, "Me, too."

Enthusiastically, Luke grabbed her around the waist, held out her right arm, and danced her around the living room, humming *Here Comes the Bride*.

"Luke? You don't mean it?" Angie realized that Reverend Wilson had been right about a wedding near her, after all.

Nodding vigorously, Luke released her. "I asked Melinda to marry me, and she said yes. Well, actually, her father did." He giggled like a little boy and spread his arms. "I asked her father if I could marry her, and he likes me. So, I'm getting married!"

Never had Angie seen Luke so elated. Hugging him to her chest, she felt his laughter rumble against her and laughed, too, at the irony of their situation. Her son thought he loved Melinda enough to marry her even though Angie wondered whether or not she could tolerate the girl.

"Can you believe it? I'm going to be a husband. A family man! Isn't it great?" Clutching her arms, Luke grinned at her. " Well, what do you think? Say something."

"Honey, I'm happy for you. This is wonderful." Angie hoped her misgivings did not show. She had a strong hunch that Luke would hurt over Melinda. Wanting to protect him, she felt a compulsion to remind him of the vision, though unwilling to spoil his happiness now. "I'm flabbergasted," she said, breaking away and going to the kitchen.

"Flabbergasted?" Luke following her with a laugh. "You sound like Grandma."

"God, I hope not. I'll never say that word again." Distracted, Angie opened the fridge door and looked inside.

"Want to invite Grandma to the wedding?"

"I suppose we'll have to." Angie propped her arm on the lower compartment door, forgetting what she had intended to take out of the refrigerator. "When's the wedding going to be?"

"Not sure. I say soon, and Melinda says small." Filled with enthusiasm, Luke spoke quickly. "I told her how great you are at organizing events. She's coming over tomorrow night so we can start planning."

"You want a beer? I'm gonna have a glass of wine." Reminding herself to stay centered, Angie took out beer and wine and set them on the counter. She wanted to avoid becoming overwhelmed by conflicting emotions.

Luke patted her shoulder. "I want you to be part of this, every step of the way. We're going to have a good life, even without Ty. You watch."

When Angie turned to ask him again if he wanted a beer, he looked so anxious she wanted to believe in his dream of happiness. Glad that he included her, she kissed him quickly, turned away, and took clean glasses out of the dishwasher. How she wished Ty were here. He would know what to do about Melinda. He had such a way with people.

"There's something I never told you, Mom. I called Grandma and asked her to come here after... you know... when you were so upset about Ty."

"Did you really?" Again impressed that her son had behaved so efficiently and considerately in handling the crisis of Ty's death, Angie asked, knowing the answer, "Grandma refused, didn't she?" Luke's impulses seemed most appropriate in spite of the fact that Angie had not been much help to him. For an instant, she feared the situation resembled hers with Barbara.

"I wanted you to know before you asked Grandma to fly out for the wedding. She might not want to come."

"My mother's not exactly been a rock in our lives, has she? When times got tough, try and find her."

Many years ago, Angie had cried night and day because of Ty's infidelity. Barbara had known how much Angie loved him but never once mentioned forgiveness. Perhaps she never understood it herself. Daddy's death could have prompted her to give top priority to her children, like Angie had when they found out about Luke's epilepsy. But no, Barbara thought first of herself, placing her children in the orphanage with the admonishment that it would only be temporary, a word that meant nothing to five-year-old Bobby and seven-year-old Angie. *Could she ever forgive Mother for that?*

When Bobby fell ill and died, Angie finally realized how much Barbara drank. Angie had taken care of him and made all of the arrangements while their mother just conveniently went to pieces then disapproved of every decision Angie made.

"Let's get off this stuff about Grandma," Luke said. "I don't want to spoil my happy news."

"You don't have to ask me twice." Angie would never do that to Luke. She must support him and approve his decisions even if they turned out to be wrong. He had a right to his life, including his own mistakes. She would set her reservations about Melinda aside but could only do so if she spoke honestly. Carrying their drinks to the table, she said. "Sit down, honey. Let me be an over-protective mother just one more time."

"What's up?" Luke sat and took a long drink of beer.

"I want you to be happy. If that means marrying Melinda, then I'm all for it."

"Good."

Hoping he would listen with his heart instead of his intellect, Angie plunged on. "But, I have to tell you that I keep remembering the vision I saw. There are powerful emotions between the two of you. I hate laying a negative on you, but I'm afraid Melinda will hurt you."

Luke set the glass down, sloshing the amber liquid. "Come on, I'm a big boy."

"I'm talking deep hurt, Luke. I don't think she's good for you. At some unconscious level that I can't explain, I recognize her. I feel certain she'll bring sorrow to both of us. Maybe she won't intend to do it, but..."

Rising suddenly, Luke knocked his chair off balance. Angie steadied it as he paced the length of the dining room, rubbed his head, and paced back.

Angie wished she did not feel compelled to continue. "The vision came as a warning, and we should honor it. I wish you wouldn't marry her."

"I love her. I want this marriage." Luke paced again.

"Just think about it for a while, that's all I ask."

"I have. I'm not gonna let one of your hunches stop me from having what I want." Luke stopped in front of her. Defiance and pleading vied for dominance in his eyes. "I'm going through with the marriage."

Angie recognized his yearning, a need as passionate as her own compulsion to merge with Ty. Just so, Luke must bond with Melinda. Tears welled in her eyes as she embraced him. Her grown son trembled in her arms. She wished she could protect him, but he must follow his own path. As his mother, Angie had to stay open and available to him, no matter how painful the process. "I understand, honey," she said. "I'll support you, and I'll not mention this to you again. You can trust me."

Luke remained enfolded a moment longer, yielding to her body as he had as a small boy. Then, with a cough he withdrew, his voice gruff. "Tell me your news?"

"Oh, some other time, okay?" Angie regretted causing him distress and did not want to diminish his news any more than she already had.

"No, tell me. I really want to know." Luke drained the glass of beer.

"I went to see a medium tonight." Angie smiled, remembering Reverend Wilson's words. "I think I got a message from Ty."

"You did? What kind of message?" Luke raised an eyebrow.

"Unclear right now. I'm going back as soon as I can get a private appointment."

"I don't like this dabbling in the occult. I'd stop you if I could."

"Don't worry about me. I'll be okay." Raising her untouched glass toward the chandelier, Angie admired the pale yellow tint.

"Be careful. Things could get weird on you. Make sure it's really Ty and not just some guy with his hand out, trying to take advantage of you and get your money."

Angie sniffed the wine's sweet bouquet and swallowed a draught, enjoying the fruity flavor. "It's not like you to be so suspicious of psychic things, Luke. What's going on?"

"You're flirting with dangerous stuff. It's not normal. I want you to quit." Luke went to the staircase, paused, and hammered on the railing. "Why in hell can't you just let Ty go? He's dead. We're alive." Dashing up the stairs, he slammed his bedroom door.

Surprised, Angie stared after him. So much change that young woman had brought into their lives. Angie thought perhaps she should try once again to make Luke understand the importance of her search for Ty, but not tonight. Like Scarlet O'Hara, she would think about it tomorrow. Leaning back in her chair, Angie savored the wine.

As Angie made coffee the next morning, she wondered how Luke would feel about their disagreement.

Luke's shoes clicked on the steps, and he came into the kitchen, hanging a paisley tie loosely around his neck. "Got to run, Mom. I'm late."

"Should I plan on Melinda's being here for dinner, or later, to talk about wedding plans?"

His morning face looked placid, compared to last night's tempestuous emotions. "She works late, so let's order pizza when she gets here."

"Okay. This'll be fun." Angie felt determined to make the best of the situation with Melinda.

Pulling two cinnamon rolls away from the package, Luke kissed her cheek. "Thanks."

"Have a good day, honey."

"You, too," Luke called as he closed the laundry room door and headed into the garage.

The easy return to normalcy made Angie smile but did not fool her. Their relationship was changing. She must be patient with both herself and Luke and try to get along with Melinda. Imagining her as a daughter-in-law took some real effort.

In a call to Reverend Wilson, Angie explained her hope to see him as soon as possible. The reverend sounded very accommodating, volunteering to see her that afternoon.

Once inside the church, Reverend Wilson took her through the meeting room filled with folding chairs and into an office so tiny, it looked like a converted closet. The only furnishings were a typewriter table, a folding chair, and a couch. Angie liked the fact that he seemed comfortable in austere surroundings, not requiring any display of showiness to contact the spirit world, like trumpets or hanging beads.

"Call me 'Hank,' please." He lay on the couch and patted the chair beside it. "Sit here. I'm simply going to shift my awareness to a different reality to see if I can contact your friend. It's no more unusual than tuning a radio to another station. After I relax a bit, just talk to me like you normally would."

Although eager, Angie felt comfortable with Hank and with the process of contacting the spirit world. She waited for him to relax and breathe deeply.

Soon Hank's face flushed, and he became more animated, speaking in a guttural tone. "I see an image, a dark circle. It is surrounded by a brighter circle. Outside is a brighter circle yet, like the sun's rays. It's a flower. Someone brings you greetings from the other side."

Her hands perspiring, Angie whispered, "Yes. Who is it?"

"Unclear. Wait a moment." His eyes fluttered rapidly beneath closed lids.

Waiting impatiently, Angie thought of the questions she would ask Ty: Where had he gone since the dreams ended? What lessons had he learned on the other side? Had his energy returned? How might they make more personal contact than through a medium?

Hank's eyes popped open. Out of trance, he said, "I'm sorry, but I can't get any communication. I see the image, sort of yellow and orange, but no message comes."

Surely the effort could not end so quickly and fruitlessly. "Could you try again?"

"That would be pointless." Hank sat up and smoothed his hair. "I feel I'm not capable of delivering a message for you. I can recommend someone else, another medium perhaps."

"Why? What's wrong?"

"I don't know." Hank sounded confused. "I feel a lot of anxiety on the part of someone in the spirit world, but there's some kind of interference I can't explain. It's like there's no one out there to contact me."

"But, Ty must be there." Angie heard the frustration in her own voice and forced herself to become calm. "I know it's possible to contact him. He told me so the last time we... .uh..." As fine a man as Hank seemed, he was still a stranger. Angie felt unwilling to say she and Ty had embraced in a passionate way. "Ty told me in a dream. We can bridge the barrier of death. We've done it before, and we can do it again."

"I'm sure it's possible." Hank seemed apologetic as well as a bit surprised. He doubtless had more luck with other clients or he would get out of the mediumship business. "Unfortunately, I don't know how to help you."

Angie wished she could hide her disappointment. "What can I do?"

"You have only two choices that I can see. You can go to another medium. Or, you say you have psychic talents. You could try to contact him yourself."

"I've not been able to accomplish that alone for several weeks."

"I know a therapist who uses past-life regression to work with the spirit world between lifetimes. Do you think it would help to try that?"

"A regressionist?" A chill passed through Angie, assuring her Hank had suggested the right course of action. The answer might lie far in the past, perhaps in another lifetime. "Yes, give me his name."

"Actually, this is a woman. She's very busy. You might have to wait several weeks to get an appointment."

"Thank you, Hank. You've been kind." Angie considered the reverend a positive marker on her path back to Ty.

A good sport, Hank laughed. "Yes, but not very psychic." He impressed her by refusing to take any money for the appointment then shyly asked, "And how is your pretty friend?"

Surprised, Angie said, "Jillian? Fine," amused at the attraction between her friend and this charming psychic. With them and her son's newfound love, romance bloomed all around her. If it flourished for everybody else, perhaps Angie could reinvent hers with Ty once again.

Fourteen

Floating in Time

Arizona high country—-the following Saturday

Through the open window of Jillian's Firebird, Angie breathed in the pristine aroma of mountain firs. Close to the road, the spindly trunks of tall, thin evergreens rose up from nearly bare ground, the litter of dried needles their only underbrush. The two-lane highway ran forward into a timeless landscape, blanketed with green. Only an occasional poison oak sported the gold and red of autumn.

"This is breathtaking." Jaunty in slacks and red blazer, Jillian swept a free arm toward the sky, crisply blue, as she drove the steep angle of the highway. "I'd skip school for this kind of trip if I had to."

"I'm glad you could go with me on such short notice." Angie smoothed the wool of her white slacks.

Reverend Hank had recommended a highly sought-after and expensive past-life regressionist. Because of a cancellation, Angie had arranged an appointment two days later, on a Saturday, thinking Jillian could probably go. In spite of her talk of ditching, no teacher was ever more conscientious or faithful to her students than Jillian.

Most people would call it luck to have gotten an appointment so quickly. From time to time, Angie perceived an undercurrent of cooperation in the progress of events, as if the universe supported her needs.

"Earth to Angie. Come in, please. If you don't talk to me, I'll turn on the radio and blast you awake with country music."

"Okay." Angie laughed. "Remember that first message I got from Reverend Wilson?"

"How could I forget?" Rolling her eyes, Jillian squeezed the steering wheel. "Somehow I've got to date that medium. Never been with one before. He's so sensitive. Bet he'd be a great lover."

"I've got a feeling you might find out."

"What? How do you know?" Jillian flushed with pleasure.

Rubbing her temples dramatically, Angie said, "I'm psychic, of course."

"Don't tease. Tell me what you know."

"Nothing really. Just a feeling. Now, stay on the subject." Angie enjoyed withholding knowledge of Hank's expression of interest. "That first message he gave me at the church encouraged me. I felt certain Ty tried to make himself known to me, maybe trying to let me know his willingness to speak through the medium. When Hank could not get any message the second time, I felt frustrated, then depressed, then excited again. Got to get off this emotional roller coaster."

"Doesn't it give you a high, though?" Jillian flashed a conspiratorial smile. "Does me. Sometimes I think I'm an emotion junkie."

Sighing, Angie rubbed her eyes. "Got to be more careful this time. If there's no contact with Ty, I won't let it wear me down. I'll just find another way, somehow."

"I'll help. Whatever it takes. This psychic trip you're on's the most excitement I've had since I met that Argentinean polo player." Jillian laughed. "Keep your chin up, kiddo. You'll get what you want."

Angie smiled at her friend, feeling gratitude and not just a little bit of awe at Jillian's ability to attract exciting and unusual lovers. "Keep giving me big doses of optimism. It was so sweet in San Diego when Ty came to me in my dreams, I just can't tell you."

"Is sex better in the astral than in the physical?"

"In some ways yes, but—"

"S'what I've heard." With mock smugness, Jillian held the car to a long curve, banked by a ravine filled with firs.

"Make no mistake," Angie spoke intensely. "If I had one wish, I'd have Ty back with me in the flesh."

"Can't blame you there. He was a beautiful man, inside and out."

Quiet fell between them. A new wave of sadness washed over Angie as she closed her eyes and focused on remembering Ty's face, letting his beloved presence fill her mind and heart.

Jillian's voice intervened.

Angie said, "I'm sorry. I didn't hear what you said."

"At least while you're here," Jillian said, her brow knitted, "you don't have to worry about Luke's wedding plans."

"You got that right." Not wanting to burden her friend, Angie rolled up the window against the cooling air and concentrated on the new topic of conversation. "It's such a drag. I took Melinda out to lunch, hoping to get to know her better. I thought maybe we could develop a relationship separate from Luke, you know?"

"Good thinking. How'd it go?"

"I've always prided myself on my people skills, thought I understood young people especially, but this time I fell down a black hole. I don't know how to relate to that girl. One minute she's all over me asking questions about my life and my thoughts and feelings. The next minute she stonewalls me."

Jillian's face took on a perplexed expression that reassured Angie of the rationality of her own reactions to the girl. "Melinda sounds like an enigma. I've got to meet her soon. What does Luke say?"

"He doesn't see a problem. Talk about love being blind." Baffled, Angie stared at her own hands and idly pushed back cuticles with a clear, round thumbnail. "In Luke's mind she can do no wrong. If I say anything about her, it sounds like sour grapes on my part. At least when he's around, she's been softer with me since that first dinner party."

"Give Luke some space. He'll come around. He's always been a levelheaded kid. Remember how mature he was when kids made fun of his seizures?"

"Yeah." The memory of Luke's brave seven-year-old face floated into Angie's mind. He deserved all the good life had to offer. "I want to get along with Melinda. I decided a long time ago no girl would ever be good enough for my son, so I'd just accept the one he chose. That's what I've been trying to do. Subliminally, there may be some kind of war going on between her and me over Luke. Don't think so, but I may be fooling myself."

"Start watching for the Stanton Road turnoff, I think we're almost there."

"Good. Can't talk about Melinda for too long. I just get pissed off."

"There it is."

Jillian turned off the highway into a winding road that became a gravel lane within a few hundred feet. Lined by well-trimmed junipers, the lane ended in a turnaround in front of an A-frame log cabin, nestled in a clump of spruce trees. Smoke curled around the chimney. A tall woman came out the front door and waved as they parked the car beside a gold Mercedes.

Anxious to meet her, Angie tugged a white jacket on, grabbed her purse, and scrambled out of the car.

"Welcome. I'm Evelyn Powers. Come in." She wore a dark green cable-knit sweater and slacks, setting off auburn hair, stylishly contoured.

After exchanging greetings, Dr. Powers guided Angie and Jillian into the cabin, decorated in mauves and beiges. Verdant philodendrons hung in baskets from the ceiling. A fire crackled in the fireplace, and a Brahms concerto played softly in the background.

"Please sit down. Would you like some tea?" Dr. Powers spoke in a cultured British accent.

"Thank you, I would." Angie's tension about the regression eased. She felt welcome, comfortable, and relaxed, immediately liking this gracious woman.

"Yes, please. Your cabin is beautiful." Jillian glanced at Angie as if to say "is this posh, or what?"

"Thank you." Dr. Powers pointed toward the dining room table, set with a bone china tea service, walked into the kitchen area off the cabin's main room, and lifted a copper kettle from the stove. After filling the dainty teapot and carefully placing the lid on it, she set out a tray laden with crumpets, scones, butter, clotted cream, and preserves.

Angie grinned at Jillian as they sat at the table. Lovable, earthy Jillian slathered cream on a crumpet and ate, licking her fingers after each bite. She went at food with the same gusto that she attacked projects at school or relationships with men. Such a contrast with Dr. Powers' quiet elegance.

"Delicious!" Jillian smacked her lips. "Where'd you get clotted cream out here in the country?"

"Oh, you like it?" Dr. Powers sounded neighborly and friendly. "I culture it myself. Cooking is my hobby."

"Thanks for your hospitality," Angie said, "especially for accommodating us on short notice."

"My pleasure." With an air of protocol, Dr. Powers poured tea in all three cups and stirred cream into her own. "Have you ever been regressed before?"

"No, but I've been hypnotized." Angie sipped the spicy tea. "To quit smoking."

"Did it work?"

"Yes, actually it did, though I was a little surprised. I hadn't expected quitting to be so easy. I'd tried several times to go cold turkey. What a relief to not have to deal with the smell and inconvenience of cigarettes any more."

"That's a sign you'll be a good subject." Dr. Powers nodded, as if she had heard that attitude many times. "You've probably meditated, haven't you?"

"I used to meditate every day, but I've gotten away from it in the last few years, I'm sorry to say." Usually more cognizant of the reasons for her behavior, Angie failed to remember why she stopped doing something she had enjoyed.

Dr. Powers' voice carried a confident tone. "I could give you a suggestion to help you renew the habit, if you like."

"Thank you. I'd appreciate that." Angie started to pick up a scone with a yellow filling, but Jillian laid claim to it with a smile. Probably apricot, her favorite, Angie thought with regret, indulgently deferring to her friend.

"What's the purpose of your visit today?" Dr. Powers inspired confidence by the quiet, friendly tone of her voice and her deft movements. "You said on the phone you were interested in contacting a dead loved one. I want to remind you that I don't do spiritualist work. By that I mean séances, but I will regress you to past lives where you might find some common ground with your loved one. Was it a husband or parent?"

"My fiancé. I had a series of dreams where we... it seemed that we came together in a place that wasn't exactly a dream world. It wasn't our regular waking reality either." Angie remembered the glowing place where she had last seen Ty—a golden floor, an archway, a staircase—all very beautiful and otherworldly. "It's important to me to reestablish that connection. Reverend Wilson told me you could take me to the spirit world. That's what I'd like you to do, so that I can find Ty."

"I understand." Dr. Powers nodded in recognition. "Many of my clients have remembered the time between lifetimes. Perhaps you can, too."

Setting down her teacup, Jillian said, "Tell her about your visions, Angie."

Angie felt grateful for her friend's sharp memory. "I've had several visions that have come true over the years. I see pictures that are exactly like the events."

"Then you should be comfortable with this process." The mantel clock struck once, and Dr. Powers rose from the table. "Shall we begin?"

Angie settled into a brown leather recliner. Dr. Powers lowered the volume on the sound system and sat in a Boston rocker nearby, a clipboard on her lap. Wiping the corner of her mouth with a linen napkin, Jillian moved to the couch. Silent anticipation settled on the room.

The rocker squeaked as Dr. Powers shifted her weight and spoke softly in her soothing British intonation. "Relax and let the chair take your weight. I am going to help you calm down before I take you on a voyage through time. As you travel you will be protected by a vibrating shield of divine energy. No matter where you go, who you become, or what happens, you will always be able to hear my voice and respond to me in English. I'll be asking you questions. Always answer with the first thought that comes into your mind, no matter how surprising. Do you understand?"

"Yes." Angie felt reassured because Dr. Powers' smile seemed genuine.

Jillian gave a "thumbs up" sign from across the room.

The clock ticked, the fire crackled, the sound of strings floated on air fragrant with orange spice. Angie closed her eyes and listened to the cadence of the refined voice beside her.

147

"Your body is completely relaxed. You feel a tingling sensation entering your toes and flowing through your entire body, causing you to feel complete peace."

An ease settled over Angie. She thought once of shifting her position to one more comfortable but decided that took too much effort.

"Imagine yourself descending a long staircase very slowly. You are going down, down, down... very slowly... down, down, down. With each step on the stair, you go deeper and deeper down."

With a sigh, Angie surrendered to the process.

"Down, you are going deeper and deeper down." After an empty silence, Dr. Powers said, "I'm going to ask you to remember certain events from your life as Angie. That will help you become accustomed to the regression process. Now, I want you to leave present time. Let go of this September day in nineteen eighty-seven. Travel backward in time through your present lifetime. Go back to nineteen eighty-six. Stop at an important moment last year and tell me about it. What do you remember?"

Angie felt as if she were floating inside her body, then the place where her body lay became insignificant. The thought occurred to her that she could remember any event, in any time, with precision. Her memory of last summer cleared.

"Where are you?" Dr. Powers asked.

"In the observatory." Angie saw images, vague at first, then clearer. She leaned against a brass railing, facing a museum exhibit. Inside the glass case sat a small black trunk, a gold key nearby.

"Are you alone? Look around. Are other people with you?"

Angie looked up to see Ty standing beside her, his arm casually around her waist. He wore a white sport shirt, his face tanned and healthy looking, and his lips moved as he read aloud to her the inscription on the exhibit.

Dr. Powers asked, "What are you doing?"

"Just a list of trinkets."

"Would you repeat that?"

"He's reading a list of trinkets contained in the trunk." Amazed at Ty's glowing face and skin texture as he spoke to her, Angie said, "He's turning to me. He's laughing. He says 'Meet you here.' I laugh too and say 'It's a date.'"

"What's the year?"

"Now?" The question confused Angie. "It's nineteen eighty-six, of course. Ty and I are in Los Angeles on a holiday. But we made a date to meet here in two thousand sixty-one."

"Are you in two thousand sixty-one?"

"No, but I will be in seventy-six years." Angie felt annoyed that Dr. Powers did not understand. Of course, the doctor could not see the images that Angie saw. Memory in the trance looked equally as detailed as her visions. The colors appeared just as bright, the atmosphere as rarified, the emotions as charged. "The Comet's coming again. Ty will know. I will know."

"What will you know?"

"To come to the trunk again." Angie resolved to answer precisely, unwilling to lose a valuable instant of the regression.

"Have you made a pact or something?" asked Dr. Powers.

"More than that. A covenant." Angie realized Dr. Powers did not understand. "We're in the observatory at Griffith Park. It's the Halley's Comet display. There's a time capsule to be opened in two thousand sixty-one when the comet comes again. I told Ty that Mark Twain had been born the year the comet came and claimed he would die when it returned. He did die the same year, in nineteen ten. Ty laughed and said Twain wouldn't outdo us. So we promised to meet again in another seventy-six years."

"I understand. Now, let's continue. You are going back again through the years."

Although she longed to stay, Angie understood the importance of following instructions. Ty's face disappeared from her inner vision. She felt propelled backward through time as if pulled through a heavy blackness. A stillness enveloped her.

"You are thirty-five years old, now thirty, now twenty-five, now twenty. Stop at an important event in the twentieth year of this lifetime as Angie."

A group of people, dressed up, stood in front of the brick church in Angie's hometown. They waved to her, and she waved back through a car window. A wedding gown with a full skirt created mounds of white lace over both her lap and Russell's. He sat beside her, shouting to the other people. He dropped his arm to her shoulder as the car lurched forward. Tin cans clattered behind them when her brother Bobby drove them down the street.

"Where are you?" came the voice of the hypnotist.

"Church. Just married."

"You're probably very happy today, aren't you?"

Angie whispered, "I pretend I'm happy, but I'm not."

"Why?"

"I should've married Ty, not Russell," Angie murmured, filled with regret. "Mother says I have to marry Russell or give the baby up for adoption."

"All right. We're moving back in time again. You are fifteen, ten. You are a child. Stop at an important event in your childhood. How old are you?"

"Eight and a half." Although dimly aware that her voice sounded childish, Angie felt no need to change it. Seeing moving-picture memories of her life delighted her.

"Where are you?"

"In the yard."

"What are you doing?"

"Playing hopscotch." Angie felt a surge of little-girl pride and bragged, "I'm champion of the orphanage. Best hopscotcher here."

"Did something good happen to you today?"

"It will. My mother is coming to get Bobby and me, to take us home."

"All right, Angie. We're moving back in time again, across the barrier of your birth, floating freely in time and space, going to a memory, another life that you remember. There's no rush. We've all the time in the world."

There was a long period with no sensation of thought or awareness of a physical body, not even any sights, just emptiness.

From far away Angie heard someone calling. Dr. Powers asked her name. Angie struggled to form a word and blurted out, "Ashley." The name surprised her, but at the same time it seemed natural to call herself Ashley.

Assaulted by the odor of her own sweat, she felt her muscles straining and held her head tucked tightly between her elbows. Her upper torso lay along her right leg, which trembled with the effort of maintaining its stretch.

"Hold, hold, hold," a familiar voice said in her mind.

"Where are you, Ashley?" Dr. Powers asked.

"At the bar." New thoughts and images came into Angie's mind, amazingly, as if she held a secret key to someone else's private life. "I don't know what 'bar' means..."

"Let the responses flow without being critical of them. Look around you. Are you alone or is someone with you?"

Peeking through the narrow range of vision that her position afforded, Angie saw the backs of several other ballet dancers, also leaning across their legs pressed against a long wooden pole attached to a wall. On the shiny floor, Angie saw the high-heeled boots and thin leotard-covered legs of the dancing mistress and heard the crack of her whip.

"Other students are here, but they're not gifted like me," Angie whispered. "The ballet mistress is here, of course. Shhhhhh. She's speaking to me. I must listen or she'll flick me."

Angie, as Ashley, leaned forward to hear the mistress's scratchy voice telling her to relax her neck and melt into the pose. Ashley wanted to please her teacher, thus Angie felt her shoulders slide more gracefully into the dancer's posture. She experienced a split awareness of herself, both as Angie lying in the regressionist's living room and as Ashley standing at the ballet bar.

This moment required a new sense of the meaning of self. She thought and felt as Ashley but at the same time observed and knew herself to be Angie. Identity meant something different from anything she had ever realized. Who was she really? And, who could observe both Ashley and Angie to ask such a question?

"We're moving forward in time," Dr. Powers said. "You are still Ashley. Dancing class is finished, and you're going home for the day."

Ashley took off her ballet shoes, pulled on low boots but left them unlaced, threw a cape around her shoulders, and went out into the evening. Raising the wool hood to keep the drizzling rain off her face, she hurried down the cobblestone city street. A carriage passed, and the horse whinnied. Startled, her nineteen eighties self noticed the strangeness of a street with no cars or sounds of engines or horns.

An old man in a cape walked down the street ahead of her. He stopped at a gas lamp and opened its globe with a long pole, reached in with another, and lit the gas jet. The city looked old but vaguely familiar.

Her boots clicked fast as Ashley hurried along the sidewalk. Rounding a corner, she climbed the stoop of a gray clapboard apartment building, turned a huge key in the lock, and entered the hallway. Opening the top of a metal mailbox, she checked but found no letters. She rushed up the stairs and let herself into a large room. The walls, covered with blue brocade wallpaper, had yellowed from time and smoke. Ashley threw her cape on an oak chair and picked up a poker.

"Describe where you are," said Dr. Powers.

"I'm in the kitchen."

"What year is this?"

"Uh... eighteen... ninety-nine."

"And the city?"

"Don't know. An 'N' comes to me."

"Nevermind. Describe what you're doing."

"Stoking the fire. I was gone so long it went out. Supper'll be late." Ashley knelt and laid fresh logs in the fireplace, wadded up paper, and struck a match. She grabbed a metal colander and threw in several potatoes from a bin. One potato rolled across the floor. She scooped it up and sat at the table. "Damn, forgot the knife."

"What did you say?"

"I hurry to peel potatoes." Ashley felt sticky, tired, and irritable. "I need to bathe."

"Why are you in a hurry?"

"Trevor will be home any minute. He'll be so angry."

"Why?"

"He wants me to stop dancing." Angie brushed away tears that trickled down Ashley's face.

"You are totally at ease and peaceful," Dr. Powers said, her voice reassuring. "You remember the events of Ashley's life with detachment."

Hoping to quell her frustration, Angie took a deep breath. "He knew when I married him that I wanted to dance. My dancing mistress says I'm talented enough for a slot in the city ballet. I intend to get it. I don't care what Trevor says. He's being unreasonable about having a child. That would destroy my body for the dance. I'll never give in. I'd rather die."

Calling her name, Trevor ran up the stairs. Night had fallen. The only light came from the fireplace. Ashley turned the small brass knob to raise the wick on the oil lamp and thrust a taper down the hurricane globe to light it. She burned her finger and wished they could afford one of the new apartments with electricity.

Trevor came into the room, took off his wet coat, and swept her into his arms. She pulled back and looked at him, a part of her curious about his appearance. Taller and thinner than Ty, Trevor had the same familiar cobalt eyes and teasing grin. Just as she was both Ashley and Angie, this man was both Trevor and Ty. Angie kissed him with the passion of lost loved, mingled with Ashley's desperation.

Dr. Powers spoke firmly, intruding on the passionate embrace. "Ashley, on the count of three, I want you to move forward in time until the next important event in your life."

"Not now." Angie hated feeling dragged away.

"You are moving forward in time. One. Two. Three. Where are you?"

Although Angie longed to stay in her lover's arms, the regressionist's command took precedence. With great effort, Angie attempted to see pictures of new events but found only a mottled blackness like a moving picture reel that needed changing.

Unaccountably, she became lighter and smaller, her identity transformed somehow. Confused about her location, Angie as Ashley looked around her. The air seemed different, brighter and thinner. Glancing down, she observed the Earth from a distance, as if she were flying far above it. "Oh, my God!"

"What's the matter, Ashley?"

"I think I'm dead."

Fifteen

Breaching the Barrier

Curiously unconscious of her physical body, Angie lay in the recliner in Dr. Powers' living room. The vague clinking of china teacups and the whispering voices of the regressionist and Jillian failed to disturb Angie's pleasant sensation of timeless awareness. Whether moments or hours passed she could not tell before Dr. Powers sat beside her, gently touched her hand, and addressed her.

"Angie, or perhaps I should say Ashley, a moment ago you told me you had just died. I asked you to rest and gain some perspective on that experience so you could describe it to me."

"Yes."

"How did you die?"

Certain only that her mouth moved, Angie felt disembodied and wondered again about the identity of the part of herself who actually answered the doctor's questions. "I drowned myself in the river."

"Tell me why."

"We had a terrible argument." Ashley's grief and outrage swept through Angie. "Trevor tried to make love without putting on his," her voice dropped because she dreaded saying the word, "you know, his raincoat."

"Raincoat?" Dr. Powers sounded matter-of-fact, obviously unaware of her ignorance on this very delicate subject.

"His protection," Angie whispered, "a... uh... condom."

"Oh, I see." The regressionist cleared her throat. "Please continue. You may tell me anything in complete confidence and without embarrassment."

Humiliating as retelling Ashley's experience seemed, Angie went on, "Trevor said he wouldn't wear it anymore. He begged me to have a child. I refused until he cried. That broke my heart, and I gave in and said I'd do it."

"And did you become pregnant?"

"No. For days, I kept imagining how deformed my stomach would look with a baby inside. Then after, how awful! All my muscle tone gone, my skills damaged forever. I'd be fat and saggy." Tears slid down her cheeks. "I couldn't bear that," Angie whispered, the words rough in her throat, "and I couldn't wait until I was pregnant. It would be a sin to kill a baby inside me." A kind of desperate resolve filled her. "So, I just did it. I just walked into the river and kept walking and went under, and it was so easy. The river took me."

As if from the sky, Ashley looked at herself lying face down on a muddy riverbank. One leg akimbo, hair drenched and tangled, skin swollen and dark, but still exquisitely formed. Her body looked beautiful, lithe and graceful, even in death.

Disoriented, Angie tried to determine her location. Certain she neither occupied Ashley's body on the riverbank nor Angie's on the recliner, she felt acutely conscious, more exhilarated than she had previously.

"Ashley, talk to me." Dr. Powers spoke in her gentle yet firm way.

"How astonishing—to die—and to know one is dead."

"You will remain calm and continue to respond to my voice," Dr. Powers said with authority. "Tell me what happens next."

"I think of Trevor, of how sorry I am that he's sad." As soon as she thought of him, Angie saw him in the living room of their apartment. "I'm floating above Trevor's head.

He just keeps crying. I've tried and tried to let him know I'm alive and okay, but he doesn't listen. He just sits and cries."

Somehow knowing that, if she thought of Ashley's body, she would be back at the river, Angie called out Trevor's name, but he did not hear her. Neither did he notice her efforts to put her arms around him. Her hands seemed to pass through him. Her spirit could think of no way to comfort him. Excited to be alive in this new form, she wanted Trevor to know and tried to tell him he would live again as Ty. Nothing worked. He kept on crying.

Although distraught that Ashley had caused Trevor so much grief, Angie viewed the episode with more perspective. Her sympathy for Trevor's grief became very personal because she had felt it for Ty. Yet, enduring Ty's long absences from her life and his sudden death had given her a kind of balance, a sense of the universe's atonement.

A new sensation came to Angie. "I'm being pulled along, up and away. I hate to leave Trevor, but they say I have no choice."

"Who says that?"

"Voices, in my head."

"Describe for me what's happening."

As Angie paused to observe the scene, she heard a Brahms concerto playing somewhere, an exquisite sound. "I seem to be traveling through a tunnel that moves up, though I can't see any walls, just grayness. I feel apprehensive because I can't control my movements, but I'm not afraid. It's getting lighter now. I can see better. There's something like a gate or a big door. People in the distance wave to me. I wave to them and feel like I should know them, but I don't. Oh, there's Emmons. Hi, Emmons. It's good to see you."

"Oh, my God, where is she? Has she gone to heaven?" Jillian's questions surprised Angie into remembering her friend also sat in the room.

After shushing Jillian, Dr. Powers asked, "Is Emmons a relative?"

"Oh, no, a friend. He advises me. My spiritual guide. He's a Brit, like you, actually." Feeling excited, Angie whispered intently, "He wants me to go with him."

"No matter where you go or what you do," the regressionist said in a calm, even tone, "you will always be able to relate your experiences. Please tell me where you are going and what you are doing?"

"Uh-oh. I think Emmons is upset with me." Feeling a bit silly, Angie worried about the gentleman's reaction, like a child whose father has caught her misbehaving. "He doesn't seem glad to see me, like he usually is when I come back from a life on Earth. I'm following him, and we're hurrying along a corridor of light."

"What does Emmons look like?"

"When he met me at the incoming portal, he wore the coat of an eighteenth century country gentleman and sported his favorite fluffy whiskers and jewel-handled cane. I feel more comfortable with him dressed like that although I can't remember why. But now he just looks like a sliver of pale blue light."

"And what do you look like?"

"Nothing much. A speck of white light." The enormity of her situation settled on Angie. "I'm beginning to feel very sad. I shouldn't have killed myself. It was wrong, a waste of a body. Emmons comforts me and tells me not to worry, that we'll talk later. I'm just beginning to feel so sad and sorry, you know."

"Try to relax and tell me what's happening. You are safe."

"I follow Emmons into a valley with white lilies and tall sunflowers growing all around. He leaves me alone. I lie down on the side of the hill and look up at the sky. A gentle shower comes down, not of rain but something like pink steam, swirling around me and through me. Even though I'm still sad, I'm calmer."

Intent on the experience unfolding in her mind, Angie stopped reporting to Dr. Powers. With Ashley's eyes, she looked around her. The shower dissolved, and the meadow looked normal again, replete with well-tended flowers. Sitting up on the side of the hill, she picked some lilies of the valley, fashioned them into a nosegay, and inhaled the sweet, heavy fragrance.

The pace of life felt different here, slower, as if nothing changed. Angie as Ashley recognized the familiar meadow as one of her guide's favorite spots. Although unable to remember any specific moments, she had often talked with him here. Idly, she smoothed the soft folds of a transparent ballet skirt that fell loosely over her legs and the grass around her.

Emmons returned and spoke with a voice she heard inside her mind. "I see you are still dressed for the dance, my dear." He stood, smiling down at her, in a long, blue velvet morning coat and white ruffled shirt. Dusting a space with his riding crop, he sat beside her. Perhaps his costume signaled a good mood. Emmons never expressed anger with her but sometimes looked discouraged.

Dreading to disappoint him and wanting him to understand, Angie stammered, "Dancing was my life, the most important thing to me."

"Unfortunately, yes, more important than anything, it would seem." Even with impeccable manners, Emmons had a way of going to the core of the subject.

Unwilling to meet his steady gray eyes, Angie smoothed the delicate petals of the nosegay, recalling her discarded intention to advance in the Ashley life. "I knew I should focus on my marriage, but I loved the dance so. My body was a perfect instrument. When I danced, I created beauty for myself and others. How could that be wrong?"

"It isn't." When Emmons smiled at her, his pink face looked warm and loving. "But to do so to the exclusion of your spiritual growth is unfortunate."

"I know. I couldn't stop myself." It seemed natural to speak to Emmons of such matters. Although Angie could not recall the past, her relationship with him felt ancient. "Why do I get so caught up?"

"There is a selfishness of spirit about you, a self-protectiveness, if you will, that you went into the life as Ashley to correct," Emmons said, matter-of-factly.

"Yes, but I can't remember how I got that way."

"Perhaps we can confront that situation another day." Although his judgment seemed stern, sincerity shone in his loving eyes. Emmons would always be on her side, no matter how foolish her errors. He asked, "Do you remember the plans we made for you to correct that imbalance? The selfishness of spirit?"

"Yes, I thought I could handle it this time. I tried to devote myself to Trevor, but I failed."

"There was little time for success." Emmons cocked a gray eyebrow wryly.

Regretfully recalling the sight of her limp body lying on the river bank, Angie said, "I also used up a human body another spirit could have made use of. That was wasteful."

"The body you chose was exceptional, strong and well-suited to long life and child-bearing. Devoting yourself to husband and children would have enhanced your spiritual development by addressing the issue of selfishness, as we had planned. Many other souls might have put the situation to better advantage." Emmons smoothed her hair back then patted her hand.

"I was wrong to kill myself. I wish I hadn't done it. I'm very sorry."

"I know you are."

Angie struggled to control her tears. This time with Emmons could best be used to augment her understanding of her problem, so she pressed on. "I've hurt Trevor, abandoned him."

"I'm glad you understand this is the critical issue. It won't be easy to atone, but you must begin that work."

"Yes. Tell me what I should do?"

"First, you must learn to place the needs of others before your own. In that way you will become less willful and selfish. A class in opening the heart will be useful. You also need to learn how to allow your finer impulses to come through and be able to discern when following them is beneficial to self and others. Perhaps some work on self-trust."

Feeling a bit sorry for herself, Angie said, "Trying to be perfect is too great a burden. I'm just a human being."

"My dear, I believe you are much more than that. You are a timeless spirit who takes on human form to learn and grow."

"Back to school." Tired but relieved, Angie sighed. "Seems like drudgery, but I know you're right."

"No need to hurry." Emmons took her hand, raised it to his lips, and kissed it softly. "Take the time you need to rest, my dear. We can speak more of this later."

Angie lapsed into dreamless sleep.

From far, far away came a female voice. "Ashley? Describe what you are doing. Ashley?" Dr. Powers called.

Breathing deeply, Angie longed to sleep but needed to continue straddling the two worlds. She had difficulty forming words to speak to the doctor. Realizing she had not repeated any of what had transpired between her and Emmons, Angie wondered how much time had gone by while she conversed with her guide in the Afterlife. She resolved to report more faithfully to Dr. Powers.

"Ashley, I'd like you to move ahead in time to the next important event. You will be able to see clearly and speak easily."

Flecks of light moved around Angie. She recognized them as other souls like herself, assembled in a lecture hall. Down front the teacher looked like purple light in motion. The classroom appeared modern with a huge movie screen across one end. A recorded music track played an upbeat love song. Emmons floated toward her from across the auditorium, motioning to her to follow him. Excited, Angie knew something important must have happened for him to take her out of class.

"You will remain focused," Dr. Powers said, forcefully, "and report details without becoming distracted or losing communication with me."

"Emmons has come to my classroom to get me, and we float to the reception hall. It's beautiful—tall, domed ceiling inlaid with rubies, emeralds, diamonds, a long staircase, and... Oh, my God, I know this place. This is where I met Ty."

"When did you meet him there?" Dr. Powers asked.

"In my dreams. After he died." Angie's voice rose in pitch. "This is the place."

"A positive sign, Angie. You're making an important contact. Please remain calm and resume your story."

Whispering enthusiastically, Angie said, "This is where we meet incoming loved ones after their lives on Earth are finished. It's the same place I must have entered after I killed myself, though I was so distracted I didn't recognize it. Now, Emmons leaves me. He's pleased because he knows this is a happy moment for me. I'm waiting for Trevor alone. I've assumed the appearance of Ashley, so he'll recognize me."

"What do you mean by assuming the appearance of Ashley?"

"I no longer appear as a fleck of light. All of us here are able to change our appearance. Those who are just returning from a life on Earth are often confused, as I was, so we assume the appearance we had when they knew us. I want Trevor to recognize me and feel comfortable as quickly as possible. Oh, he sees me. He's waving to me." Angie waved her arm widely, striking the back of the recliner. "Hello, darling. Welcome home."

Dr. Powers said, "Please calm yourself and report."

"I wave and he comes into my arms. I hold him. I want to spread my love around him. I want to warm and nurture him. He's exhausted from his life as Trevor, grieving for me and fighting the war. He died when his biplane crashed in Germany. Very little time has gone by, but many changes have taken place on Earth. When I died there was only talk of airplanes. They'd not been invented yet. Oh. Trevor has to go now."

"Where is he going?"

"With our guide. I can't go there. I must wait for his rejuvenation."

As Angie watched Trevor follow Emmons, she felt sorry to see him leave but knew they would be together again soon. Turning back toward her classroom, she thought how lovely it would be to have him here with her.

"Please move forward until your meeting with Trevor. You will succinctly describe what takes place."

Angie felt herself being pulled gently forward. Her vision cleared, her mind came into sharper focus. She felt distant, like an observer of her own thoughts and feelings. Her throat relaxed as she willingly shared her wisdom. "After some healing time, my loved one and I were able to be together for a while. I have grown between lives and understand myself better. I apologized for the emotional pain I caused Trevor, and he forgave me. The class work has helped me clarify the direction of my life plan, and I was able to explain to him."

"Could you describe for me the new direction you speak of?" Dr. Powers asked.

Imbued with a knowing calmness, Angie spoke from her soul's perspective. "I have volunteered to accept responsibility for the Ashley life when I return to Earth as Angie. I must learn to keep my heart open in spite of abandonment by others in order to develop sensitivity of spirit. I will be aided in this effort by Emmons who will provide me with flashes of insight. That way I'll know major events in advance and won't be overwhelmed to the extent of committing suicide again."

"And when will he do that?"

"My guide warned me when Luke fell ill at camp. Emmons also showed me Ty's plane crash in advance. Though I was depressed and thought of suicide, I felt strong enough to survive and decided not to take my life. As Angie I am regaining ground I lost as Ashley."

"You have a right to be proud." Dr. Powers sounded sympathetic. "And what about your search for Ty? Have you learned all you need to console yourself?"

"Because the First World War interrupted his goals, Trevor wants to go back and continue his life learnings. He will be reborn as Tyler Beckman. He agreed to participate in my life by abandoning me as many times as necessary, though freely showing his love for me. In the process he will learn the opposite, to be the cause of the grief he experienced as Trevor. We are both paying off some old karma."

Dr. Powers said, "This is a rather overwhelming agenda the two of you have set out for yourselves."

"Yes, but we are strong. We share a great love." Feeling proud of their relationship, Angie said, "We are what people on earth consider soul mates because we are committed to each other's spiritual growth. We willingly do whatever the other requires without judgment."

"And what does he require of you presently?"

"One moment please," Angie murmured. "My loved one comes to me. He holds me and reminds me that I am not finished with the lessons of this lifetime. I must accept his absence and learn to value my life on its own terms. He tells me he must leave to experience another avenue of existence."

"Do you mean he is being reborn?"

"Not into this world," Angie said, analyzing their lifetimes from an expanded viewpoint. "He is going to a dimension I've never experienced. He will be inaccessible to me, but it is necessary for him to develop his soul. As Ty, he completed a cycle of learning in Vietnam when he encountered another version of himself."

"Please explain."

"He has spent many lifetimes involved in war, one as an English soldier who came to hate fighting."

"Indeed!" Dr. Powers sounded fascinated. "Could you tell us his name in that lifetime?"

Cascading pictures flashed across Angie's mind—Ty in a loincloth with a spear, Ty again as an ancient Celt, then Ty in knight's armor, and Ty in a scarlet longcoat, brandishing a rapier. "Lieutenant Thomas Whitfield, in the service of His Majesty, King George the Second.

"What year was that?"

"Seventeen hundred and forty-five." Angie's heart swelled with ardor at the sight of the dashing officer.

"And were you with him in that lifetime?"

"I must have been." Although she waited patiently, no more pictures came, nor did more knowledge. Angie's eyes fluttered, and she lost focus, coming to ordinary consciousness despite her desire to remain in trance. Hurriedly, Angie related what more she knew. "Ty's soul self wishes to advance into other endeavors. His special gift lies in developing humanity's potential for flight. Because of my love for him, I want him to have what he needs, in spite of the cost to me. He says I must trust in myself, no matter how difficult that is to do."

"Perhaps we can return to the seventeen hundred and forty-five lifetime for a moment and gather more information."

"No." A disappointed sigh escaped Angie's lips at the loss of trance. "We are finished."

"All right." Dr. Powers took Angie's hand. "On the count of three, you will become awake and alert. You will remember everything that you have experienced here today. Whenever you wish to meditate, you will be able to return effortlessly to your present trance level. You are awakening. One. Two. Three."

As Angie sluggishly sat up in the chair, Jillian stared at her with a look of dismay. Dr. Powers opened the blinds to evening half-light. Angie wished to smile at the two women or say something, but both responses required too much energy.

Feeling empty, Angie drained the glass of water Dr. Powers handed her.

Jillian knelt beside Angie's chair and rubbed her hand, smiling. "It seems that you found what you came here for."

"Maybe." A bit lost, Angie cleared her throat, her previous expansiveness of spirit gone. "Right now I don't know what that means. Who said good-bye to me? Trevor or Ty? Will I ever see him again?"

With a questioning look at Dr. Powers, Jillian rose and put her arm around Angie's shoulder.

"You've gained a lot here today," Dr. Powers said. "You need time to sort things out. Be patient with yourself."

Glad for Jillian's support, Angie leaned against her friend. "I feel like my heart's been wrenched open."

Sixteen

Special Days Don't Work

The chords of *Oh, Promise Me* played on an organ blended with the scent of bayberry from red and green votives burning on the altar. Standing between Father Garcia in a white robe and one of Melinda's tux-clad brothers, Luke wished he could pull down the front of the red cummerbund or adjust the sprig of holly on his lapel one more time. Embarrassed to have anyone see his hands shake, he clasped them behind his back and took a deep breath.

On this day, like no other, Luke savored the excitement. He wanted to make Melinda happy. They would build a life together, a marriage filled with meaning. He wondered how his bride would look in her wedding gown. How he wanted to make love to her. Waiting the last six months had been easy, compared to the last few days. He'd better get off that thought.

Wooden statues of Jesus and the saints stood in niches around pews where the guests sat—Hispanic families on the west side all the way back to the vestibule and his own people on the east. Three of Melinda's little girl cousins passed out candles and strewed red rose petals on the carpeted aisle. Luke's gaze settled on his mother, looking great in a sea of pale blue—dress, hat, and eyes. She smiled and nodded to him, making him feel loved and approved.

With Melinda working so many hours the last three months, his mother had been a godsend, attending to the details of the wedding. Nobody could put together a project like she did. When she had been teaching school and getting a newspaper out, she had organized the hell out of her students and met every deadline with time to spare. Same thing happened with her own wedding, splitting vendors between Phoenix and San Diego. Once Ty teased that she would arrange for an astronaut to do an errand on his way home from a moon shot, if she thought she could get away with it.

Despite his gratitude, Luke worried from time to time. Occasionally, Angie seemed to miss a beat, not her old self. The grief for Ty no doubt still brought her down. What would she do with her son gone, too? He and Melinda would visit often. Maybe someday his two ladies might become like mother and daughter.

At Angie's side sat Grandma, fidgeting with a fur cape and whispering to her current husband, Gerald Fox, whom they'd just met the night before at the airport. He seemed nice enough, a retired something or other from a big company. The new husband had gushed about how thrilled he was to finally meet them and how happy to have Grandma—he called her Miss Barbara—as a golf and tennis partner. In the car on the way to dinner, Luke worried that Angie and Barbara might start in on each other, but they didn't. Melinda had captivated his grandmother. The two chatted as if they'd always known each other, and they all had a great time together.

In the rows behind Luke's family sat some buddies from high school and college, Ted and the women from the law office, Angie's friend Jillian and her new man, the notorious medium Hank Wilson, who'd turned out to be a reasonably nice guy. They all sat quietly, smiling and watching bridesmaids come down the aisle.

On Melinda's side of the church, kids climbed up on benches and called out to bridesmaids, who winked and grinned as they passed. Aunts and grandmothers whispered to each other, and men laughed. Although Melinda had wanted a small wedding, Luke insisted all her people should be there, and they were. It took the first four rows just to seat her immediate family. He felt vindicated at insisting on getting married in this barn of a church in South Phoenix. All of the bride's relatives fit inside just fine.

At first, Melinda's family had been reticent, acting like Luke was some rich kid from uptown, too sophisticated for them, but before long they had warmed to him. If he had not already fallen for Melinda, he would have done so after the first Sunday dinner with her family. They ate in the kitchen at a long wooden table, covered with some kind of oily cloth, chairs and stools carried from all over the house and pulled up to corners, kids at a card table alongside. Passing endless bowls of steaming rice, beans, baskets of warm *tortillas*, and *salsa*, everybody talked at once, getting up *burritos* in hand, even telling jokes. The atmosphere, so different from his quiet dinners in the dining room with his own mother, charmed Luke. Once Melinda's dad offered him a bowl of *menudo* then guffawed when Luke gagged on the nasty-tasting soup. He loved being part of a big family and hoped to have one with Melinda. Sometimes it worried him, though, that she never wanted to talk about children.

A short, plump bridesmaid stopped before the altar, her face bright. In a red gown, she held a white mum in a circlet of holly berries and ivy. Luke had lost track of how many young women had come down the aisle. With a brushing of wool sleeves, six groomsmen arranged themselves beside the best man. One coughed.

Then, the music stopped. In the silence that fell over the room, the organist pushed buttons. Restlessly, the Hispanic multitude turned toward the aisle. Demurely, the reserved Anglos looked back. The first chords of *The Wedding March* boomed out. This was it—their wedding day. His bride would come to him. Luke held his breath.

At the end of the petal-strewn aisle stood Melinda, stately as a Mayan princess—gold-sequined streamers threaded through her long black hair, her supple curves revealed beneath the slim white satin gown. In one hand she clutched a bouquet of red roses, trailing ivy. The other lay lightly on her father's arm. Mr. Chacon, well scrubbed and clean shaven for once, grinned proudly.

As Melinda glided toward her groom, her black eyes glistened behind a shimmer of white veil. With a fond smile, she looked straight at Luke. For a moment, they were alone in the room, aware only of their love for each other. Then Melinda arrived beside him in a fragrant blend of musk and flowers. Her breast rose and sank against his arm with each breath she took.

Overwhelmed with love for her, Luke feared his knees would buckle. He squeezed her trembling fingers tucked under his arm and mouthed, "Love you." They turned toward each other, and the music died away.

With a serious nod of his steel-gray head, Father Garcia said, "Dearly Beloved, we are gathered here today... *Queridos, estamos reunidos aqui...*"

Angie watched Luke turn to the bride and etched his glowing expression in her memory. Never had he looked so happy, so fulfilled and hopeful. Since birth his tiny face, round and dark-eyed, always bore an intense look, as if he struggled to figure everything out. In childhood the seizures rendered him helpless and afraid until he gained courage. Today he appeared self-assured, confident of his path.

How Angie would miss her son and feared he would never again be her champion. Such thoughts might make her cry, so Angie looked past the latest stepfather to Barbara, who smiled and appeared absorbed in the ceremony.

The night before, Barbara had disapproved of using both Spanish and English in the ceremony, but Melinda won her over by saying some of the relatives did not understand English and would miss everything. Melinda obviously fascinated Barbara. How unlikely that two women, so totally self-absorbed, could have bonded so quickly!

Angie hoped that was not sour grapes. Even though she and her mother had not seen each other for over a year, Barbara had not been in Arizona more than three minutes when she said Angie's hair was too long and needed to be cut. Why must her mother always criticize so much? Angie resolved not to let such unkindness get under her skin today, hating for happy occasions to turn out badly. She vowed to hold her temper for Luke's sake. After all, pathetically as it often turned out, Barbara always did her best.

Holding that thought helped Angie deal with Melinda, also. In the past few weeks, the tension between them had diminished. Angie hoped they might become closer in the future. She understood some of the qualities Luke loved in the young woman—her commitment, an almost messianic zeal for success, and a deep-seated vulnerability, as if she had placed her soul in jeopardy.

Melinda certainly made a stunning bride as she floated down the aisle. Six sets of attendants seemed pretentious, but Christmas colors had been the right choice with bridesmaids in red satin and the flower girls in forest green taffeta. The altar banked in poinsettias and gold candelabra wound with pine garlands created a perfect setting.

Right after the regression with the hypnotherapist, Angie had been astonished by the extent of psychic forces involved in her life and had not known how to sort her thoughts and feelings. The wedding preparations could not have come at a better time to let her get perspective. Glad that Melinda worked so much overtime, Angie enjoyed doing the details of the wedding, but it took a great deal of energy, and she often felt tired. Angie liked going with the bridesmaids to shop and fit their dresses, almost like having students again. Maybe she should go back to teaching.

Only six months before, in planning her own wedding, Angie had assumed she would feel the same happiness Luke felt today. How suddenly her hopes ended in that plane crash.

Luke deserved something better. Angie wished she could believe his marriage was the right thing, yet the vision of Melinda running away still haunted her. Today the bride looked at Luke with an expression of great love on her face. Angie hoped her prophecy would prove wrong this time.

"I pronounce you man and wife. Whom God hath joined together, let no man put asunder." Father Garcia commanded solemnly. *"Los declaro marido y mujer. A quienes dios ha unido, que nadie los pueda separar."*

A young Hispanic man stepped to the microphone and asked the guests to light their candles. As the overhead lights dimmed, the tenor sang *You Light Up My Life.* Radiant in the flickering candle glow, Luke stood with Melinda in a circle of attendants. Angie prayed his happiness would endure, that he would receive the love he longed for in his life.

When the room lights came back on and the recessional blared, Luke and Melinda kissed. The audience applauded, whistled, and shouted. The bride and groom dashed up the aisle, followed by grinning bridesmaids and ushers.

Sniffing, Barbara dabbed at her eyes with a handkerchief. Angie wondered whom her mother considered the audience for her performance. Barbara never cried for anyone except herself. Maybe she intended to impress the new husband or Melinda's family, certainly not Angie, who resolved not to get sidetracked by her mother.

Hoping the hors d'oeuvre trays had been set out, Angie rose and hurried up the aisle on the arm of an usher. In the stone-floored vestibule, bridesmaids surrounded Melinda. Luke stood beside them and grabbed Angie in a bear hug when she arrived.

"Congratulations, honey," Angie said. "I'm glad you're happy,"

"Thanks for everything, Mom." Ebullient, Luke pulled her to his right and Melinda to his left. "Line up everybody, here we go."

Poignancy filled Angie's heart. The boy who had accompanied her at her brother's funeral and the youth at Ty's no longer existed. A man stood beside her today. Angie trembled at the fleeting nature of the moments in their life together. Shoulder to shoulder, they greeted the wedding guests who poured out the doorway.

When the priest motioned the couple to the sanctuary for the signing of the license, Angie slipped between Luke and Melinda and hugged both their waists. "Got to check the table service. See you later."

"Okay." Luke kissed her cheek.

Melinda turned to the little girl cousins who clutched her ring finger and yelled, "Let us see!"

Assuming Melinda had not heard her, Angie walked next door to the reception hall. There, she checked the food and drink trays, helped the band find extension cords, and unfolded some chairs still stacked in a corner. The room had filled quickly, everyone in a partying mood—laughing, talking, reaching for crustless sandwiches and drinks. Angie poured a glass of wine and sat down at one of the round tables. She moved the gold bells into the exact center of the holly wreath then glanced around the room, making certain the other centerpieces looked right.

"Mind if we sit with you?" Barbara asked, as she and the new husband sat down.

"Of course not." Angie quelled a sigh of relief when the best man asked her to dance. She agreed, although a bit nervous about dancing the *Cumbia,* but her partner held her firmly and led her through the wide swings of the dance. Secure with his broad hand against her waist, Angie tilted her head back and smiled at the whirling face of Melinda's brother, as handsome as his sister was beautiful. The rhythms of the combo—piano, guitar, bongos, and castanets—pulsed with an enthusiastic Latin beat. Many other couples came onto the floor and danced, calling to each other and laughing.

When the music ended and the best man returned Angie to the table, Melinda sat with Barbara, their heads so close together they could have been planning a bank robbery.

"Beautiful ring, darling." Barbara stroked Melinda's hand. "At least a carat, wouldn't you say?"

"More." Her smile dazzling, Melinda nodded and fluttered her fingers, drawing Angie's attention to the diamonds, which Luke had probably paid a great deal for, lovely, if extravagant.

"Oh, really! You're very lucky," Barbara purred.

"Luke's quite a guy." Flushed, Melinda grinned and spoke intensely, "I'm lucky to have him," then turned to Angie. The smile vanished, and her words became curt. "The lady from the bakery says she can't find the cake-cutting knife, you know, the one with the satin streamers tied to it?"

"It's in the box with the champagne glasses." Angie felt surprised by the fact that the baker had spoken to the bride. More importantly, Melinda's annoyed tone appeared out of keeping with the minor quality of the problem.

"I told her you'd take care of it." Melinda rose and hurried toward a bridesmaid who passed by them. "Rosalie, wait for me." She behaved as if she considered her new mother-in-law the hired help.

Angie cautioned herself not to make assumptions. Melinda was probably just excited and thoughtless, an understandable reaction on such a special day. Angie drained her wine glass and picked up a carafe.

"Better go easy on that stuff." Barbara pointed to the goblet. "You know how wine makes you giddy, Angie."

Oppressed by the insensitivity of both mother and daughter-in-law, Angie wondered how to keep on absorbing their barbs. Suddenly, unwilling to play the martyr even to a small degree, she held up her glass to the new husband and said in a low voice so that people at nearby tables could not hear, "Gerald, your wife says I can't hold my liquor. Now you sleep with her every night. You tell me how many glasses she drinks before she goes to bed."

Laughing in a high pitch, Gerald asked, "What do you mean by that?"

"Don't tell me she's changed," Angie baited the nervous husband. "Doesn't she drink a quart every night after supper? To settle her stomach?"

Shaking a finger so hard her bracelets rattled, Barbara leaned toward Angie. "Just because your new daughter-in-law doesn't like you, that's no reason to attack me."

"Mother, there's a difference between attack and retaliation." Her annoyance temporarily soothed, Angie hoped her mother might shed some light on the difficult relationship with Melinda. "What makes you think she doesn't like me?"

A smirk on her over-made-up face, Barbara said, "It's obvious. She's sweet and charming to everyone else."

Glad to know someone recognized the situation, Angie said, "I know, but I can't figure out why." *Maybe Mother could help.*

"If you had one shred of sensitivity to the needs of other people, you'd know Melinda's afraid of you. You're so judgmental and unkind—"

"Mind your own business." Angie rose abruptly, unwilling to listen one more time to the litany of her shortcomings from Barbara's perspective. "I've got to go find that knife."

Angie strode toward the kitchen. When would she learn to keep her mouth shut? Arguments never changed anything. At the kitchen door, she turned to look back and realized Barbara had crossed the dance floor right behind her, determination on her reddening face. Rummaging through a box of extra glasses on the floor, Angie found the knife and handed it to the lady from the bakery.

"This is my business. Don't tell me it's not." Hands on hips, Barbara stood before Angie. "Luke's my only grandson, and he loves Melinda."

"Mother." Angie glanced at the bakery lady, who smiled and went into the reception room, closing the door behind her. Relieved to have the chance to vent her anger, Angie snarled, "Since when has it mattered to you what happened in his life?"

"Melinda's a nice girl, but it's clear to me she doesn't like you. What'd you do?"

"Nothing!" Angie brushed back a stray lock of hair. "God, Mother, why do you always assume I cause the trouble?"

"You probably went off half-cocked like you always do." Barbara's skirt swished as she bumped against a tiled counter and turned away, faking the wiping away of tears. "Not giving people a chance to explain. Like ending your engagement to Ty without ever giving him a chance to explain about his other girlfriend."

"You mean when we were young? All those years ago?" Nothing had ever gotten resolved between Angie and her mother in a lifetime. Perhaps this argument was healthy, even if poorly timed. "He broke my heart, Mother. Why didn't you help me?"

Gerald came through the kitchen door and patted his wife on the shoulder. "Miss Barbara, come out and dance with me."

"Not now, Gerald," Barbara shouted. "Leave us alone." As he shrugged and left, she wagged her finger at Angie.

"The same with Russell. He might've stayed and helped raise Luke. But no, you had to do it yourself. Our ideas weren't good enough."

"To put Luke in an institution? My God, Mother, does he look incapacitated?" Careless now if anyone heard, Angie shouted, "If you'd had your way, he'd still be locked away there instead of getting married. That's your solution to everything. Get rid of the person. So you won't have to see the suffering. Like Bobby and me. Put us in an orphanage so you wouldn't have to be bothered."

"Angela, will you ever forgive me for that? Why won't you understand?" Barbara's voice broke, but it was impossible to tell whether with real emotion or pretense. "I was distraught after your father died. I couldn't take care of you and Bobby."

"If it were only Daddy's death, I could forgive you. What about Bobby's? You made me do everything. And with Ty, you didn't show up at all. Guess I was lucky you sent flowers."

"You never even try to see my side."

Angie folded her arms, half-heartedly willing to try. "I'm listening."

"I've just had so much." Barbara rummaged in her purse, pulled out a handkerchief, and dabbed at her eyes. "I can't deal with death and funerals. I'm not strong, like you are. I decided a long time ago the only thing to do is take care of myself. I don't go to funerals. I refuse to ever go again."

"Even to your own?"

"Angela! Don't be macabre."

Luke burst into the church kitchen. "So this is where you're hiding. Come on. We're gonna cut the cake." He grabbed Barbara around the waist and herded her toward the door. "Grandma, did I tell you you're looking foxy today?"

Dabbing her eyes, Barbara giggled and kissed his cheek. Luke winked back at Angie, who followed them through the doorway, wondering if he had noticed the argument. His laughter rose above Barbara's as he escorted his grandmother to her seat. He met his bride at a long table set with a five-tiered white cake, red and green paper plates, and clear plastic champagne glasses.

Angie leaned against the kitchen doorframe, watching Melinda and Luke feed cake to each other. His happy face reminded her of herself as a kid at Christmas, always sure the holiday would be perfect. She would get the gifts she wanted, and everybody would be happy.

But that had never happened. With Daddy gone on his perpetual military missions, Angie was sent to bed early and lay awake listening to her grandparents and her mother argue downstairs. At the time, Angie believed adults did not like Christmas and did not care if they spoiled it for her.

Now, grown up, she could not make special days work either. She also knew that, like in the family of her childhood, her arguments with her mother never led anywhere. They just dredged up old troubles to hurt each other again. They could never attain closure.

Angie's heart hoped this marriage would turn out like Luke wanted. Her head told her not to expect a miracle. Her sweet son was headed into misery and Angie with him.

Seventeen

Search for Connection

Late the morning after Luke's wedding, Angie awoke and fumbled for her notebook on the bedside table, still open to the same blank page after many months. Difficult as it was to write lying down, she did not want to sit up and risk dispelling the dream before capturing it on paper.

> *Dreamed of walking in a wood, holding up the hem of a gown so long it covered my bare feet. Gnarled, grayish trees grew close together, shutting out the moonlight. In the distance stood stones, vaguely rounded, shrouded in mist. Ty ran in front of me and disappeared behind a tree. I wanted to hurry to catch up with him but had to step carefully to avoid stumbling on gleaming crystals, jutting out from the damp earth. I kept searching for him, always hoping to find him beyond the next tree, but never saw him again. It seemed I should know this place, but it looked like nothing I've ever seen before. I felt lost and alone.*

Throwing off the bed covers, Angie trudged into the shower and let the hot water pour down, trying to forestall the grief rolling over her. She had postponed her search for Ty while preparing for Luke's wedding, refusing to admit to herself that she did not know what to do next. The past life regression with Dr. Powers had brought up more questions than answers. What did the lives as Ashley and Trevor mean? If Ty had really gone to another dimension, would she be able to find him at all? How could she deal with her bereavement if she gave up her search? It seemed there would be nothing to live for any longer.

The pelting water relaxed her. After stepping out of the shower and wrapping herself in a bathrobe, Angie sat in the rocker and willed herself to slide into a meditative state. The effort to visualize Ty's face as it appeared in her vision on the hospital wall failed.

Resettling herself to perhaps improve concentration, she thought of his appearance as Trevor in the regression. How distraught he had been. Angie recalled the way he hugged her at the incoming portal. She wanted to experience that love again.

Although she waited patiently for many moments, no trance or any other altered state of consciousness happened. The addition of Baroque music on a cassette tape failed to help. Angie seemed capable only of visualizing pictures as memories from the past, unable to re-experience events the way Dr. Powers had helped her to do.

With a sigh, Angie admitted she could not enter a trance on her own. Rummaging through her purse, she found the phone number, then ran into the kitchen and lifted the receiver. Her fingers drummed on the counter through four rings and the answering machine. She left her message, hoping the regressionist had not gone back to England.

Afterward, Angie roamed the house, looking for something to do. Deciding to redecorate her bedroom, she hurried out and bought yellow paint. Surrounding herself with the colors Ty loved might bring him closer. When she got home, the message light failed to blink, so she left another request for a return call.

As Angie worked on the decorating project, she rehearsed the explanation of the plan taking shape in her mind. Painting made her perspire, so she came down off the ladder, sat down to rest, and drank iced tea. Where had her energy gone? Formerly, she could paint a room in a day. To avoid leaving the house and taking a chance on missing the regressionist's call, Angie ordered a rose floral bedspread and drapes through a catalog.

Late that evening, while Angie watched a boring comedy on TV, Dr. Powers called and said, "If you're ready to process the information you received in your regression, I'd be happy to make an appointment."

"That's not quite what I had in mind." Angie turned off the TV, so delighted to be talking to Dr. Powers that she rushed ahead without considering the doctor's suggestion. "I want you to take me forward in time, so I can meet Ty and plan what our next life is going to be."

"What do you mean?"

"In the regression, I remembered reuniting with him after his death as Trevor." Pacing, Angie explained patiently, "But, when we met in my dream reality it was after his death as Ty."

"Yes, of course." Dr. Powers' British reserve came through clearly in her tone and her accent.

"I really don't know where he is today or where he will be in the future. He said he intended to go to another dimension. Was that after the life as Trevor or is he there now?" Angie reminded herself to slow her words. "There are lots of things I'd like to find out."

"Why don't we take you back into the past again? That way we can ask those questions." The doctor's suggestion seemed off the point.

"I'm concerned about the future. What about when I die? Will he meet me at the incoming portal?"

"I would think so, if he's not reincarnated already."

The prospect that Ty might go into another lifetime without her concerned Angie. "If I can regress myself forward, maybe I should call that 'progress' myself, into the time after my own death, I should be able to talk with Ty again. Then, we could plan what's going to happen in the next life as we planned after we were Ashley and Trevor. I've got to get myself into the future."

"I'm afraid the future isn't for us to know, Angie." Dr. Powers sounded resolute. Perhaps other patients had made the same request of her.

"Maybe I'm not making myself clear." Sitting on the blue and green couch, Angie picked up her wine glass, then set it back down, annoyed at finding it empty. "You know how I remembered planning with Trevor what would happen in our next lifetimes as Angie and Ty?"

"You mean that you would atone in this life for committing suicide in the last?"

"Right. Well, I just want to do more of that planning, only forward in time. If I can go back, I can go forward." Because Dr. Powers remained silent, Angie plunged on. "I believe I'm capable of that. Ty and I could plan who we want to be in our next lives. He'll do whatever work needs to be done in the spirit world to get ready. I can do some things here." Remembering the visit to the observatory where she and Ty had made their covenant to meet again, Angie laughed. "Like leave a message in a trunk, for example."

"I don't think you should try," Dr. Powers said, her tone fearful. "It's dangerous. There's much we don't know about the future or God's plan for us."

"Well, not literally a trunk." Angie wished she had not tried to joke. "I just thought it would be possible to leave a trail. I don't know what, maybe write a diary or set up a trust fund. I'm brainstorming here." Angie's free hand fluttered in all directions. "If I knew who we would be next time around, maybe I could leave some markers to go by, you know, so Ty and I can recognize each other. Maybe we could decide what city we're going to live in. Or, what kind of work we'll want to do. What we'll look like—"

The doctor's shallow breathing indicated her hesitancy. "What makes you so sure you'll reincarnate with him? Maybe that's not the best thing for you to do."

"Of course, it is. We love each other." Discouraged at failing to persuade the doctor, Angie felt tense. "I'm trying to help us create new lives together. What could be wrong with that?"

"It's not right, Angie. You should focus on the life you're living now. I wouldn't feel right about helping you plan your next life before you've finished this one."

Pacing the living room, Angie threaded the coiled phone cord through her fingers. "What are you saying?"

Her voice harsh, Dr. Powers said, "You want me to try to help you manipulate the future."

"Not—"

"Please, you're putting me in the role of God, whether you intend to or not. We might interfere with the divine plan for your lives. I can't do that." In soft, even tones, Dr. Powers conveyed anger expertly controlled.

"You wouldn't be interfering, you'd be helping me," Angie pleaded.

"No. I'm sorry. I can't help you," Dr. Powers said, voice flat with her own kind of judgment.

In the silence, Angie picked up the glass and walked to the kitchen, stretching the phone cord to its limit. There, she retrieved a bottle of Chardonnay from the refrigerator and poured another a drink while trying to recover from her disappointment. Like a good counselor, the doctor remained silent. "Why?" Angie finally asked.

"It's wrong, unethical. It might even be immoral. Angie, you're an excellent regression subject, when your hypnotist is responsible and in control. I caution you against any involvement in spiritualist work, which is obviously what you're speaking of here. You're psychologically, uh, shall we say 'delicate' from your paranormal experiences and your loss. Please don't try to go through with this plan. It's dangerous."

"Dangerous?" Stunned, Angie needed time to think through the doctor's response. "There's nothing to fear except doing nothing. Please help me."

"No. I'm sorry if you thought I'd willingly participate in such a project. Give it up, now. I want to help you sort all this out, but I can only feel good about doing so in a counseling situation. Will you do that?"

"But, that's not what I need."

"I hope you change your mind. Call me if you do." Dr. Powers' voice sounded kind despite her refusal. "Get some sleep. Good night, Angie."

"Good-bye." The phone line hummed in Angie's ear. How could the doctor believe the search wrong? She should know better than anyone—it's a need, a soul need—and what the hell did she mean "delicate?" Did Dr. Powers think Angie was crazy? And why use the word "dangerous"?

Determined to find another way, Angie flipped through the yellow pages. An ad for Madame Bella promised communication with deceased loved ones. With nothing to lose, Angie phoned and made an appointment for the next evening, relieved to have a plan, even though not the one she had hoped.

Walking into the darkened dining room, Angie sipped the wine and stared into the backyard at the wavy aqua reflections from the pool light. In the silent house, she missed Luke and wondered if he felt happy five days into the honeymoon. Hopefully, Mother and Gerald got home to Florida all right. Angie felt lonely and called Jillian to ask how school went the past week.

"Nothing exciting to report," Jillian whispered, her voice gruff in a pleasantly puzzling way. "Could I call you back later?"

"Sure. Is Hank there?"

Jillian's laugh sounded delightfully wicked. "Yes."

"Why don't the two of you go with me to Madame Bella's. I've got an appointment with her for tomorrow night?"

Speaking briskly, Jillian said, "I'll ask him and let you know. Talk to you later."

The call might have interrupted their lovemaking. Smiling at the thought, Angie walked toward the stairs as the phone rang.

Hank's voice boomed, "My God, Angie. Madame Bella? You're scraping the bottom of the barrel."

"Not a good reputation, huh?"

"That woman is a quack. She materializes toy horns that dance in the air, supposedly to announce the presence of spirits. The manufacturer's labels are still on the horns."

Although sheepish in the face of Hank's authority on this subject, Angie felt frustrated. "Oh, come on, Hank. I've got to find somebody to help me, or I'm never going to connect with Ty."

"Don't go to that woman. She's been arrested I don't know how many times, a disgrace to the society of mediums. In fact, the organization's been trying to get her out of Phoenix for years."

"You couldn't help me," Angie shouted angrily. "Now, Dr. Powers refuses. This woman says she will, so I'm going anyway. Don't try to stop me."

Just as Hank asked something about Dr. Powers, Angie slammed down the phone, aware that she acted irrationally in hanging up on him. Hank had done nothing except try to warn her, and he probably told the truth. Sensing she would have to give up on Madame Bella, Angie regretted her rudeness but decided to call back later to apologize. No point in interrupting their lovemaking twice.

The sweetness of those times with Ty filled her memory as she trudged upstairs and fell asleep, desolate.

The next day in a rundown section of South Phoenix, a pink neon sign announced "Madame Bella, Psychic Counselor" in front of a bungalow with discolored stucco—the only residence left on a street with a pawn shop, a convenience store, and a check-cashing business. Once inside, Angie found her sinuses overwhelmed by the bitter smell of dime-store incense.

In the semi-darkened living room, Madame Bella herself failed to inspire confidence with her fleshy face and long, painted nails clicking on a card table. She spoke in generalities then pretended to swoon and gave Angie a message from an "Uncle Henry," not a family member that Angie had ever heard of previously.

After the session, she thanked the medium, paid her fifty dollars, and called the whole episode "a learning experience." Hank had been right.

From there, Angie drove to the public library and checked out all the books she could find on reincarnation— The *Nature of Personal Reality: A Seth Book* by Jane Roberts, *The Search for Bridey Murphy*, and a new one, *We Don't Die* by Joel Martin and Patricia Romanowski, among others.

Angie spent many days and nights lying in bed, reading. *The Tibetan Book of the Dead* indicated that people who had recently died might stay bound to the earth. If a living person read certain instructions, the deceased soul would hear and take courage in accepting death. The situation did not quite fit Angie's because she was clinging to Ty, rather than he to her. Needing to keep her search alive, she did not know what else to do, so she read aloud to him, hoping he would hear and come to her.

Alone, she grew more frustrated with each passing day. The dream of herself gingerly stepping through the woods with Ty always out of reach became a metaphor of her lost self-confidence. Angie did not know how to regain the calm center she had experienced while in trance and when Ty met her in the dream reality. Nothing worked.

One night Angie threw down the Tibetan guidebook and covered her face with her hands, wondering why she persisted on this quest. Did she think she could deny death? Unwillingly, she faced the dread that there was nothing but the grave. Perhaps she had deluded herself in every way. If she called on her guide for comfort, she might learn that Emmons did not exist. Had she imagined the reincarnation memory of Ashley? In her dismal scenario, she could have made up the whole regression.

How could she know for sure? With no sense of contrivance, pictures and responses had simply appeared in her mind at the suggestions of Dr. Powers. Perhaps they had always lain dormant there, waiting for remembrance. If Angie had unconsciously made up the past-life memory, she might be as crazy as her mother, a fear so great Angie's thoughts fled from the idea.

The painful episode of Ashley's short life came to her— the dread of childbearing, the obsession for dance that had given her life meaning, so like Angie's own compulsion to find Ty. To commit suicide and end her young life seemed a desperate act, but Angie understood what despair could provoke. In those first days after Ty's plane crash, she had awakened from a Valium fog and thought death preferable to the grief. She had conquered her anguish well enough to go on living, maybe because of Ashley's mistake.

Whether others named the psychic experiences insanity or not, Angie must honor her own mind. A baseline integrity told her they had great value, even though not yet discernible. At the least, intuition had warned her and kept her alive. At the most, supernatural insights might imbue her soul with meaning.

Unwilling to accept defeat, Angie wanted to go on believing she would find Ty somehow but could not figure out what to do next. She missed Luke and wanted him to come home, but he would not come home to her, not anymore. Melinda would be with him, her nose self-importantly in the air.

Angie sighed, too tired to make the effort to cry. Certain morning would come, no matter how much she wished it would not, she fell into a trance-like sleep, carrying her sorrow into another place.

Angie dreamed that she sat on bleached earth, a white gown spread about her. Mournfully, she leaned against a large, rounded stone, a forest of gnarled oak trees beyond dimly visible through the mist.

In a pale blue morning coat, Emmons came to her, a loving smile on his face. Dusting a spot with his riding crop, he asked, "May I join you?" Without waiting for her response, he sat beside her. "My dear Alma, I came to restore your faith in yourself."

His use of the name "Alma" transfixed her. That was her soul name, Angie knew instinctively. She listened, unable to reply.

"You have been here many times before in many lifetimes. I have always loved you, as has he." Emmons pointed toward Ty's blanched corpse lying atop one of the rounded stones.

A shudder of sorrow and loss passed through Angie when she gazed toward the bier on which lay the empty shell that had once been her lover.

"My dear Alma, this is not the first time you have grieved his passing into the other world. Once, you abandoned him, and he died because of your pride. One of your soul tasks is to atone to him."

A cold wind rustled across the silent moor. Angie felt gratitude. Her guide told her what she needed to remember.

"As Alison in my time," Emmons tapped his eighteenth-century coat, "you accomplished much,

overcoming haughtiness and devoting yourself to the welfare of both your son and Thomas. In that manner, you gained balance. Your recent soul memory showed you the opportunity to advance. Unfortunately, you complicated the task by the suicide as Ashley. In the present lifetime, you have accomplished much but still give up too easily. You must learn to endure and accept the needs of others as equally important as your own."

Angie felt confused because she knew she had honored Ty's and Luke's needs in this lifetime. Regretfully, her lack of charity toward her mother and Melinda made his point. When a gratified look spread across Emmons's face, Angie understood that she need not speak to communicate with him. He knew her thoughts.

Emmons said, "In different guises, your lover, Taliesin, has remained faithful to you through many ages, yet he faces a persistent struggle for belief in the Divine. A demonstration of his challenge is preoccupation with war, recently mitigated by his choice to work for the public good."

Eager to learn of Ty, Angie listened to her guide's words.

"As Thomas, he allowed his multi-dimensional self more play and vicariously experienced union with Ty across two centuries. In an insightful moment, the duality of the Battle of Culloden and the Vietnam War merged into one and the same effort. The creative definition of his soul work sprang from this experience of time displacement. He wanted to help the human race to learn to fly. At the present time Ty is learning about space travel from discarnate beings on Alpha-Centauri and neighboring planets. His new skills will benefit Earth in years to come.

Now aware of why Ty no longer came to her, Angie felt proud of her lover's spiritual growth.

"You have always been strong and independent, my dear Alma. Teaching the youth as both Alison and Angie benefited them and you. Your psychic experiences have helped many to expand beyond their limited perceptions. Your soul force compels you to teach spiritual ideas as you learn them yourself. Now, you are coming to understand generosity of spirit as your lover learns to trust his budding faith. You are bound to each other in eternal love. I trust my message has served you."

Emmons stood, bowed to her in a quaint and courtly fashion then vanished into the mist.

The next morning, her heart warmed when Angie awoke. The golden sun shone brightly through the bedroom window, giving the rose-colored coverlet a glow. At peace with her grief, Angie felt a new willingness to accept whatever life brought her.

Eighteen

To Live a Life

Luke and Melinda's apartment, May, 1988

Leaning against the bedroom doorframe, Luke watched Melinda apply makeup. The vanity lights suffused her lovely face in an irresistible glow, and the rich black waves of her hair seemed to float around her beautiful shoulders. Proudly, he finished giving her the account of his oral argument in court that day.

"I'm sure you gave a great closing, darling." Melinda snapped a lipstick shut and straightened her floor-length, sleeveless, black gown.

"You're gonna knock 'em dead at the party tonight, babe." Luke loved her sleek, modern style.

After dabbing heavenly smelling musky perfume behind her ears and between her gorgeous breasts, Melinda went into the bathroom, calling out through the partially opened door. "I intend to tell your boss what a treasure she's got in you."

"Tell her one more raise and I'll be as upwardly mobile as my wife." Luke knew their competition excited Melinda. She loved making money and spending it. They lived at the limit of their combined salaries, but not over it. Melinda handled their budget so well they contributed to a portfolio and sent her family a check every month.

Their Siamese cat rubbed against his leg. Luke picked him up. "Hey, Diablo, what's happening?"

"Oh, damn." Melinda came out scowling. "I was sure I'd started my period. But no. Five days late."

"Really?"

"Yes, and if I'm pregnant, we won't have to look far for the culprit, will we?" Grinning wryly, she gave him a quick kiss then rubbed a mewing Diablo's head. Donning a bugle bead cape, Melinda said, "Let's go."

Luke brushed cat hair off his suit coat and followed her out to the hallway. Even though they'd agreed to postpone having children until their careers were in full swing, the idea that Melinda might be pregnant thrilled him. She wouldn't like it, though. "Five days isn't much. You've been that late before haven't you?"

"Never!" Melinda sounded horrified, a hint of panic in her eyes. "I told you I didn't want to have sex that night after we went to my folks' house for dinner."

"Are you serious?" Luke had the notion they might be having a more important conversation than he had realized.

"I told you I was in my fertile time then. But no, you insisted." Did anger flicker in her eyes, or did she merely tease?

"Oh, honey, don't worry." Luke laughed, uncertain which of them remembered correctly. "That was the only time we ever broke your rhythm schedule. I doubt you're pregnant. Hey, I'm always willing to use a condom, but you won't let me."

Melinda hooded her eyes in a way that made Luke feel shut out. "You know the Church doesn't allow anything except rhythm."

The elevator doors opened, and an elderly couple wearing tennis outfits nodded in greeting. Luke smiled back and stepped inside with Melinda. When he put his arm around her waist, she trembled. They rode to the parking garage and walked to the car in silence. Inside his new Trans-Am, Luke cupped her face in his hands. "I love you."

"I'm scared," Melinda whispered.

"I know. It'll be okay." Luke kissed her gently.

The next morning, Melinda bought a pregnancy test kit at the supermarket. The directions said it was not effective unless two weeks had elapsed since the missed period. She grew tenser and quieter every day as the time for the test approached.

Meanwhile, Luke imagined the headline: ACCOUNTANT BIRTHS WORLD'S BEST BABY. In daydreams he cuddled the child in his arms, watched it learn to walk and talk, met its teachers, played ball with it. Mom would love a baby. There would have to be brothers and sisters also. Luke had gotten the child all the way through college graduation more than once before reminding himself Melinda might not be pregnant.

If she were, she could insist on an abortion. Luke would hate it but could not in good conscience stop her. It was her life and her body. Still, this would be his child, too. The idea of surgically removing it grated on Luke. He wanted to know and love his child. Time dragged by until the test day.

The following Saturday, Melinda awakened nauseous, went into the bathroom, and remained there a long time. Since she had complained the previous two mornings, Luke felt certain the test would prove positive but could not predict her reaction even though he knew his wife pretty well.

Luke made a pot of coffee and pretended to read a brief. After an hour he could not stand the tension anymore and opened the bedroom door. In a pale green gown, Melinda lay on the black and white checked sheets, one hand across her stomach, staring at the ceiling. When he sat beside her, she did not move. "Positive, huh?" he asked softly.

Sighing, Melinda covered her eyes and whispered, "Yes."

Loving her more than ever, Luke lay down beside her in silence, wanting to sympathize but consumed by a rush of joy. When he cradled her in his arms, she cried, and he said, "I'm glad we're going to have a baby. Don't worry. Everything'll be okay."

Shaking her head, Melinda pushed him away, swung her legs over the side of the bed, and strode to the door. Holding the doorknob for a long moment, she wiped her eyes then turned to him, her impeccable face calm, as though she had made up her mind. "I can't have this baby, Luke. My promotion will go out the window."

His stomach churned. Luke needed to convince her to want it, too. "I know the timing is bad, babe, but we'll face that all right. I can get a loan to cover bills while you're off. You can go back to the office right away. We'll find a good sitter."

"No, it won't work." Melinda wandered into the living room.

Leaping off the bed, Luke followed her. "You know your boss will give you leave. You're too important to the company. It won't hurt your career."

"This isn't about a few months off from my job." Her voice wavered, and she ran one hand back and forth along the white leather couch. "This child will be my responsibility afterward. I can't have that kind of drain on my time and energy. I've got to build my career." Melinda punched a large red pillow. "I'm so close to being able to go on my own. This will set me back, maybe keep me from ever making it."

"Now, wait, Melinda. This baby's my responsibility, too." Luke knelt on the couch and took her hands in his. "I want it. I'll take care of it. Hell, I'd be happy as a house husband. Think you can support me?" He laughed, but she didn't.

"You don't mean that."

"Yes, I do." The thought charmed Luke. Practicing law could wait. His wife did not understand him as well as he had thought. When her expression indicated disbelief, he feared her determination and asked, "Why don't you talk to your mother before you decide about an abortion?"

"She'd be horrified. Making babies was her whole life. She'd think I was going straight to hell, then she'd tell Dad." Shuddering, Melinda turned away. "He'd never understand."

"How about your sisters?"

"No. This is my problem. I don't want to talk to anyone."

Wanting to be included, Luke hoped using "we" would jog her into thinking of this as a joint decision. "Why don't we go see your doctor before we make any final decision?"

"Not a chance. His office is in the same block where my folks live. It'd be all over the barrio in fifteen minutes. Might as well send my family a telegram."

Frustrated, Luke stared out the window. Under a rain-soaked sky, Phoenix stretched out for miles, dark and ugly. Melinda systematically eliminated anyone who might argue against abortion.

Angie would know what to say, but he did not suggest her. Even though he had hoped his two ladies could become friends, Luke had noticed coolness between them since Christmas. They sidestepped each other, as though by agreement not to engage in any meaningful conversation. Luke said, "How about this. Go see Dr. Gutierrez. Have a checkup. Talk to him."

"Does he do abortions?" Melinda's chin quivered, indicating she might not be as sure of herself as she sounded.

"I don't know, but I trust him. He's been my doctor as long as I can remember. Will you see him?" Her hesitation angered Luke, and he shouted, "Melinda, for God's sake. This is my baby, too."

"Oh, I know." Wrapping her arms around his neck, Melinda looked into his eyes, their noses almost touching. "You're such a lover. I wish you had a harder edge to you. Guess it's up to me to be strong for both of us... to demand the excellence and the sacrifice we need to really make it."

Her musky scent enticed Luke, but her words repelled him. He hated knowing his wife thought of him as weak. "Success isn't worth this."

"You want the baby, don't you?" When he nodded, Melinda said, "Okay, I'll talk to your doctor. At least he's Hispanic and a professional. Maybe he'll understand what I'm trying to do."

The day of the appointment, Luke waited impatiently in Doc Gutierrez's reception area that always smelled of crayons. Looking very sad, Melinda opened the office door and motioned with her finger for him to come in. Throwing a tattered magazine down, Luke followed her through the familiar whitewashed rooms. The last time he'd been here, when he'd stopped taking his epilepsy medicine, Doc gave him a stern talk about responsibility. Would he be friend or foe today?

Stocky, middle-aged, with gray hair and mustache, Doc sat at his dark wood desk. Framed licenses and pictures of his wife and children hung on the walls behind him. Luke and Melinda sat in Indian-print barrel chairs on the other side of the wide desk. Doc removed his glasses and rubbed his eyes for a long time, as if the act were part of his thought process.

Just as he'd done so many times over the years, Doc spoke to the core issue. "Your wife says she wants an abortion. What do you want?"

Luke trusted Doc to know what was medically safe and to give the best advice. "I'd like to have the baby, Doc, but, bottom line, it's not my decision. I know it's not for me to say. I wish it was." Luke wondered if he would be able to support Melinda should she actually decide to go through with an abortion. Would he still love her, or would he come to hate her for killing their child?

"You'll pardon my asking," Doc said, "but why didn't you use birth control if you didn't want to get pregnant?"

When Melinda's face flushed scarlet, Luke held her sweaty hand and tried to cover for her. "Well, we thought it would work. You know 'rhythm'? She'd never had a sexual relationship or been to a gynecologist, so she... This probably sounds silly to you, Doc. Sounds silly to me now. We should've been more careful." Luke fell silent, wishing they were not considering abortion. They should be happy, anticipating the baby.

"Dr. Gutierrez, it was my idea," Melinda said. "Luke wanted me to go on the pill, but it's not the way I was raised. You understand that, I'm sure."

"What about abortion?" Doc went relentlessly on. "Would you feel okay with that?"

"No. I'd feel guilty." Melinda's shoulders trembled, and she dropped her head. "There's no way this can turn out that I won't feel bad... and guilty. I know abortion is wrong, and I don't really want to do it. It's my job as a woman to have a child. It's what God created me for... at least that's what I was taught to believe."

"Abortion's too important to act on someone else's beliefs." With a stern look, Doc said, "Do you know what yours are?"

"I think so. It's my body, and until the fetus is viable, I've got a right to abort."

Leaning back, Doc folded his arms and asked, "What about its soul?" Maybe the doctor sided with Luke after all.

"I don't know. I just know I feel trapped," Melinda whispered. Her hand flitted up then dropped restlessly into her lap. "That's not all there is to it. I have a career to consider. For myself and for others who are... depending on me. Hispanic women who'll come to work for me and gain self-esteem from my success. They won't be defined by their bodies, just like I can't let myself be."

Although Melinda seemed powerful and certain, Luke knew the little girl part of her felt afraid and longed for Daddy's approval so much that she'd remained a virgin until twenty-three. She had even refused to take birth control pills because he might find out. Luke wondered whether her commitment to the marriage was as strong. These few months had given her a glow. She loved their sex life and learned quickly. Luke had thought they had storybook happiness. Now, he no longer felt sure.

Giving Luke a tiny smile, Melinda said, "Luke wants the baby. Seems like there's no way out."

"What does your mother think about this, Luke?" Doc asked.

Regretfully, Luke said, "We haven't told her." Angie had been a part of every important event of his life, up till now. He missed her advice and support.

"Well, she's an intelligent woman who's had a career," Doc said. "She might have some good input."

"No, I don't think so," Melinda shook her head vigorously.

Impatient with her intransigence about his mother, Luke asked, "How much time do we have to make a decision?"

"Tentatively, I'd project a due date in mid-January. So, you've got till July. The sooner the better, if you're going to abort." Doc handed Melinda a business card. "This is an excellent family planning counselor. I hope you'll talk with her. If you decide to abort, let me know as soon as you can. I'll recommend a doctor."

"Oh, you don't do them?" Melinda seemed disappointed.

"No. Catholic upbringing too strong in me. Guess you know what I mean." Doc smiled disarmingly at her and pushed back his chair.

"Thanks, Doc," Luke said. The two men stood and shook hands, then Luke and Melinda walked out of the office without speaking.

Once in the corridor, Melinda said, "I don't want you to talk to your mother about this."

"Why not?"

"I don't want her to know about the abortion at all. Promise?"

"Why?" Keeping such a huge secret from her seemed dishonest to Luke.

"She might put a hex on me."

"God, Melinda, my mom's not a witch!"

"I can't help it. Sometimes when she looks at me, those blue eyes drill right into my soul. She scares me."

Luke felt an impulse to laugh, but his heart hurt too much. "Okay, I won't tell her."

The next Saturday, Luke lay in bed, listening to Melinda make her early morning sounds—shower, electric toothbrush, hair dryer, but she did not hum today. When she came out of the bathroom and leaned over him, the combined scents of perfume and hair spray stung his nostrils. He pretended to be asleep. She touched his cheek with her fingers. Then he heard the bedroom door close.

Rolling over, Luke stared at a wall painting of red, orange, and pink, its chaotic brush strokes reflecting his own confusion. Should he consider himself a coward, a cad, or a goat? He could not bear to go with his wife because he hated her intention. She had refused to talk to the counselor. The more he tried to change her mind, the greater her determination grew. They had ended in a dreadful argument and had barely spoken for the past two days.

In good conscience, Luke could not stop Melinda from doing what she felt she needed to do, but neither could he support her. He had begun to doubt he would still be able to love her afterward. What could he say to her when she returned, "How was your day?" He'd always thought epilepsy the worst thing that could happen to him, till now.

Conversation in the kitchen interrupted his introspection. *Is that Mom's voice?* She never came to visit without an invitation. Curious, he leaped out of bed, pulled on his jeans, and opened the door, zipping up as he ran.

In the middle of the black and white kitchen floor stood Mom, hands on hips, glaring at Melinda, who looked like a five-year-old who'd gotten caught pulling down her panties to show the boy next door.

"Why won't you tell me where you're going?" Angie scolded as Melinda cast a pleading look at Luke.

"Hi, Mom." Luke kissed Angie's cheek, but she didn't seem to notice. God, was she on a tear! Somehow, she knew, he'd bet any amount of money.

Angie felt as if she had just disciplined an unruly student. Hating the awkward moment, she reminded herself to stay calm. She had too much at stake to lose her temper. "I want to know where you're going." Although Angie had already dreamed her daughter-in-law's destination, verification seemed important. "Melinda, I'd appreciate a civilized response from you for once. I've never pried into your life or pushed my presence on you in any way. You might give me the benefit of the doubt just once and assume there's a valid reason for my asking."

"It's really none of your business, but I'll tell you anyway." Despite the higher-than-normal pitch of her voice, Melinda spoke in measured words. "I was on my way to a doctor's appointment."

"Are you pregnant?"

Melinda laughed nervously. "Of course not. That's ridiculous."

When Angie glanced at Luke, his expression of surprise told her that Melinda lied. "God, you are. I knew it. I just knew it." Sitting on a black lacquer stool, Angie folded her arms and shook her head, relieved to know she had been right.

"What's going on, Mom?"

Pointing at Melinda's mid-section, Angie said, "Let me tell you when that baby's due—January 16th."

Melinda's mouth dropped open. "How'd you know?"

"Ty's birthday. I had a dream last night. I was in a dark, scary place, kind of feeling my way along a wall. I could hear a woman crying and tried to get to her. I came around a corner, and there was a bright light shining on a table. You lay on the table, Melinda. A man stood over you, and I knew he intended to hurt you. You begged him not to cut on you. He sneered and laughed, a horrible snigger. Then he pointed at your stomach and said, 'This could be Ty.'"

"That's a hell of a dream," Luke said.

"What does that mean, 'it could be Ty'?" Melinda asked.

"That his spirit could be reincarnating in a different body." Angie caught her breath. "He could be coming back as your baby." The words thrilled her.

"That's crazy." As if to protect her unborn child, Melinda crossed her arms over her abdomen. "You can't believe that. Luke, do you believe that?"

Shrugging, Luke said, "Could be. Never thought about it much."

"It's true whether you believe it or not." Angie tried to take Melinda's hands, but the young woman pulled back. "You have something very precious in your body. If it's not Ty, some other spirit wants to come to live with us. I'm sorry we've not become friends, but I'll help you through this, whatever it takes."

Briskly, Melinda moved to the glass table and grabbed her purse. "There's not going to be any pregnancy. I didn't want you to know, but under the circumstances— "

"Not an abortion!" Now, Angie understood the whole import of the dream. She had to save Melinda from doing something they would all regret for the rest of their lives. "You can't do that!"

"She intends to, Mom. That's where she's going." Luke's husky voice revealed he wanted the baby.

Horrified, Angie asked, "How can you allow this?"

"I don't want her to do it, but I can't talk her out of it." Luke sounded defeated. "I've no legal right to stop her."

His haughty wife gave him a withering look as if his opinion were the last one she would consider. Flushing, Luke took a step toward Melinda then stopped and banged his fist on the red tile counter. Angie's heart went out to him.

Melinda glanced at her watch. "I'm late."

Convinced the young woman had no notion of what the repercussions would be, Angie said, "Please, this is such a final step. Can't we talk about it?"

"Okay. What do you want to say?" Melinda stared down and drummed her fingers on her purse in a manner obviously designed to annoy her mother-in-law.

Refusing to rise to the bait, Angie calmed her voice, imagining she spoke to a troubled student the way she had done many times at school. "I want to know why. Tell me how you feel."

"I've told you before that building my own business is the most important thing in the world to me." Although she sounded defensive, Melinda spoke earnestly. "A baby is too much interference. I'll always be second rate. You have to sacrifice to make it big. I'm willing to make that sacrifice."

Appalled that her daughter-in-law considered a baby's life a reasonable sacrifice, Angie tried a different tack. "What about Luke? Don't his needs count?"

"Yes, but I told him before we got married I didn't want any children. Not for several years, if ever. He knew that." Melinda did not act like she loved Luke at all.

"It's one thing to agree when you're planning the future. But this is his child now. He already loves it and has a right to know it. I can't stand to see you hurting my son like this."

"Mom, she's got to do what she thinks is right. She deserves my support in that... " Luke stumbled, obviously unconvinced by his own rhetoric.

"Right now," Angie said more gently to Melinda, "you might think your job's more important, but how are you going to feel about this next week or next year? I'm afraid you're going to think back and wonder what the baby would look like. That cannot help but make you feel sad. You'll wonder what he'd be—"

"You don't know it's a boy." Melinda's black eyes narrowed in a defiant stare.

"Yes, I do." Angie saw the young woman blanch and suddenly realized that Melinda feared her. Only a fool would fail to take advantage of such an edge. "What if you can't get pregnant again someday? Sometimes that happens after a woman's had an abortion. Then what? You'll regret it then."

"Don't do this to me." Melinda hurried toward the door.

A flash of despair swept through Angie as she remembered facing Melinda's dilemma in the lifetime as Ashley. Unable to resolve those issues, she had drowned herself. Angie wanted to help Melinda avoid the same fate. The dream could have many interpretations besides a message of Ty's return. It could have been a suicide warning. Angie refused to allow her daughter-in-law to kill either the baby or herself. Grabbing Melinda's arm, Angie spoke in her most commanding voice. "No, you can't do this. I won't let you."

"Mom."

Melinda's words came in a high, fast pitch. "It's my body. You don't have any say in this."

"That's where you're wrong." Tightening her grip, Angie leaned close to Melinda's face and snarled. "You're a well-brought up young woman, smart, too. You know damned well abortion is wrong, and I know you don't really want to go through with it."

"That's your opinion." Melinda jerked back and grabbed the doorknob, attempting to shake Angie's hold on her.

"It's yours, too," Angie roared.

"Don't tell me what I think."

"This isn't just about you. It's Luke's child too, and mine. We're a family. You know what that means. Why, surely your mom and dad don't condone your having an abortion." Melinda's eyes fluttered, and she glanced away with such shame that Angie knew the truth. "You haven't told them either, have you?"

"No," Melinda whispered.

"Of course not. You know what they'd say." Angie's captive remained silent, shuddering beneath her hand. Now was the moment to save the child, save a channel for Ty or another soul. Especially, this was the moment to save Melinda. "Right this minute you're terrified that you're doing murder. You're afraid you'll always regret it. Aren't you? Look me in the eye and tell me I'm wrong." Angie released her hold on the young woman.

"No, no." Falling forward, Melinda beat on the door. Her shoulders shook and she sobbed, hovering as if her legs had lost their ability to support her. Then she slid to the floor, crying, "How can you know what I feel?"

Responding to the fear and shame in Melinda's contorted face, Angie embraced her. "I do understand, dear, in spite of what you think of me."

Luke knelt beside them. "Let me take her, Mom."

"Don't touch me." Melinda scrambled up and ran into the bedroom.

Holding his arms out in a gesture of supplication, Luke looked so downhearted that Angie wished she could make it all right, as she had when he was little. His wife seemed equally as needy today. Angie squeezed Luke's hands. "Go to her, honey."

With an anguished nod, Luke followed Melinda, who fell crying across the bed. He tried to hold her, but she would not turn over.

From the doorway, Angie hoped her voice conveyed the compassion she felt. "You can't do this, Melinda. You'll kill your own spirit if you do."

"I know. I know." Raising her head of glossy hair, Melinda moaned, "I can't kill my own baby. I'd be a monster."

Luke engulfed Melinda in his embrace, crying, "Oh, thank God, thank God," and rocking her. When he laughed out loud, she pulled back and looked at him, as if searching for forgiveness. She must have found it because they clung tightly together.

As Angie hugged both of them at the same time, Melinda glanced up. Her huge eyes gave her face the haunted look of a de Grazia painting, vulnerable and, for once at least, like a lovable child. Angie kissed her cheek, then Luke's and walked out, stepping so lightly she almost danced through the bedroom doorway.

"Thanks, Mom!" Luke shouted, his voice finally merry, like a prospective father's should sound.

As Angie let herself out, she said, "Call me 'Grandma.'"

Nineteen

Birthing

January, 1989

Although Luke felt awkward about knocking at the home he had grown up in, he did anyway because Angie needed space. More private than before, she never seemed to have company. These days his wife behaved the opposite, calling him at work every few hours, depending on him for support.

Melinda worried him all the time. Had she gained too much weight or maybe not enough? Would she be okay? How badly would the delivery hurt her? He often had unsettling dreams of a stillborn baby and prayed for a healthy one, especially with no epilepsy. A boy. Mom's idea of Ty's returning might have been off the wall, but she had been right about the sex. The ultra-sound confirmed her prediction.

The little boy would need a good father. Since Luke had never known his own, he hoped he could fill the baby's needs. He pondered whether or not they had put enough money into the college fund. This being an expectant father had turned out surprisingly unsettling. At work, he always felt calm, even enjoying the tension of courtroom conflict. How could one little baby undo his self-control?

Even though Melinda waited impatiently for Luke at home, he needed to spend a little time with his mother but promised himself he would not burden her. Missing the security he always felt with her, he entered the living room, calling, "Hi, I'm here."

"Come on up, honey." Angie's happy response made him feel guilty for visiting so seldom. They had not talked since Christmas Eve, almost three weeks ago.

The main floor of the house looked neat although a layer of dust covered the tables, something that never happened when he was a kid. They'd cleaned every weekend, and Mom had taken great pride in their home. Even though it was modest by his standards today, she had done well for them on a teacher's salary.

Out of habit, Luke picked up a stack of towels from the stairs, carried them up, and set them on the sink in Angie's bath adjoining her bedroom. It looked nice since she repainted and added bookshelves, but she spent too much time there. Wearing an old robe, Angie sat in her rocker with a book on her lap, her black hair streaked with gray she no longer dyed. Luke kissed her warm, moist forehead. "You okay? Got a fever?"

"No, I'm fine. What's up with you?"

"Not much." Luke wanted to tell her the turmoil he felt, but he had promised Melinda not to confide any details of the pregnancy to her. Once his wife decided to have the baby, she acted as if it had been her own idea. He suspected she still feared Angie might be part witch. "What you reading?"

"*The Bridge Across Forever*, Richard Bach's new book." She dropped it on a stack beside her chair. "How's Melinda?"

Unable to pretend for very long, Luke wished he had not come. Maybe he worried too much. The closer the due date, the more volatile Melinda became, one moment withdrawn and sullen, the next tearful and needy. Getting through the pregnancy seemed to be her focus, not bringing a child into the world. Luke sometimes wondered whether she would love the baby but reassured himself she would be okay once it arrived. Even so, he dreaded going home to her.

"I said, 'how's Melinda'? Okay?"

Luke grinned and resolved to put on a better face. "Never better." Relaxing, he sat on the bed and loosened his tie as he told Angie about his oral argument earlier in the afternoon and how excited he had felt in court. Then he described one of Ted's antics with the secretaries. She listened, smiled, and laughed at the right places but stared at him in a peculiar way as he stood to leave.

Reaching up, Angie touched his cheek with a warm hand. "Where are you these days, Luke?"

"A little preoccupied, I guess." Feeling dumb, he scratched his head in an exaggerated way, to demonstrate. "Shows, does it?" When she laughed, Luke felt relieved. At least Angie did not act angry with him. He had never been able to hide much from her and never wanted to previously. Maybe that was the real reason he had come to see her, so she would help him face his demons like she used to do. She always knew what went on inside him. He might as well tell her and use her intuition. "I'm scared to death, Mom. It's hell being an expectant father."

"Waiting's probably getting to you." Angie smiled in a comfortable way as if glad to slip into their old roles. "Just remember, no matter how bad it gets for you, it's a lot worse for her."

"God, I know. I try to imagine how it would feel to have a child growing inside me, but it's just too ludicrous. When I touch the baby, Melinda's skin feels so taut and tender, like it must hurt all the time, and she sure looks uncomfortable. She holds her back, and it's hell for her to walk across the room. Sometimes, she even cries and tries to keep me from hearing. I feel sorry for her."

The phone on the bedside table rang, and Angie grabbed it. "Hello. You all right? Yes, he's here." Shoving the receiver to Luke's ear, she said, "I'll get dressed," then jumped up and dashed into the walk-in closet.

Luke's neck muscles contracted as he listened to a terrified Melinda. "No, don't call a taxi. Of course, I want to take you. Be there in ten minutes. No, five." Slamming down the phone, he yelled as he started toward the door. "Shit, Mom, this is it. You coming?"

"Right behind you." Angie yanked up her slack's zipper and slid into shoes at the same time. Her face flushed. She caught her hair back in a clip, grinning. "I wouldn't miss this for the world."

Ignoring the speed limit, Luke drove while Angie stared straight ahead and shoved her own foot into the floorboard each time he pressed the brakes. They dashed inside his apartment.

Sprawled on the couch, a sweaty Melinda looked as panicky as he felt. Moaning in an effort to rise, she hauled up her massive and unwieldy load of a stomach. Luke and Angie helped her out of the apartment and into the back seat of the car. Angie climbed in beside her, and he scrambled behind the steering wheel.

Luke could see the headlines now: EXPECTANT FATHER SAVES WIFE AND UNBORN CHILD. Somewhere down the column of the newspaper story, they'd describe how he careened around corners on two wheels, sideswiped cars, leaped tall buildings in a single bound, and got to the hospital in the nick of time.

When the car turned the corner onto Camelback Road, a light drizzle dampened the windshield. In the rear view mirror, he saw Melinda's head as she leaned forward and panted. She seemed to welcome Angie's help. Luke winced, wishing he really were Superman so he could rescue her.

"Oh, God," Melinda groaned.

Rubbing the back of Melinda's neck, Angie murmured, "It's okay, honey. We'll be there soon. You're doing great."

Angie's soothing tone had carried him through many seizures, but Luke felt disconsolate now. Sweat stood on his forehead and trickled down his shirtsleeves. What if Melinda died? Or the baby? It would be his fault. He had caused her pregnancy. She did not want it, but he had let his mother stop the abortion. There could be no doubt that Melinda hated him. His wife would never love him again. How could she, after what he had done to her? Luke did not care if she never spoke to him again, just as long as she came out of this okay. He prayed she and the baby would survive. Then, if Melinda wanted him to go away, he would gladly go, just so they were all right.

With a terrifying scream, Melinda cried, "I think it's coming."

The stoplight at the intersection ahead turned red. Through the early evening traffic, Luke saw the cars in every direction, like he had X-ray eyes. None headed into his path. His hands clamped down on the steering wheel, and he sped through the light.

Mind clear of all other thoughts, he focused on getting to the hospital. He felt powerful, as if he could drive his Trans-Am through hell itself and bring his precious passengers out alive. Pressing the accelerator down, he dodged between cars, ears tuned to hear a siren over Melinda's screams. The police would have to give him an escort once they saw his wife's condition, but no cops appeared. Luke swerved past a bus. Horns honked, but he ignored them.

"Luke," Melinda screamed.

"Almost there, babe." Pulling into the lighted turnaround of the emergency entrance, Luke slammed on the brakes, and jumped out of the car. Angie put the seat up while Melinda cried and panted. Taking as much of her weight as possible, Luke helped her rise.

Uniformed orderlies met him with a wheelchair. "We'll take her from here, pal," one of them said.

When Luke tried to set Melinda in the chair, she arched up as if her body no longer remembered how to bend into a sitting position. Another contraction spread anguish across her face. Luke felt like a knife stabbed into his heart.

"You bastard. This is all your fault." Tears rolled down Melinda's face. "Get away from me."

Stepping back, Luke extended his hands in the air, like a criminal surrendering, to show her he was not touching her. He did not blame her one bit. What a hell of an invasion, to have her body totally out of her control. Yes, he was to blame, all right. If he had not wanted to make love to her so much, especially that one night, she would not be going through all this. She would never love him again, or the baby.

An orderly turned the wheelchair and started down the bright, antiseptic-smelling corridor toward white double doors. Luke followed until someone pulled on his arm from behind him.

A nurse about his age smiled at him. "We need you to sign your wife in. Then you can go upstairs and be with her."

The nurse looked so sympathetic, Luke relaxed. For a moment he observed the split emotions within him as he watched Melinda and the orderlies disappear behind the double doors. Dreading the distressed look on her face, Luke would gladly take the suffering on himself if he could. At the same time, he felt relieved that he had something else to do.

"I'll wait for you here." Angie headed toward a black marble bench.

"Would you call Melinda's folks? They'll want to come down right away."

"Of course."

Luke turned to the nurse. "She's pre-registered. Her name is Melinda Brock." When he finished, he and Angie rode up in the elevator together.

What agony did Melinda face upstairs? Luke feared it might press her beyond her endurance. Maybe she should've had the abortion. He felt guilty about interfering with her rhythm system. Although unwilling to admit it at the time, he had known what he was doing. Part of him wanted to override her objections so they could have a baby.

How could he have been so selfish—making her go through this to satisfy his desires? If only he had supported her in the abortion, Melinda would not be in such misery now.

Angie patted his back. "She's doing fine, honey. Don't worry."

"How long you think it'll be?"

"Hard to say. Soon." Angie spoke as calmly as though they waited for Melinda to come out of the hairdresser's.

When the elevator doors opened, Luke rushed to the nurses' station and asked where to find his wife.

A nurse with iron gray hair said, "Birthing Room Five, down the hall to the left."

"I'll wait for you here." Angie sat on another black marble bench.

With a deep breath, Luke walked through the door of the birthing room. Under the fluorescent overhead light, Melinda lay still, her hair a tangled mess. Her mounded bare belly pulsed restlessly. Dressed in a green shower cap and gown, Doc Gutierrez bent over her. The nurse walked around the bed and checked the blood pressure monitor. Melinda stared vacantly toward him, her face pallid. What was happening? In the scary silence, Luke moved toward her and took her hand.

Firmly, Doc said, "Now, push, one more time."

Melinda strained so hard her cheeks flushed and sweat bubbled up on her forehead. Her long red fingernails bore into Luke's palm. He felt relieved to experience some pain himself. The nurse handed him a cloth, and Luke wiped Melinda's forehead.

"Come on, *mi ja*." Doc's voice sounded gruff despite the endearment. "You're doing it. Here he comes."

With a grimace, Melinda groaned long and loud. Then her head jerked. Luke held his breath. Doc beamed at Luke and, miraculously, held up the glistening, ruddy baby with a shock of black hair. The baby let out a shrill cry, louder than his father thought such a tiny body could produce, and everybody laughed.

"This is your job, son," Doc said as the nurse put scissors in Luke's hand.

Squeamishness he had thought he might experience dissolved the moment Luke cut the cord. He enjoyed the task with an illogical conviction that he had done it many times before this.

When Doc laid the naked, crying baby in Melinda's arms, she stared in what seemed like shocked surprise for a moment, as if part of her mind refused to believe in the baby's reality. Then her face broke into a huge smile. Melinda loved their son. Luke felt like someone had removed a stone from his heart.

Joy swept through him as he kissed his wife, and she kissed him back. That must mean she loved him again. Everything would be all right. He hugged Doc, who clapped his back and laughed. Luke thanked the nurse then watched the radiant mother and son. Only moments ago there had been two of them. Now they had this exquisite new person to love. A real family! "May I hold him?"

"Sure," Melinda murmured.

As Luke nestled the little warm body in his arms, the baby stopped crying. Luke gazed in awe at his perfect face and sweet round head, noticing a tiny mole on his shoulder.

Then, time seemed to stretch into a static moment. Luke's vision blurred. The hospital room and the people in it faded.

Dream-like surroundings replaced them, looking very old with latticework cupboards, like an antique apothecary in a museum.

Transfixed, Luke saw the faces of two babies, then three, then one again—all wrapped in a strangely familiar white cloth. He felt a sense of completion, like coming home.

The nurse's intrusive voice disturbed the reverie. "May I take the baby now, please?"

Confused, Luke glanced at her white-capped head and blinked. "Yes, okay."

Lifting the baby out of Luke's arms, the nurse asked, "What do you call the little guy?"

"Aaron," Luke whispered. When Melinda had suggested the name, he had agreed with little interest. Now, it sounded like a prayer.

"Come along, Aaron," said the nurse, "and we'll get you cleaned up and put a diaper on you." The baby cried as she carried him out of the room.

After Doc offered congratulations, he closed the door behind him. Shaking off the feeling of disorientation, Luke knelt by his wife. "You did great, babe. I'm proud of you."

"Thanks."

"I love you."

Melinda turned her face away. "I need to sleep."

"Course you do. You've done your part. Now I'll do mine." Tenderly, Luke tucked the covers around her, smoothed her hair, and kissed her forehead. "Sleep tight, Mommy dear." Melinda smiled weakly acknowledging the title, and Luke decided he liked the sound of it very much. He went out into the hall to look for Angie.

Still under the spell of the waking dream, Luke thought he might tell her about it. Certainly she would understand, but somehow the experience seemed too precious and private to tell anyone, something just between him and Aaron.

As Luke rounded a turn in the off-white corridor, he saw Doc sitting beside Angie and holding both her hands. Doc spoke to her softly. With her face averted and eyes closed, she obviously did not want to hear what he said. Neither of them seemed to notice Luke's return, and he felt awkward announcing himself. Angie and Doc had become friends over the years because of Luke's illness. He and Angie had been to Doc's home, mostly to Christmas parties, and knew the wife and kids.

"Don't shun me, Angie." Doc spoke in a tone of gentle command. "If you won't do it for me, do it for Luke and that new baby. I'm telling you, you don't look good. Your skin color is off. I want to run some tests. Just come in anytime. You don't need an appointment. You've been through a lot in the last year and a half, and it's taken a toll on you."

Opening her eyes, Angie looked startled when she saw Luke. Freeing her hands, she leaned toward Doc and kissed his fleshy cheek. "You're a dear, but right now you're keeping me from my grandchild." Rising, she hugged Luke. "Congratulations, Daddy. You got through it, too."

Conflicted about what he had just heard, Luke said, "Wait till you see him. He's beautiful!"

Angie took Luke's arm. "Let's go see our baby, okay?"

"Whatever you say." Luke agreed, thinking Doc must suspect something or he would not have spoken so intensely. That validated Luke's recent concern for her health. Later, he would insist she go for a checkup. Right now, she had to see the new baby.

Father and grandmother strode down the hall to the nursery and found Melinda's mother, father, brothers, sisters, and several cousins huddled around the glass window, pointing and laughing. Even the fourteenth grandchild seemed to be a big event.

Twenty

The Vision Understood

On the short drive from her house to Luke's, Angie rolled the car windows down and ran the air-conditioner full blast in an effort to cool the interior, an almost impossible task in August. The constant heat added to her tension in wondering what emotional atmosphere she would encounter on arrival.

Angie strove to keep her relationship with Melinda affable. It would hurt Luke if his two women could not behave civilly toward each other. Perhaps problems steadily worsened between Luke and Melinda, or Angie's ability to cope with the situation had lessened. She didn't know which.

The disc jockey said the temperature had already climbed to a hundred and one degrees by seven in the morning. Another news story focused on the Resolution Trust Company.

Angie had had some success recently selling feature articles to magazines, and she considered writing about the growing embarrassment Arizonans felt regarding the savings and loan scandals and impeachment proceedings for the governor. Marketing the idea would probably be easy, but where would she find the energy to do the work?

Turning the radio off, she pulled into the underground garage and parked. On the elevator, she wished again that Luke and Melinda had moved to a house in the suburbs after the baby's birth. Instead they had rented a bigger apartment in the same high rise. Although not a place she would choose to raise a child, their home was beautiful and conveniently close to hers.

Baby-sitting had not been in her life plan. At first she had refused to take any pay. Melinda and Luke had both insisted since they'd have to pay a daycare center. Because all three of them adored Aaron, she had hoped the arrangement would end the hostility. Some days she believed things had gotten better. Other days, she felt less hopeful. Difficult to read, Melinda blocked Angie's every attempt to understand her.

In spite of the anxiety, Angie did not regret agreeing to take care of the baby because he brought her such joy. It seemed ironic that, with the baby-sitting, the articles, and Ty's life insurance, she had more money than she ever had teaching school. In some ways, life had improved. Angie wished she could take more pleasure in it.

What might she be doing today if Ty were still alive? They might go sailing or perhaps work around the house. Whatever her day held, she would spend the night in his arms. Sadness filled her to think he would never hold her again. A lifetime of going to sleep by herself lay ahead, and she must endure the loneliness.

When Angie let herself in with a key, Melinda stood at the kitchen counter, eating toast and reading the paper. The new mother had worked hard to get her perfect figure back. The svelte fit of a gray pinstriped suit and red silk blouse revealed her success.

"You look pretty this morning, Melinda. Good colors."

"Thanks, are my bags showing?" Melinda pulled on the skin under her eyes.

"No." Angie laughed, appreciating the casual level of conversation they'd been able to achieve, in spite of its artificial quality. By unspoken agreement, they'd not talked about anything important since Melinda agreed to have the baby. In spite of accepting Angie's help before the birth, Melinda still feared her mother-in-law. Angie accepted her daughter-in-law's disdain and never forgot that Melinda had the power to hurt Luke and Aaron.

"Aaron cried... seemed like all night."

"Not sick, is he?" Angie looked down the hall toward the nursery.

"Don't know. We should probably have him looked at. When's his next checkup?"

Angie tugged her daybook out of her purse and flipped to the day. "Tomorrow at ten."

"Okay. I'm out of here." Melinda popped the last bite in her mouth, picked up her shoulder bag, and left.

"Have a good day," Angie called after her and walked down the hall.

No matter how bad she felt, Aaron's nursery made her feel better. She and Luke had painted its sky blue walls with a Cat-in-the-Hat mural from a preprinted design. In the center of the white baby bed sat Aaron with a big toothless grin. His black eyes sparkled when he saw Angie, and he flapped chubby arms on the quilted yellow blanket.

Swooping the baby into the air, Angie jiggled him back and forth. "You glad to see Grandma? I'm glad to see you." Laughing, she gave him a noisy kiss.

Luke came in, tying his tie, and rubbed Aaron's belly. "Hey, little guy, how's it going?" He kissed Angie's cheek. "Melinda leave already?"

"Uh-huh." Angie wished Melinda treated Luke more politely, like saying she was leaving. In a futile attempt to make up for the slight, Angie hugged her son. "How're you today?"

"Okay. Little tired. This guy kept me up half the night, didn't you, buddy?" Luke rubbed the baby's head. "When you see Doc tomorrow, tell him Aaron's been waking up more than he used to. Got to be a reason for that."

"Maybe needs more solid food."

"Could be." Luke nudged her shoulder. "While you're there, why don't you get a checkup, too?"

"I'm fine." Angie tried to disguise her annoyance with a teasing tone. "How'd you get to be such a worry wart?"

"Inherited it from you, I guess. Got to run." Picking up his briefcase, Luke headed toward the door, looking weary, more tired than one sleepless night's worth.

With the baby on her hip, Angie walked into the hall. "Luke, you okay?"

Pausing as if about to say something, he picked up his jacket. "Yeah, fine." With a quick kiss for the baby, Luke went out the door.

When Aaron whimpered, Angie said, "It's all right, baby. Daddy'll be home soon." Opening the refrigerator, she grabbed one of the formula bottles she had filled the previous day and heated it in the microwave. "Let's get you some breakfast, okay?" Holding the wriggling baby on her lap, she fed him cereal, studying the contours of his little round head and full cheeks. She loved to make him laugh by holding his pudgy toes and saying, "This little piggy went to market."

Today Angie sensed his beautiful little soul looking out at her—one she loved dearly without recognizing it. As Aaron's own intelligent light grew within him, she knew for certain he was not Ty. Although disappointed that she could not see Ty in the baby's eyes, she gave up fooling herself. Ty lived in her mind. They would meet again someday, somewhere.

After she bathed and dressed Aaron in an aqua shorts set, they drove to the public library, a place the baby loved. Already at seven months, he seemed to understand the idea of a quiet place. When she carried him down an aisle, he put his round forefinger to his mouth, short arm barely reaching. Angie laughed at his serious appearance, with his black hair, ears like little saucers, and brows furrowed exactly like Luke's.

No doubt Aaron would choose for his life's work something to do with study—maybe not the law like his dad, but definitely graduate work of some kind. Angie visualized him living among bookshelves. She checked out some books on metaphysics and Bishop Pike's book about receiving messages from his late son. Perhaps she would find a new clue to help her contact Ty. At the very least, it pleased her to know others succeeded in communicating with the dead and wrote about it.

Back at Luke's place, Angie put stew in the slow cooker and settled down to read while Aaron napped. Tired herself, she fell asleep and did not wake until Luke turned the key in the lock at five. Hastily, she picked Aaron up, hoping his long nap would not make him fussy later to keep his parents awake all night again.

Because Melinda did not return, they waited dinner until past seven while Luke paced and looked at his watch. Feeling weary, Angie wanted to go home but hated to leave her son looking so discouraged. Although she had not eaten all day, the idea of food sickened her.

Finally at seven thirty, Luke said with downcast eyes, "Guess we may as well go ahead and eat."

"I'll reheat the stew. Maybe she'll be here by the time it's hot."

"Melinda didn't say when she'd be home?" Luke asked. After Angie shook her head, he muttered, "She didn't tell me where she'd be, never does," and laid his head on his arms as if lost in thought.

Melinda had not appeared by the time Angie reheated the dinner. She and Luke ate in silence. Rising, he walked to the playpen, rubbed the baby's head, then strode back into the kitchen and leaned against the refrigerator. Angie waited patiently, knowing motion helped him control his anger.

"She's always working late or attending some conference."

"Her career's a lot more important to her than it is to you." Angie's explanation sounded weak.

"That's for damn sure."

"Ever tell her how you feel?"

"I'd like to throw something, that's how I feel." Luke picked up his china dinner plate and jostled it before dropping it into the sink with a clang.

"Talk, man." Angie smiled indulgently. "Dishes are too expensive." She shoved a kitchen chair toward him.

Straddling the chair and resting his arms on the back, Luke teetered on the legs. At the age of nine, he had practiced that trick to show off for his friends. His face looked drawn and sad. "Mom, our marriage is falling apart. I feel like Melinda's become my enemy, she's so cold and careless. When I try to think about her or figure out how to improve things, I just feel angry and betrayed. She likes the baby okay, but she doesn't have time for him either."

"Have you tried talking to her?"

"Yeah, lots of times. I've used my whole bag of tricks. Can't romance her. She won't argue. Can't even get her drunk. It's like the woman I married is gone. Her body's still here, but her heart sure as hell isn't. She likes you better than she does me these days. At least she talks to you."

Wishing she had some positive suggestion, Angie carried the rest of the dishes to the sink and loaded the dishwasher. Things were worse between them than she had thought. "It's different with me. She and I relate on a superficial level. I don't live with her, sleep in her bed."

"Me, either." Luke dropped the chair with a clang and paced. "Melinda's making damn sure she'll never get pregnant again. I used to feel guilty for trying to distract her from the rhythm method. Secretly, I hoped she'd get pregnant. But I'm not sorry anymore. She doesn't care about my needs, so why should I care about hers?"

Angie understood and felt responsible for the episode over the abortion. She feared she had manipulated her daughter-in-law. These days anyone could see Melinda's coldness toward Luke. Angie wished she could protect him but knew he had to learn his own lessons.

"Think there's some kind of karma going on with us?" Luke's face sagged, adding years to his appearance. "Maybe I owe her some debt from a former life."

"Could be. You have any gut feeling about it?"

A strange look crossed his face. Luke might have been surprised by his own thoughts. Perhaps he wanted to tell Angie something but feared betraying a confidence. "Not really. Maybe I'm rationalizing. Guess my manhood can't handle how easily she shut me out. No. It's more than that. I worry about whether we'll be able to go on living like this. Aaron's got to come first, but it's pretty dismal to think of living with a hostile stranger till he grows up. I'm not sure I can do it." Sitting on a chair at the table, he laid his head on crossed arms.

Angie massaged the knotted muscles of his shoulders and neck. Luke had changed in the past few months. He felt more deeply and thought more carefully. Encouraged by his open-mindedness in considering reincarnation, Angie wanted to share her search with him. Maybe that would put a new light on his problems. "Sometimes I wonder how much of my own sorrow is karmic, about Ty, I mean. I'm pretty certain a lot of it is from my Ashley lifetime. Remember I told you about how I abandoned him then? Now he's returned the favor. Course he didn't need to, not with my mother so willing to drop out of my life. Knowing all of that should make it easier, but it doesn't."

"Yeah, I know. Thinking about this business with Melinda gives me a headache." Stretching, Luke walked to the playpen. "Look, Aaron's crashed." The baby lay asleep, his backside still in the air from trying to crawl.

Melinda came through the door. She kicked off her shoes, threw her jacket on the couch, and plopped down.

"Hi, hon," Luke said.

"What a day." Propping her feet on the coffee table, Melinda rubbed her forehead.

Because Luke and Melinda had so little time together to talk, Angie thought she would leave them alone, even though pessimistic about their chances for resolving the problems between them. For Luke's sake, she hoped they would prove her wrong.

After kissing Aaron's sleeping face, Angie patted Luke's arm, said, "See ya in the morning," waved to Melinda, and opened the door.

Aaron awoke. "Ma, Ma."

Picking him up, Melinda cooed, "S'okay, Mama's here."

Not to be mollified, Aaron leaned over her shoulder and cried, holding his arms out toward Angie, "Ma, Ma."

A worried look on her face, Melinda spoke loudly. "I'm your mama, not her." She jiggled him in the air before her face. She probably thought to make him stop crying through the force of her will. "You know that, don't you?"

Aaron shrieked louder.

"Let me take him." Luke moved toward Melinda, but she jerked away and walked around the living room. Aaron's crying escalated.

Such uncharacteristic jealousy surprised Angie, who had not thought Melinda cared so much about the baby's feelings. Maybe there was hope, after all. Melinda's techniques probably scared the baby. Angie squelched an impulse to take him in her arms. She wanted to leave but could not ignore Aaron's terrified screams. Even though she waved to him, smiled, laughed, cooed, nothing deterred him.

Melinda's face reddened, then she plopped him into Angie's arms. "Do something with him."

The baby stopped crying as Angie carried him into the nursery. After closing the door, she held him tight, her heart pounding against his chest, which quivered with his gasps. What would Melinda do? Angie felt angry with

Melinda for provoking her own fear, for hurting Luke, and for scaring the baby. Did she have a grudge against all of them?

After Aaron calmed and fell asleep, Angie nuzzled his sweet-smelling neck, laid him in the crib, and headed toward the front door. Only their mid-sections visible between the counter and the cabinetry, Luke and Melinda stood in the kitchen, obviously unaware of Angie's presence.

"This is it, Luke," Melinda said, her voice harsh. "He goes tomorrow."

"No, his doctor's appointment is tomorrow."

"Monday, then, at the latest. I can't take this anymore."

"Shhh. She'll hear you." Luke whispered angrily.

"I don't give a fuck if she hears me."

"I said we'll talk about this on the weekend."

"There's no reason. The decision's final." Melinda's voice carried a chilling authority.

The memory of Angie's vision returned. The significance of the bundle she carried became clear for the first time.

Picking up her purse, Angie left the apartment, so exhausted she worried she would not be able to get herself home. She leaned against the elevator, waiting for the doors to open.

On the way home, she drove as if the car carried dynamite in the trunk. To avoid being overwhelmed by tears, Angie refused to dwell on the possibility that Melinda would take Aaron out of her care. Tomorrow was soon enough to find out what mischief her daughter-in-law had planned.

Twenty-One

A Test of Faith

Two weeks later

Anxiously, Luke sprinted up the concrete steps of the parking garage in the superior court building. His case had run longer than anticipated, so he doubted he could get to the doctor's office before Angie arrived. Unsure why Doc wanted him there, Luke assumed bad news and wished she had gone for a checkup right after Aaron's birth. Since then, she had lost a lot of weight. Luke could not remember her ever so thin before.

Since the first day Melinda sent Aaron to daycare, Angie had not come to the apartment. Aaron adapted easily. Fascinated by other babies and little children, he did not seem to notice his grandmother's absence, but she sounded depressed on the phone. Luke missed having her in the apartment when he came home from work. He had gotten used to sharing his days with her, since he could not with Melinda. Angie's absence brought the barrenness of his marriage into full force.

Climbing into the Trans-Am, Luke drove toward Doc's office. With Angie not coming to the house every day, Melinda seemed more relaxed, and Luke hoped she would warm to him. He missed the touch of her skin against his. More and more distant, now she slept in a nightgown and never rolled into his arms to cuddle. Admittedly, he felt less willing to understand.

Angie had taken her loss of Aaron without a word, getting good at stifling her words about Melinda. Luke could imagine what it cost her emotionally because he had seen the anger in her eyes many times. Sometimes he felt like an acrobat, walking a tightrope between them.

His stomach churned when he thought of what Doc might say. Angie had had too much grief to handle. She had never recovered from Ty's death. Sometimes Luke wondered if she had adjusted to his moving out of the house. Now Melinda had taken Aaron from her. It did not seem fair for her to be sick, too.

Luke pulled into the stall next to her car parked in front of the hacienda-style office. Damn, she'd beat him there. He slammed the car door and ran inside the familiar white-washed office. Angie sat in one of a row of armless chairs with a closed magazine on her lap. Across from her, a young woman and a toddler sat at a child's table and chattered over a coloring book.

An expression of fear crossed Mom's face. "Luke, why are you here?"

"Doc called and asked me to come. I don't really know why." Luke squeezed her hand as he sat next to her.

"Oh, God." Angie dropped her head and put her hand over her mouth.

From his private office, Doc Gutierrez called, "Angie, Luke, come back now." Holding the door as they passed through, Doc looked troubled and clapped Luke on the back then sat at his cluttered desk. A new baby picture had joined the family gallery behind him.

As long as Luke could remember, Doc had always fixed the problem—pills for the epilepsy, flu shots, Angie's allergies. Doc explained about birth control to Luke as a teenager, although they agreed not to tell his mother. Today Luke hoped for some kind of reassurance in Doc's face but saw none.

One hand resting lightly on the upholstered arm, Angie sat on the edge of the worn barrel chair, poised as if she might fly out of the room on a moment's notice. Wisps of gray crept out of the hair clip fastening the black shaft of her hair. In white sun dress with full skirt flowing over pale legs, she looked pretty and frail. Luke wanted to shield her from what Doc might say.

"There's no way to say this gently, Angie. The biopsy and the chest x-ray confirmed the diagnosis." Doc coughed. "Lymphoma."

"Cancer?" Angie half rose, then fell back, bloodless fingers gripping the chair.

"Technically Hodgkin's Disease, but, yes."

Luke could almost touch the stillness in the room. No one breathed. The situation felt as surreal as a science fiction movie. This could not be happening to his mother, the indestructible force in his life.

"How bad is it?" Angie asked, her voice measured.

"There are some other tests, but the diagnosis is firm."

Angie could have been talking with an auto mechanic about car repairs. The only clue to her inner turmoil was her stranglehold on the chair arms. "Do I have a chance?"

"There's been a lot of success with this particular strain. A seventy to eighty percent remission rate. It won't be easy, but there's a good chance you'll be okay."

Only a chance? Luke felt like he had been kicked in the stomach.

"What should I do?" Angie whispered.

"There are treatments indicated, but every case is different." Doc handed her a card. "I've made an appointment for you to see an oncologist."

Nodding, Angie took the card and stared at it. Perhaps she could not think of any more questions. None came to Luke.

"I'll be with you every step of the way," Doc said in his most reassuring doctor's voice. "Any time you need me, don't hesitate to call to talk or visit. You know I'm your friend. I want to help you through this."

Although Luke wanted to grab Angie and run away, he rose and stood behind her, holding her shoulder. "She's gonna get well, isn't she, Doc?"

"We're going to do our best. We'll monitor her progress carefully." Doc's jowls jiggled as he flipped through some papers. Was he avoiding making eye contact? He looked old, handing Luke a prescription. "Get this filled right away."

Wanting to shout that they did not need pieces of paper, they needed a cure, Luke whispered, "Thanks."

Angie fumbled with her purse, which fell off her shoulder twice before she anchored it.

Doc lumbered to his feet. "I'll talk with the specialist after your work up. We'll stay in touch. Don't worry."

Unable to listen anymore, Luke had to take action. He held out his arms to Angie. She came into his embrace like a child afraid of a dog, one hand barely touching his chest. In his grip, she felt tiny and smelled of Chanel. She lifted her head and gazed at him, sea blue eyes watery. She looked as defenseless as Aaron.

Luke could think of no way to rescue her. Cancer sounded like a death sentence. Angie had raised him alone, putting him first as long as he could remember. Now, he would do the same for her. Her body sagged against his. "Don't worry, Mom. We'll beat this. I'll help you."

"Why? Oh, God, why?"

With a forlorn smile, Doc came around the desk and encircled both of them with his arms. Luke squeezed Angie tightly, hoping to infuse her with a comfort and relief that he did not feel coming from Doc's hug.

Releasing them, Doc sniffed and opened the door. "I'll call you tomorrow."

Outside, Luke remembered they'd come in two cars. "Why don't I take you home and come back for your car later?"

"I drove myself here. No reason why I can't drive home."

"This has been such a shock. I don't want you to be by yourself."

A look of wry annoyance on her face, Angie said, "I'm not an invalid."

"Mom, let me—"

"No. I need some time alone." She bent to get into her car then straightened and stared at him. "Thanks, honey. Try not to worry." Drumming her fingers on the open car door, she lifted an eyebrow and said, "I'm not dead yet," then climbed in and took off in a hurry, going over the curb as she turned into the street.

"I'll be there in a few minutes," Luke yelled after her. As her car merged with traffic, he wished he had been able to stop her. What were they really up against? He sensed Doc had not been completely open. Luke went back inside and asked the receptionist for a moment with the doctor.

Doc stepped into the hall a few moments later. "All I can tell you is to have the tests, get the treatments. That'll help. But it's just a matter of time. I'm sorry, Luke."

"What about this eighty percent recovery?"

"In younger people, when it's caught early. Not in your mother's case."

The calamity worsened each moment. "How much time has she got?"

"It's hard to say." Doc took off his glasses and wiped his eyes. "She's had this condition for quite a while."

"Whatever it is, just tell me."

"She has a few months, a year. Maybe two, if we're lucky."

On the drive home, Luke felt as if he had lost control of his life. He tried to imagine seeing Angie suffer and living on without her. No headline could define this moment. He wanted to hit something.

Luke felt compelled to handle details to try to reverse the downward spiral into disease. He reasoned that, if he took care of everything, she would be all right. One part of him knew he was reacting erratically. Another part felt reassured by physical activity.

First, he called his secretary and canceled his appointments for the afternoon. Usually he had sympathy for his clients, but he would never be able to listen to them whine about their unfaithful spouses or thieving partners today. Then, he phoned Melinda, but she was on another line, so he left a message saying he would pick Aaron up from daycare. Luke needed the comfort of the baby's presence.

After leaving Tiny Tots Nursery with Aaron, Luke drove to Angie's. She had not returned, so he went inside and waited, wishing he had gone with her. Maybe the shock of the news had been too much for her.

When Aaron whimpered, Luke gave him a bottle, impatiently calculating that Angie had left him almost five hours earlier. He phoned Jillian, but she had not heard anything. Explaining to Jillian about the cancer made it a reality. Luke felt heaviness in his chest. His heart felt like it had grown too large and strained at the walls.

Jillian offered to visit that evening. Even though he did not want Angie to stay by herself, Luke needed some time alone. Jillian said Hank could try to locate Angie by doing a trance. Luke had not thought of that as a possibility, but it strangely comforted him to think of connecting with her psychically. Nevertheless, he told Jillian such extremes did not seem called for, but he might change his mind if Angie did not return soon.

When Luke hung up the phone, Aaron cried. Luke laid him on his belly in the middle of the floor and set toys around him. A car engine stopped outside, and Luke adjusted the shutters to peer out the front window. Angie got out of her car and waved to him. Her hair cut short and black again, she looked dazzling in a long red dress. Her necklace and earrings glittered in the sunlight.

As Luke opened the front door, Angie passed through and kissed him on the cheek. She looked so beautiful he felt like crying. It was not fair for her to have an ugly cancer inside her.

"It takes more than a few stupid lab tests to keep this woman down." Angie held out her arms and whirled around gaily. "I've been done over. How do you like my new look?"

"Love it!" Luke wondered whether she should go out shopping by herself but wanted her to do whatever she felt like, anything to bring her joy.

Up on all fours, Aaron called, "Mama." When his grandmother swung him into the air, he squealed.

Pressing the baby to her breast, Angie stared at Luke intently. "I have to watch this baby grow up. Nothing is going to stop me."

Luke trembled at the thought that she probably would not. "I need to get home. I called Jillian trying to find you. She'll be over tonight."

"You told her?" Looking surprised, Angie put Aaron into Luke's arms and said gently but firmly, "I can take care of myself, honey."

"I know." Luke thought she probably denied the truth of her condition but did not blame her. She would need help before long, and he had to face his responsibility. No one would ever be taken care of better. Luke would make certain of that. Hugging her, he said, "See you soon."

On the drive home, Aaron fell asleep in his car seat and did not stir when Luke carried him inside and laid him in the playpen. Luke called his grandmother, intending to ask her to fly out, even though he knew Angie would never ask her. Barbara was their only family, and he wanted her with them. When he told her about the cancer, she broke down sobbing and could not talk anymore.

Gerald came on the line and said he would make sure she called back when she felt better. He assured Luke she would want to be with her daughter, but Luke thought the offer insincere because of the way Barbara had stalled him when Ty died. Angie had not been surprised, had not expected any help from her own mother. Funny, how they'd turned out so different. Luke had been lucky to have Angie for a mother.

Melinda came in as he hung up the phone. "Who was that?"

"I've got bad news, babe." Luke plopped on the couch and covered his eyes with his hand. This had been the longest day of his life. He could not remember getting up that morning. "Mom has cancer."

"No." Melinda set her briefcase and purse beside the couch.

A lump appeared in Luke's throat. Saying the news aloud the third time turned out to be as difficult as the first. "Doc gives her two years at the most."

"I'm so sorry, Luke. Your mother and I don't agree on a lot of things, but I'd never wish something like this on her." Melinda sat on the coffee table and took his hand, rubbing her fingers across his knuckles.

His wife had not touched him so gently in a long time. Luke felt reassured. "Grandma probably won't come through. It's up to me to figure out how to take care of Mom."

"Is she going to the hospital?"

"Not now. I don't know what'll happen later."

"Why don't you hire a nurse? I'll help you find one."

"I can't leave her with a nurse night and day. Mom won't be around very long, and she needs us."

"She has medical insurance and Ty's money."

"I wasn't thinking about how to pay for it. There's so little time left. She's not going to get to see Aaron grow up." Luke imagined how awful he would feel if he could not watch his baby become a man. He should have stayed with Angie instead of coming home.

"You'll visit her, of course." Patting his hand, Melinda rose and folded her arms.

"Melinda, she's my mother. We have to be with her in the time she's got left."

"You don't mean you're going to bring her here?"

"I don't know what to do. Maybe we'll have to go there." Luke wished she would help him think this through instead of obstructing him. "I don't know what'll happen."

"You can't bring her here." Although her voice remained quiet, Melinda shook her head vigorously. "This is no place for a sick person."

"I'll do whatever it takes. What the hell do you think?"

"Don't you raise your voice to *me*." When the baby cried, Melinda picked him up and set him on her lap. He stopped crying and twirled strands of her hair in his fingers.

"I'm sorry I yelled," Luke said, feeling very alone. "I'm upset."

"Of course, you are." Melinda sounded conciliatory though she frowned.

"It's too soon to talk about this." Luke took a beer from the fridge and came back. "Look, I don't mean this is gonna happen next week, maybe not for several months." He paused, dreading to say the words. "Eventually she's not going to be able to stay by herself. I may have to move in with her. Maybe have a nurse while I work in the daytime."

Fear registered in Melinda's face. "You mean move out of our apartment?"

"Well, yes. Or maybe we could all move into her house. This isn't an inconvenient commitment in our daybooks." Luke slugged down the beer.

"No." Melinda paced the room, jostling Aaron. "There must be another way." Aaron grabbed a handful of her hair and stuck it in his mouth. She jerked back, "Ouch," and he cried.

"Here, let me have him." Luke took the baby out of her arms and cuddled him, pacing the room. "It's okay, big guy.

Everything's gonna be all right." Luke wished someone could tell him that.

Melinda followed them back and forth with her eyes, as if watching a tennis match. "I can't stand to be around sick people. It gives me goose flesh to think of it." She blurted out the words, like a confession

Luke turned his back on her and walked into the kitchen. "Let's talk about this tomorrow."

Stiffening, Aaron cried harder and rubbed his face across Luke's shoulder. Luke jostled him with one arm while warming milk with the other. Melinda slammed the bedroom door.

What a colossal nerve she had to think her squeamishness had any importance at all, compared to his mother's problem. He had always thought Melinda brave. How wrong could he be? How could he have ever thought she would be a good wife? She didn't have a fucking clue how to act. There was no point in being married if it didn't mean he would have a friend to lean on at a time like this. Far from making things better, his wife made them worse.

Nestled in Luke's arm, Aaron smacked and took quick little breaths as he sucked on the bottle, the sweetest sound in the world. His long black eyelashes lay on pink cheeks. Luke kissed the baby's forehead and inhaled the enticing scent, like the smell of his own skin. "Looks like it's just you and me, boy."

Easing the baby into one arm, Luke juggled the bottle while he sat at his desk and pulled open the drawer. Maybe writing would help sort his feelings. He took out a spiral notebook and flipped past yesterday's entry. It seemed he had poured his soul into his journal lately.

Tonight, the words flowing off his pen failed to unburden his heart.

Unwilling to think, Angie felt weary of her own inclination to try to figure out meanings, the trait she liked least about herself. Right now, she needed action—to go somewhere and do something wild. Smoothing her hands over her silk-clad hips, she remembered the titillating feeling of a climax rippling through her. Over a year had gone by without one. No wonder she had become ill.

Luke had been out of line to tell Jillian about the illness, not giving Angie time to absorb the news. But then, he probably did not know how to do so. She did not know herself and wondered wryly if the Navy had protocols for dealing with a person dying of cancer. What comforting words soothed one into accepting the end of the mortal self?

Waiting for Jillian to arrive, Angie flipped on the television and surfed through the channels. A weatherman predicted a break in the hot spell, under one hundred tomorrow for the first time in over two months. Pitiful choices appeared—a talk on the habits of mountain lions, an Andy Griffith rerun, a soccer game. Hitting the off button, Angie threw the remote on the couch. She would go to church and say a prayer if she could think of anything to say.

Wandering around the room, she folded her arms then unfolded them and swung them aimlessly. Should she eat something? Her gaze fell on the vase of dried sunflowers sitting in the corner. They'd been so beautiful in Ty's living room but suddenly looked out of place here. She carried them to the dining room and stood them in a corner. Judging the change not much better, she stashed the vase in the hall closet.

"Yoo-hoo, anybody here?" Jillian's voice rang out from the entryway.

When Angie opened the front door, her friend beamed a glorious smile, full of love. Relieved to see no visible sympathy, Angie hugged Jillian. "I'm so glad you're here. Let's go somewhere, okay?"

"Feel like sinning a little?"

"Only if it's followed by a hot fudge sundae and some dancing." Angie winked. "Maybe I'll treat myself to a cowboy tonight."

Jillian drove them to a bistro where they'd often had dinner together after school. Angie ordered her specialty, lobster with drawn butter, and ate all of it. She listened to Jillian's tales from school, for a while transported back to her teaching days when they were colleagues with a common mission. They made jokes at the expense of poor assistant principals, who, because they'd been winning coaches, received promotions past their ability to perform their jobs.

Dessert came, and Angie dived into delicious chocolate. "Yummy. Almost as good as sex."

Laughing in agreement, Jillian asked gently, "What's going on with you, Angie. Talk to me."

"Well, I'm bulging the seams of this dress, and I just bought it today." Angie tried unsuccessfully to hook her finger in the belt to demonstrate how much she had eaten.

"You know what I mean." Jillian's kindly expression made talking about the problem a bit less awful.

"Thanks for letting me slide for a while." Angie put down her spoon and smoothed the napkin on her lap. "You know, it's funny. All these months I've been searching for Ty, it never occurred to me I'd have to die to find him."

"Oh, Angie, maybe you won't. You're going to get treatment, aren't you? Chemotherapy?"

"Probably. I'll do whatever the specialist suggests. But, I saw the look on Doc's face. He didn't fool me for a minute. He believes I'm going to die."

"How do you feel? That's the most important thing."

"I am so angry I can't tell you. I don't want to leave Luke and Aaron." Angie grimaced at her first consideration of how difficult life would be for them with her gone. "I intend to stick around to keep them out of Melinda's clutches."

"Angie, don't be glib." Years of honest friendship gave Jillian the right to insist.

"I don't want to die, and I'm scared of the pain." Fumbling, Angie wadded her napkin and threw it on the table. "Let's get out of here." She opened her purse and laid a few bills on the table then went to the restroom. Jillian would have to take care of the waiter.

Her image in the bathroom mirror looked a little puffy, but not too bad. She straightened her freshly colored hair, liking it short and sassy, and applied fresh lipstick. She preened from side to side, surveying the new look. Satisfied of her appeal to a new lover, Angie wondered whether it would be a man or death.

Jillian and Angie drove a few blocks to the Okay Corral and walked into the cavernous country nightclub, its dance floor lit by a rotating mirror ball. Men in Levis, boots, and Stetsons leaned on the bar. Most of the women wore tight jeans and cleavage-revealing T-shirts. The air smelled of beer and cigarette smoke.

A shapely woman in a yellow lamé pantsuit held the microphone like a lover and sang a mournful song about missing a husband or a train, or maybe both. Two guitar players and a drummer accompanied her.

Several men at the bar noticed their arrival as Angie and Jillian sat at the table nearby and ordered wine. With her blond hair, tall, voluptuous figure, and teasing eyes, Jillian always drew men's attention. Now that Angie had created her new look, she imagined they made an attractive pair.

Two smiling men headed toward Jillian at the same time, and the older gallantly stepped aside while the other asked, "Would you like to dance?"

"Very much," Jillian said and preceded her partner to the dance floor.

Exhilarated, Angie wanted to feel desired. She laughed, delighted when an attractive man asked her to dance.

Rising, she walked into the arms of the smiling cowboy. His embrace sturdy, he drew her to him with practiced ease. He smelled of pungent aftershave freshly applied, his plaid shirt rough on her cheek. His closeness made her tense.

"I'm Matt. What's your name?" His smile was wide and open. Curly brown hair fringed a fortyish face. A slight paunch hinted at a few beers too many, but he looked unblemished by any emotion stronger than lust—perfect for Angie's plan.

"Angie." She liked the casualness implicit in first names only, an unspoken agreement to take pleasure with no obligation to share pain. The tempo picked up, and they whirled in a country swing dance. Angie missed a step and said, "I'm sorry. I don't know how to do this."

"Just make it up as you go. That's what I do."

Through the end of the tune, then several more, Angie danced, thrilled by the sensation of the music's rhythm, occasionally seeing Jillian with a different partner in the crowd. Matt's strong arm guided Angie in turns and reels. He must have lied about making up moves since he seemed certain of where he led her. She abandoned herself to the dance. Finally, he took her back to the table and excused himself with thanks.

Fanning her glistening skin, Jillian ordered wine from a passing waitress. "Having fun?" At Angie's nod, Jillian said, "Me, too."

"Seemed like you danced with a different partner every time," Angie teased. "What'll Hank think? Will he be mad at you?"

"Naw, I'm not going home with these guys. Hank knows he's got a corner on my market." Grinning wickedly, Jillian pointed to the line of men at the bar. "I've set a goal to dance with every single one."

Invigorated, Angie dabbed her shoulders and arms with a tissue, glad to feel alive. She drank more wine and watched Jillian, who jumped up and danced with eyes closed as she threw her body into the swaying rhythm. Her wide hips slowed against her partner's. The cowboy pulled her close, his arms quivering, and Jillian gazed into his face, as if mesmerized. Angie laughed, enjoying her friend's outrageous flirting.

When a slow song played, Matt came up behind Angie, took her shoulders in his large hands, and whispered, "Let's dance." She went into his arms gladly, warmed by his presence and the wine. "You feel good against me."

Something familiar in Matt's blue eyes haunted Angie. Her life energy coursed through her, and she yearned to spend herself in his arms, to pour out her desire and become one with him.

"You make my blood race." Matt pulled her closer. His stiff jeans pressed against her thin silk when he rasped, "Come home with me."

Unbidden, words came from deep inside Angie's mind. *He can't help you forget. He's not Ty. Comfort yourself.*

Disengaging herself, Angie said, "I'm sorry. I can't do this. Please forgive me." She walked back to the table and sat down, laying her hand on her heart.

Matt followed her and leaned on the table covered by a red and white checked tablecloth. "What'd I do?"

Fondly, Angie touched his cheek. "You didn't do anything wrong. You put me in touch with myself. You helped me see what I have to do."

His open face looked disappointed. "You're telling me no?"

"I'm sorry, but thanks." Angie recognized herself again. She would do whatever it took to face the cancer. Death, her old enemy, would not defeat her.

After Matt shrugged and walked to the bar, Angie waited impatiently for Jillian to return to the table. "I'm ready to go, are you?"

"Sure." Picking up her purse, Jillian smiled and waved like a prom queen toward the bar, then drove Angie home.

Before getting out of the car, Angie hugged Jillian. "You're the best friend I could have. I love you."

Once inside the house, Angie dropped her purse on the couch and retrieved the sunflowers from the closet. Plumping up the blossoms, she set the vase in the corner of the living room and said aloud, hoping Ty could hear, "Our love is too powerful, my darling. It would take more than cancer to betray it."

Angie hoped she could maintain the strength she felt tonight. Facing death was the scariest thing in the world.

Twenty-Two

The Clearing of the Mist

Angie came awake slowly, remembering indistinct images of Luke flying an airplane. In the dream, she sat beside him and wondered why he looked so wrinkled. Did that mean she would live to see him get old? What a lovely thought.

Afternoon shadows fell deep in the shape of palm trees outside her bedroom window. Shuffling through the bottles on her bedside table, she searched for the pain pills, not recalling how long it had been since she took one. Thank God, Luke would arrive soon.

With her body aching constantly, the days seemed endless, broken only by restless nights and awakenings from undefined nightmares. Only in the evenings with Luke beside her did Angie find comfort and peace. No doubt, Melinda resented the time he spent away although he never mentioned it. Angie felt guilty about wanting his presence so much and feared her illness would break up his marriage.

Angie struggled out of bed, pulled a fluffy pink housecoat around her, and held the railing as she placed each foot carefully on the stairs. She stopped to pant halfway down. In the kitchen, a sharp pain doubled her over the sink. With shaking hands, Angie took two glasses from the cupboard, for herself and Luke. She poured eggnog, added brandy, sprinkling the concoction with nutmeg, then carried the glasses to the coffee table.

Sighing, she pushed aside a new stack of library books—
Madame Blavatsky on reincarnation, Ralph Waldo
Emerson's writings, and Thomas Troward with his
farfetched theory on man's capacity to live forever. Angie
settled on the couch to sip the drink.

Her hotheaded ideas in the days after Ty's death had
been the height of egotism. Then she had believed in the
possibility of denying mortality. Yet, the cancer came after
she gave up the search to make contact with her lover.
When Doc gave her the death sentence, such anger and
defiance might have sustained her health. Now, she could
only accept her condition and pray for a miracle cure.

In earlier years, she had detected the onset of illness
and often intercepted the process with vitamins and rest. It
seemed perverse that she did not recognize the cancer
inside her until it grew too advanced for treatment.

Now, it did not appear she would be able to conquer
death at all. Just as she could not prevent Ty's plane crash,
she could not intervene in her own destiny. Accepting her
mortality had been tougher than Angie had anticipated.

The chemotherapy exhausted her and seemed to have
very little impact. How much longer could she function on
her own? She should probably call Doc and ask him about
getting a nurse or helper of some kind, but where would the
energy come from to interview them? Maybe Luke could
handle that, the way he did almost everything else.

At least she could still study. Angie picked up Elizabeth
Kubler Ross's book on the stages of dying then gazed
outside at the unpruned rose bushes, bleak and bare in
December. She sipped the tepid eggnog and lay back on the
cushion, closing her eyes and drifting.

The sound of a key in the lock awoke her. Night had
fallen, and Angie flipped on a light. Imagining she looked
terrible, she patted her hair, the new growth thin and
almost all gray. The dark sockets around her eyes grew

larger every day, and her body seemed to shrink. She wished her son did not have to see her this way.

Later than usual, Luke came in carrying his cat. He dropped Diablo on the floor and kissed the top of Angie's head. "How's it going?"

"Better, now that you're here." Angie touched his bristled cheek. His face looked careworn, as if he had reached the maximum burden his heart could carry.

"Be right back." Luke went outside.

Diablo circled the room, cased the side chair, and leaped into it, licking his black paws. Angie watched him, disturbed without knowing why. When Luke returned with suitcases, she sat up straight, understanding. "You're moving in?"

"Don't you remember the last time we saw Doc, we decided you shouldn't be alone?"

"I know but... is this okay with Melinda? Is she coming, too?"

"Uh... no. I'll stay at night, and we'll hire someone for the days."

Angie did not know which upset her more—needing a babysitter or realizing Luke would have to live separated from Aaron and Melinda. "Are they staying in the apartment without you?"

"Well, uh..." Luke pointed to the eggnog. "Is one of these for me?" When Angie nodded, he downed the thick concoction like water.

"Something's not right."

"Why don't you quit worrying?" Picking up his suitcases, Luke headed toward the stairs. "So, can I have my old room back, or have you rented it out already?"

"Not yet, but I've had some good offers." Her attempt at humor sounded hollow. These days were not quite like old times for either of them. Following him, Angie stopped to stroke Diablo's sleek fur. "Why are you here, cat?"

After a slow trek up the stairs, Angie reached Luke's room where he had already opened all the drawers and stuffed clothes in. She leaned against the door frame and sang, "'It's beginning to look a lot like Christmas.' Wonder why things always seem to go wrong at the holidays?" When he stared at her as if he had not heard her, she sat on the bed, folded her hands in her lap, and said, "Tell me the truth about Melinda."

"There's nothing to tell."

"Then why did you bring Diablo with you?"

Restlessly, Luke tossed a pair of rolled socks back and forth. "I didn't want you to know. You need to concentrate on getting well, not dealing with my problems." He threw the socks into a drawer and paced the room. "Might as well tell you, you'll figure it out anyway. We're giving up the apartment. Melinda's going to stay with her folks, at least temporarily. She wants a divorce."

Angie hated feeling like a burden to her son. She had brought anguish down on him as much as Melinda had. "It's because of me, isn't it?"

"No! We've been headed toward this for a long time. You know that."

"Can't you talk to her and get her to change her mind?"

"I don't think so. She says the marriage interferes with her career." A melancholy look crossed Luke's face. "I think she just doesn't love me."

"Oh, honey, I'm so sorry."

"Me, too. I didn't want to believe you were right about Melinda, but in my heart I think I always knew. We want different things out of life. I don't know why I was so blind to that." His voice rose with anguish. "But to take Aaron to live in someone else's house? How can she do that?" Luke slammed the maple drawers shut with such force that the hardware clanged, then he stared at the curtained window.

When in doubt, tell the truth, Angie sighed. "The baby's the bundle Melinda carried away in the vision. It isn't happening exactly the way I saw it. The details are different."

"But your responses were right." Luke's apologetic expression tore at her heart. "I should have listened to you. I'm sorry now that I distrusted your vision."

"It was a blessing and a curse for us both. Neither of us knew what to do with the information. Now I know it was a warning, to help prepare both of us for this moment."

"I should've known after Ty's death that you were right about Melinda. I should never have married her." Sinking down beside Angie, Luke dropped his head in his hands.

"The marriage hasn't been all bad." Angie rubbed the knotted muscles in his back. "Without her, Aaron would never have been born."

A look of determination crossed Luke's sad face. "I want him with me."

"I do, too." Angie wanted to distract him. "I dreamed about you today. You were flying an airplane, taking me somewhere, and you were old. I think that means you're going to become a pilot some day."

"Always wanted to get a pilot's license." Luke sounded amazed. "I figured I'd not be eligible because of the epilepsy."

"Guess you were wrong. Can't fight my prophecies, you know." There was much she did not understand. Feverish, Angie hoped she would live long enough to realize the full potential of her gift. "I wonder why so many of them involve airplanes?"

"Don't ask me."

Angie's gaze fell on the intersection of the living room walls, and she remembered Ty's face in the hospital room the morning after he died. When she had made her promise to him, she had no idea of the price she would pay to fulfill it.

"I don't have any control over the visions," Angie explained, grateful that Luke let her talk about her psychic experiences now. "When they come or what they're about. I used to feel like I had some obligation to do something to change the events. Now I believe they are gifts for me. To prepare me for what's going to happen to the people I love. Ty was destined to get on that plane. The vision helped me through the grief."

"And what about my destiny?"

"You had to marry Melinda. It would've been pointless to argue with you."

"That's true," Luke said with an ironic smile. "Are you saying I wanted to bring this trouble down on myself?"

"If we knew in advance everything that was going to happen in life, where would the adventure come from? I think that's why I can't see my own future. Maybe life on Earth is a school for everyone." Angie took Luke's hands in hers. "I don't know if you can accept this right now, but I know it's true. We're all connected—you, Aaron, me, Melinda, Ty, Bobby, Daddy, Grandma, even your father. In time or out of time, we're all joined in love. We're never any farther from each other than a thought, and thought is all there is."

"Nice words, Mom, but they don't keep me from feeling damned rotten inside."

"Your beliefs will change, as time goes by. I intend to prove it to you."

Luke furrowed his brow. "How can you do that?"

"I'll come to you after... " Speaking of her own death unsettled Angie. "I'll make myself known to you, if I can."

Luke looked puzzled for a moment, then the old impish grin broke across his face. "You mean you're gonna haunt me?"

Angie laughed. "How lucky can you get?" She bent forward, seized by a coughing attack. Luke rubbed her back until it subsided. Then he helped her to bed. She lay back and closed her eyes, sorry he had to take care of her but pleased that he wanted to do so. "You'll be a handsome old codger," Angie whispered as he tucked the light blanket under her chin. "And I'll be there with you. I promise."

"What?"

"My dream, you know." Wanting to give them both hope, Angie smiled.

"Here, take these." Luke placed capsules on her tongue then held the straw and glass to her mouth.

Swallowing, Angie let the painkiller carry her away into the sluggish void.

Jarred awake by the sound of the vacuum cleaner, Angie wondered who would be cleaning in the middle of the night. Or was it daytime? Struggling into her robe, she started down the stairs.

An unfamiliar voice called, "Whoa, there, Mrs. Brock, where do you think you're going?" A large red-haired woman in a white uniform pushed the vacuum cleaner out of Luke's bedroom.

"Who are you?"

"Didn't mean to startle you, ma'am." With a kind smile, the nurse said, "I'm Hannah Stockett. Mr. Brock hired me to see after you while he's at work. Don't you remember we spoke on the phone last night?"

"Sorry." Many of life's details were slipping out of Angie's awareness.

"He wants me to cook and clean, help you get your bath, see to your pills."

"Oh, of course." Angie vaguely recalled a mention of the subject. Maybe with Doc? Or was it Luke? A coughing spasm hit, and the nurse eased Angie back into bed.

The sharp pain cleared Angie's head. She had to become more awake and aware, even if that meant feeling more discomfort. She made herself a promise—more meditation, less pharmacology from now on. She would only die once, at least as Angela Brock, and did not intend to miss a minute of the experience.

Enjoying Hannah and the bustle the nurse created, Angie allowed herself to be plumped, coifed, and coddled. When Luke came home from work that night, she told him about her decision to curtail the use of painkillers.

Luke sat on the coverlet beside her and loosened his tie. "Sounds good to me. You can always change your mind later if you need to."

"She's done very nicely today, Mr. Brock," the nurse said, looking proud of her patient.

With a boyish smile that belied the formality of the title "Mister," he said, "Call me 'Luke.'"

"Thank you, Luke," Hannah said, "See you both tomorrow," and closed the door behind her.

"Now, tell me, why this new attitude?" Luke asked.

"It's important that I keep my wits about me so I can experience everything. I want to be present with you in the time we have left to be together. I appreciate the sacrifices you're making for me, moving in here so I won't have to go to a hospital."

"It's okay, Mom." He rose.

"Stay, please." Laying a trembling hand on his arm, Angie smiled. "Let me say this. It's one of the perks of having cancer." Her son settled beside her and took her hand. "My greatest sadness isn't that I'm going to die. It's that I'll be separated from you and Aaron. I want to see him grow up and watch you raise him. He's going to become a beautiful young man, just like you. It breaks my heart to think I'll miss that."

Luke glanced away. "Melinda's thinking of taking him to California."

"You won't let her do that," Angie said angrily. "Even if she tries, you'll get him back, and you'll be a better parent to him than I've been to you. I want to be with you and help you."

"Mom, please."

Her voice cracked but Angie went on. "I feel like I've burdened you with my grief and my dependency, especially now with Melinda so angry." She wiped away a tear. "I'm sorry."

"You did the same for me when I was sick as a kid. You didn't desert me, like my father did." Luke's voice carried unresolved hostility. "You took care of me."

"I'm afraid I contributed to the breakup of your marriage. I never liked Melinda very well. I think we were in competition for your love from the first day." With an effort to mask a painful spasm, Angie breathed deeply. "I believed the vision would come true so much that I may have helped make it happen. That's a tricky line to walk. Now I feel sad that she's gone, and we don't have a chance to work at making our relationship better. For your sake and Aaron's."

"None of this is your fault."

When Luke stared at her, something about the planes of his face struck her in a different way. The mottled green and brown eyes looked dark as moss agate stones and very old. They seemed to peer at her from some brooding past. Angie wanted to call her son by another name, but the sound of it escaped her. Certain that he was a kindred spirit through many lifetimes, Angie felt even more determined to set her heart to rights. "I've always meant well, and I believe I've acted out of love. Though the truth is I've meddled where I didn't belong. Maybe even with the abortion, but I'm not sorry about that. It was the right thing to do. It's just that sometimes my love creates confusion and anxiety. It's not my intention. Luke, I want your forgiveness."

"You have it." Luke enfolded her in an embrace.

Angie could have remained there for a long time, consoled by his strong arms, but he laid her back on the pillow. Perhaps her son felt awkward or embarrassed. Even so, she felt glad to speak her mind. "You know, dying is as much an adventure as living is. I can do it without the pain pills. But more than that. I believe I'll survive consciously afterward. I wasn't kidding when I said I'd make myself known to you. I want you to stay alert, hear me if I can only whisper to you from the other side."

"I may not be any good at it. I've never had a psychic experience." A vague expression crossed Luke's face as he glanced toward the ceiling. "Well, maybe once I... oh, never mind."

Although Angie waited, Luke had a closed look, like he did not want to talk about something. She did not press him. "Sometime, you'll learn to see with psychic eyes. You're my son." Grinning, she ran her hand through his wavy blond hair. "I've got faith in you."

"Sounds like a curse." His groan indicated Luke had much to overcome before he felt comfortable with such experiences.

"You'll recognize me, just like I did Ty. I know he's still out there, waiting for me. Just think of that. Dying can't be too awful if I'll get to be with him again."

Luke expelled a long breath and sprang up. "Gonna change clothes and get some supper. You hungry?"

"Actually, I am. Surprising, huh? Soul baring's good for the appetite." Angie picked up a book and opened it.

"Something new you're reading?"

"No, it's the *Tibetan Book of the Dead*, instructions on dying. I read them to Ty, hoping he'd come to me. Now I want to read them for myself."

With a quick intake of breath, Luke said, "I could read them, too. If it would help?"

"Thanks, honey," Angie said, knowing he did not really want to do it. "Supper'll be fine."

Hearing Luke's steps on the stairs followed by the clang of dishes, Angie could not focus on the book. A poignant solace came to her. All along, finding Ty and reuniting with him had been the important goals in her life. Now, she cherished her life with Luke even more.

Unable to save Ty, Angie could only know his fate and steel herself. He walked a different path now and had the right to go his own way. Even though her vision did not keep Ty alive, it had sparked her own spiritual search, and she felt grateful for the peace she had found.

Angie let go of the past and with it went her obsession.

Thankful, too, for her visions, she forgave herself for not trusting them in the past. She had had to learn to be connected to her power of prophecy, to trust her inner self. It had not come naturally. She thought of herself as a beginner mystic and wondered how many lifetimes it would take to gain the kind of confidence that would give her conscious control over psychic processes.

In spite of everything, Angie sensed a richness about her life, perhaps even a heroism in her unwillingness to let love die. Some people probably thought her insane—tilting at windmills—in her search for Ty. She could accept that label but knew the truth.

A line from a Robert Browning poem came to her: *Man's reach should exceed his grasp, or what's a heaven for?* Smiling, she thought, make that "woman's reach," then drifted into a quiet place in her mind, somewhere between wakefulness and sleep. Her body cooperated, the usually throbbing nodes lulled into comfort.

Angie dreamed she walked through a thick mist. In the distance atop a tall hill stood Emmons in a gray morning coat. The sun shone brightly from the other world as he held out a hand, beckoning to her. Angie labored to reach the summit, her steps sluggish as if countering an unseen force that would prevent her from making contact with her guide.

Finally, she arrived, and Emmons took her hand, "Come, my dear, I want you to see the way you've come."

When Angie looked down into the valley behind her, the mist cleared, and she saw herself as part of an old sepia tone print. She wore a mauve Martha Washington-style dress. Throwing off a straw hat, she knelt beside a marsh where a man, mired in the sludge, flapped his arms wildly to keep himself afloat. A tiny child who looked exactly like Luke sat on a log, watching the man drown. The images, though exceedingly distinct, looked like old photographs.

The snapshot changed. Angie stood beside a great body of water. The tide lapped against an embankment where twisted trees grew. She wore a hooded cape, as did her husband, an older, stockier version of Ty.

Luke. a grown man now in the breeches and bloused shirtsleeves of a colonist, sobbed over the body of a woman, unmistakably Melinda, who lay dead on the bank, her soaked gown and cape spread out around her.

"'Tis not your error, my dear," Emmons said, his voice powerful. "You know the ones drowning. They are the same soul in need of care. Before I depart, one word for your son—remain open to Spirit and loving to all.

The ringing phone and Luke's angry shouts awakened Angie. His side of the conversation indicated Melinda had not done something she had agreed to do. She should have brought Aaron for the weekend but did not.

The incident, so close in time to her dream, told Angie that the souls she loved had been together in the eighteenth century. Now, the circle was closing on them again.

"Let there be time to ease the suffering and right the wrongs," Angie prayed.

Twenty-Three

Bye, Mama, Bye

Although he tiptoed, Luke's shoes creaked on the stairs when he went to his bedroom after work. He remembered fondly the game of running up and down as a six-year-old. In high school he had always tried to sneak in so Angie would not know how late he had been out. He had fooled her too, sometimes. She might have been psychic, but she used to be a heavy sleeper. Not anymore. He intended to change clothes then relieve Hannah for the evening.

So far they'd avoided a hospital, and he still hoped for improvement. Angie had insisted Doc remain her primary doctor, but Luke knew Doc consulted with the oncologist. Even though Doc hinted that remission was probably out of the question, his decision to end chemotherapy agreed with her. She seemed better in the past few days.

The week had been fairly uneventful. Thursday already, and Aaron would arrive tomorrow— his presence better for his grandmother than any medicine. She always brightened and even managed to go downstairs last weekend and play pat-a-cake with him.

When Melinda brought Aaron for his weekend visits, she avoided going upstairs to see Angie. Luke had long since lost his opinion of her as self-controlled and strong. Seeing the valor in his mother's suffering, he felt appalled at Melinda's immature fears.

Luke threw his jacket on the bed, removed his tie, and flipped open the black leather briefcase. He quickly proofread Aaron's custody papers to make sure there was not any loophole Melinda could use for a court battle. With any luck, Luke could keep the paper trail to a minimum and have Aaron here in the house permanently within a few weeks.

Luke changed into jeans and a sweatshirt then hurried down the hall to Mom's bedroom. A healing tape of muted strings played softly on the cassette deck. A basket of philodendrons sat on the night table beside vials of tablets and syrups. Luke glanced at the bureau and noticed the absence of the bouquet of red roses he had had delivered last week. He must order more. Never should his mother be without something beautiful in her line of vision.

Hannah sat in the rocker. Laying a book in her lap, she pressed her finger to her lips.

Propped up with eyes closed and hands folded, Angie wore a pink satin gown and lay against pillows on the rose-colored sheets she had asked Luke to dig out of storage boxes from Ty's house. A cap of short gray hair curled around her face, her skin porcelain white. She must have sensed his presence because she turned and opened her eyes, bright and shiny, though dark-rimmed.

"Oh, good, you're home." Her voice sounded weak and raspy, but she smiled in acknowledgment of his kiss on her forehead.

Hannah closed the book with a snap and rose. "I finished my homework, Mrs. Brock."

"Homework?" Luke asked.

"Your mother's got me reading that reincarnation claptrap." The nurse straightened the bed covers with a practiced air then squeezed Angie's foot. "See you tomorrow. Sleep well."

"Always the teacher." Laughing, Luke said to Angie, "I'll see Hannah out." As he and the nurse walked downstairs to the dining room, he asked, "How'd she do today?"

"Rather melancholy, didn't eat much." Hannah's voice, though brusque, sounded kindly. "Seems to lose a little more ground each day."

"This February's been the bleakest I can remember." Knowing how his mother disliked the winter, Luke said, "So much rain. Suppose some flowers would cheer her up?"

"I threw out the roses. They were completely wilted."

"Right. Would you mind ordering some more before you leave? The florist's phone number is on the fridge."

Silently, Hannah trod across the parquet and picked up the card. "You always get roses. How about lilies, for a change?"

"Sure, okay." What did the variety matter if the flowers brightened Mom's thoughts a bit?

Moving to him with a warm smile on her wide face, Hannah touched his arm. "You're a good son, Luke."

"Thanks." He went upstairs, remembering his old brag, "world's best son," never thinking he would have to prove it like this. As he walked in the bedroom, his mother coughed, then lay back and sighed. "How you doin'?"

"Maintaining." Angie held the spot on her side where a node grew. "Cancer's tougher than I am."

"You don't have to be a hero. Take the morphine." Her insistence on enduring the pain frightened Luke, but his respect for her integrity had grown during the past few months.

"Not yet." Angie patted the mattress. "There's something I want to tell you."

"What's that?" Luke rubbed out a spent incense stick in an ashtray on the bedside table, peppermint to ease her breathing, then sat beside her.

"Remember that first weekend I went to visit Ty in Los Angeles, right after we got back from Bobby's funeral?"

"Your wild weekend of sin? What I remember is discovering I had a racy mother."

"Sons don't get details about some things." Angie chuckled mischievously. "Ty and I went to the observatory at Griffith Park and saw a time capsule that'll be opened when Halley's Comet comes again." Her face was so animated she looked like her old self again. "You know, the Comet returns every seventy-six or seventy-seven years. Mark Twain was born the year it came. He predicted he'd die the year it returned, and he did. Did you know that?"

"Really?"

Nodding, Mom coughed. "Ty and I made a pact to meet there again in two thousand and sixty-one. Just a joke at the time, but the memory of it came up in my regression. It's funny that I didn't put the pieces together until lately. I believe we might incarnate together in the next life."

"How would you recognize each other?"

"I don't know for sure. Maybe by saying 'right, red, returning.'" Her face softened. "I need to feel safe because I'll be returning home soon," she whispered.

Hoping to keep her involved in the story, Luke asked, "What does that mean?"

"It's the way sailors remember how to find their way home in the dark and stay safe in the channel." Angie coughed and gagged.

Fearing the worst, Luke reached for her, but she recovered her breath. He dreaded the sight of her suffering and struck a match, lighting another incense stick. Angie slipped away a bit more every day, and there was nothing he could do to stop her. Her feather-light touch on his arm brought his attention back to her.

"Luke, I'd like to be buried back home in Indiana."

As if a fire alarm had gone off, Luke strode across the room. All her focus had been on reincarnation and the future, never mentioning the details of her own death. He did not want to respond to her request.

"It's where I grew up," Angie went on, "where Ty and I fell in love, and where you were born. I have a lot of good memories of my hometown." She smiled, her face gentle and loving. "It seems like a lot to ask after all you've done for me, so I won't hold you to it, but I'd like it if you could take my body there, after I'm finished with it."

Opening the Venetian blinds, Luke gazed out into the darkness, imagining life without her—no hugs, no long talks, no psychic events. Poor little Aaron would grow up and never know her. Luke had depended on her unconditional love all his life, had accepted it as his due for only having one parent. How could he face the long years without her? On the other hand, he could not hope for her to live on suffering like this for his security. Luke turned to her and tried to say "okay," but no sound came out. He cleared his throat. "I'll do it. I'll take you back to Indiana."

Tears stood in her eyes. "You know the very best thing that happened to me in this life?"

Luke shook his head, unable to speak.

"Being your mother."

Luke couldn't look at her because he would surely cry. Turning back to the window, he idly closed and opened the blinds, telling himself he would go on without her because there was nothing else to do. That's what it meant to be alive—to lose people you love. Suddenly unable to contain his anguish, Luke hurtled toward her and held her, sobbing, "I love you. I don't want to lose you."

Kissing his cheek, Angie said, "You never will. I'll always be a part of you. Just look around." She gestured in the air around the room. "I'll be there."

Luke squared his shoulders and vowed he would not lose control again. He would be strong for her.

"You know what?" Angie smiled. "I'm jealous of you."

"Why?"

"I wish I could kiss my mother."

A welcome anger washed over Luke. "I've tried to get Grandma to come out here, but she won't. I'd like to throttle her."

"You too? I even wish she wouldn't call. I pretend to be getting better so she won't feel so bad. I feel guilty for being sick and causing her to worry."

"You've been a good daughter. Don't feel like it's your fault."

"Some people won't stay when the going gets tough." Angie shrugged. "My mother's always been like that."

"So's Melinda. I had the idea marriage would create a strong bond, something to depend on, you know? I couldn't have been more wrong. She doesn't know how to be a friend." The irony of his botched marriage grated on him. "She not only let me down. She's mad at me because she did."

The New Age music tape ended. In the silence Angie's breathing sounded more pronounced. "We're not responsible for other people's behavior. It's taken me a long time to learn that and be able to forgive Mother. Now I feel sort of grateful to her."

"Grateful? You're kidding. What for?"

"For my life lesson. On the day she put me into the orphanage, she set me up. I couldn't have learned to accept abandonment without her. Mad as I've been at her, the truth is she's always done the best she could." Angie lay back and sighed. "I had to forgive her for not being a perfect mother."

The idea of forgiveness stuck in Luke's throat. He could barely speak civilly to his grandmother on the phone. As far as forgiving Melinda, he could not even consider it. "How can you?"

"I finally realized she wasn't mean to me on purpose. She's afraid of death or living, maybe both." Angie gazed softly at him. "It's hard to stay mad at somebody who's terrified." She coughed and rubbed her side with a trembling hand. "Besides, I've been a very headstrong daughter."

Luke hoped to end the difficult conversation. "You're tired. Why don't you sleep for a while?"

"No, I've got a lot to say to you. I feel strong tonight." With a smile, Angie patted the bed. "Melinda made me face something in myself, too."

"What?" Luke settled beside Angie, fascinated with her effort to wipe her emotional slate clean.

"I resented Melinda's obsession with her career. I didn't want to see my own selfishness, so I projected my anger at myself onto her. She's always talking about her mission to create a place where Hispanic women can be successful. How could she be so high-minded and treat you so badly? And neglect Aaron?"

What a stretch to consider Angie and Melinda alike. Luke had no trouble agreeing to his wife's selfishness, but his mother was an angel.

"The truth is I've been as preoccupied with my search for Ty as Melinda's been with her career. I focused on connecting with the dead, not the living. I could've made a new life for myself. Instead I got cancer." Angie lovingly touched her side as if the cancerous node were an old and trusted friend. "Melinda and I are more alike than I want to admit."

"But she's been a total shit!"

"I have to forgive her or I can't forgive myself." Angie took his hand, and he saw challenge in her faded blue eyes. "You'll have to forgive her, too, honey."

"Hah! I'm thinking more in terms of getting even." Annoyed with his mother despite his intention to treat her gently, Luke paced at the end of the bed. He tread on a squeaky floorboard. "Forgive her? It's out of the question. Maybe Grandma. She's old and not too smart. But Melinda? Never."

"Judgment will consume you, if you're not careful. You've got to let go of anger and forgive both of them. Otherwise, you're stuck yourself."

Shaking his head, Luke stopped pacing and stared at her. Clearly, his mother's condition prevented her from understanding the scope of Melinda's transgressions. "I'm gonna take her to court and make her give me my boy back."

"Besides, you never know what you might have done to provoke the situation."

"Me?" Luke could not believe his ears. His mother thought he had done some harm to Melinda? "I never did."

"In a past life I think you did, honey. There's no way to prove that, but I wish you would stay open to the idea." Mom's hand shook as she pushed her hair back. In a voice tiny even for her, she asked, "You suppose you could heat me up some soup?"

His watch said seven-thirty. Surprised at the lateness of the hour but relieved to end the conversation, Luke did a sweeping bow. "Supper'll be fashionably late tonight, madam."

"And one more thing," Angie called after him. "I have a message for you from my guide, Emmons. In his words, 'remain open to Spirit and loving to all.'"

Uncomfortable with the idea of spirit communication, in spite of Mom's evidence, Luke went down to the kitchen and fixed soup, sandwiches, and hot cocoa. How could she possibly think she caused the cancer? He must've misunderstood. Forgiving everybody seemed overboard, too. Whatever happened to good old-fashioned responsibility? He had a right to expect help from his wife and his grandmother. Why should he have to do everything for Angie himself?

As Luke started upstairs with the tray, the doorbell rang. Maybe Angie expected company. "Be right there," he yelled, ran up two steps at a time, and put the tray in front of Angie, then dashed back down to the front door. Melinda stood on the porch holding Aaron, their black eyes glittering under the porch light.

"Da," Aaron squealed and held out his arms.

"Hi, big guy." Luke took the boy and hugged him. "I didn't expect you till tomorrow. Something wrong?"

"I'll be right back." Tossing the diaper bag on the couch, Melinda ran to the car and returned, carrying the car seat and two suitcases. She set them in the living room. "I'll get the rest later."

"Rest? This is plenty for the weekend. It looks like everything the kid owns."

Twisting her hands, Melinda said, "Luke, uh, I've changed my mind about the custody. You don't have to go to court." She touched the baby's back as he lay against Luke's shoulder. "I'm leaving him with you."

Her words took Luke's breath away.

"Aaron's better off with you." Tears welled in her eyes. Melinda looked more vulnerable than Luke had ever seen her. "I love him, and I love you. I know that now, but it's just not enough."

Her sadness unnerved Luke. He leaned toward her to touch her shoulder. "Melinda?"

Quickly, she stepped backward, raising her arm and warding him off as if she were crystal. "Please don't touch me. I won't have this courage very long. For some reason, it's not in me to be a wife and mother, even though I want to."

Melinda's words echoed his thoughts. Maybe she had finally come to her senses. Luke tried to think of something to say and failed.

"I don't expect you to understand. I'm not even sure I do myself." Melinda turned away as if about to leave, then stared at him, intensity on her haggard face. "Even though I love both of you, I can't be with you. I've got to accept myself the way I am. Whatever drives me, my career comes first. You're a nurturer, and I'm not. Aaron belongs with you." She expelled a long breath, and her shoulders drooped.

The suffering Melinda exhibited at giving up her child showed a perverse kind of courage that wrenched Luke. He said, "Maybe we should try to work it out, get counseling or something."

Aaron stuck his fingers in Luke's mouth. "Coo-kee, coo-kee."

"It's too late. I'm leaving for Los Angeles in the morning. I've found an investor who's willing to finance my business. It's the chance of a lifetime. I've got to do that, for the sake of the women who'll be depending on me."

"I don't understand you. How can you say you love us and then take off for California?"

"This is my work, my duty, what I have to do with my life. I hope someday you two can be proud of me."

Aaron cried out and reached for Melinda's hair.

Ducking away from the baby, she ran up the stairs, calling, "I want to say good-bye to your mother."

Overwhelmed, Luke trudged into the kitchen and found a cookie. Aaron took it and stopped crying then held the cookie to Luke's mouth. From habit, Luke took a bite, encouraging the baby to speak. "Mmmmm, good."

Pursing his plump lips, Aaron said, "Mmmm, good." He spoke as clearly as his daddy had.

"That's right, son." Wishing he could feel happy with the baby's little success at talking, Luke carried the boy upstairs. Melinda had never acted this way before. What the hell would she say to his mother? At least he had his boy back. Why didn't Luke feel happy about that? He hesitated in the doorway.

Melinda sat on the bed, head bent. "I was afraid you'd see through me. You know that Mexican legend of *La Llorona?*"

"The devil woman." Angie nodded. "She's in all of us, that need we try to satisfy at any cost."

"I'm afraid there's a part of me that can harm my child." Melinda spoke with great sadness.

"I think we all hurt our children, even though we don't intend to." Angie laid her hand on her daughter-in-law's cheek. "I think you saw that desperation in me, too."

Miraculously, Melinda did not pull away. Tears shone in her eyes. "You scared me. I thought you'd know how empty I am when I'm not working." She took Angie's hand in both of hers. "But I'm not afraid of you anymore."

Angry that this was the first time the two women he loved had spoken honestly to each other, Luke lamented what they had all missed. Finally, he sensed a peace between them and hoped Angie was right, that they would have another lifetime to make up for this one.

"We're not so very different, you and I," Angie said, kindly. "Just different obsessions."

"I never meant to hurt Luke or you. Please forgive me." Melinda seemed unashamed of her tears.

With obvious effort, Angie reached across the bed, pulled a tissue out of a box, and handed it to Melinda. "I need your forgiveness, too. From the first day I met you, I let the vision interfere with my opinion of you. I don't think I ever gave you a fair chance, and I'm sorry. I always felt like I bullied you about the abortion, but—"

"No, you did the right thing." Melinda blew her nose.

When Aaron whimpered, Luke crushed the warm, sweet smelling baby to his face and whispered, "Shhh, Daddy's here."

With a tender look toward father and son, Angie turned back to a sobbing Melinda. "We'll always see you in Aaron's beautiful eyes." Her hand shook as she brushed Melinda's flowing hair back. "Will you accept one word of advice from a tired old psychic?" When Melinda nodded, Angie said, "Out there in California, stay away from the ocean. I'm afraid you'll drown."

"Thanks, but you don't need to worry. I'm petrified of water." Melinda hugged Angie then carefully laid her back on the pillow. "Good-bye." Going to Luke and Aaron, she enfolded them in one embrace. Tears poured down her face. She kissed both of them on the mouth then turned and ran down the stairs.

"Mama," Aaron cried.

Anguished, Luke followed Melinda and watched her dash out the door. She sobbed while she set Aaron's highchair and stroller on the grass. She jumped in the car and drove away without looking back.

Aaron screamed and bumped his stomach against Luke's chest.

Luke waved Aaron's little arm at the departing car. "Say 'bye-bye' to Mama."

"Bye, Mama, bye," Aaron called, his baby words heartbreaking.

Luke hated her, wanted to make love to her, felt glad to be rid of her, but missed her already. In spite of Angie's advice, he reproached himself because he could not forgive Melinda. He would have to live to be a hundred to wrench peace from this night.

Twenty-Four

A Promise Kept

Having barely slept, Luke rose early. Every time he closed his eyes, Melinda's tortured face filled his mind. Even though she could not help what she did, he blamed her for the loss of their marriage and for abandoning him and Aaron. He had looked in on Angie several times in the night. At about three, she felt so exhausted from fighting the pain that she accepted a morphine tablet.

On impulse, Luke called the office and left a message saying he could not come in, telling himself he had too much to do to get his life reorganized. Then, he called the daycare and said he would not be bringing Aaron today. The baby's presence always comforted Luke, and time with Angie became more and more precious. Luke did not want to waste a day.

Jillian made an unexpected visit just as Luke finished the phone call. "Hi," she said, fresh and sophisticated in mint green slacks and blouse. "I know it's early. Is it all right if I see Angie before school?" With a grin, she flashed her hand before Luke's eyes, showing off a diamond ring. "I've got some good news to tell her."

"Of course," Luke said, "go on up. It's all right if you wake her. She always dozes right off again. And congratulations."

"Thanks. I'll only be a minute." Blond hair bobbing, Jillian dashed up the stairs, her health and vitality a tormenting contrast to Angie's condition.

Jillian's arrival must have awakened Aaron because he cried out. Luke poured orange juice into a bottle and hurried up to retrieve the baby before he tried to climb out of his crib. In the spare bedroom, Aaron had successfully negotiated the railing and sat on the floor, chewing on a paperback book.

The orange juice went down quickly. Then, Aaron splashed happily in the tub, chasing plastic boats while Luke shaved. Someday he would teach his son how to shave and watch him get ready for ball games and dates. What sport would he like best? Football? Baseball? Soccer like his dad?

The child needed a mother's presence. Luke intended to make certain Melinda did not drop out of Aaron's life like Luke's father had done. Maybe they would not have an ideal family with her in California. Who knew what "ideal" meant, anyway? Whatever Melinda did, Aaron would be the core of Luke's life just as Luke had been for Angie.

The bond with Aaron seemed critical, perhaps even preordained. When Angie had predicted that Luke would have psychic experiences of his own, he had had the impulse to tell her about the brief image where he had seen Aaron like triplets. She would not have laughed at him as he had sometimes laughed at her. Even so, something held him back. That moment had been too precious to share in words, to risk diminishing it.

Whether he understood the vision's meaning exactly or not, he knew something timeless had happened between him and his son. In any event, he could sympathize with Angie's struggle to come to terms with interpreting psychic events.

Whisking the baby out of the tub, Luke rubbed him in a towel, powdered, and diapered him. Aaron babbled the whole time. Sometimes Luke wished he could figure out what ideas the baby tried so hard to communicate. His precious face certainly looked expressive. Aaron probably knew some secret language his dad should understand.

Luke carried Aaron into Angie's room where Jillian stood beside the bed. "Hey, big guy, make your grandma and Jillian smile." When Luke set the baby down on the coverlet, he immediately crawled to his grandmother and hugged her.

"Good morning, honey boy," Angie murmured and laid her hand on the baby's bare back. She offered Luke a frail smile. Faint blue veins threaded through her transparent skin.

"Morning, Mom."

"What a darling." Jillian looked wistfully at the baby.

Angie obviously did not have the strength to hold Aaron. Luke took him and set him on the plush beige carpet, arranging his favorite stuffed toys within reach. The baby picked up a teddy bear and chewed on it.

"Well," Jillian said with a sigh, "I've got to go to school, but I couldn't let the day go by without saying thanks. Without you, I would never have met Hank."

"Yes, you would." Angie smiled. "You've known him before."

"How do you know that?"

Shrugging, Angie said, her voice thin but confident, "This close to the veil, the barriers are weak. There are moments when I feel as though I know everything."

"How lovely for you to get to have this experience." Jillian squeezed Angie's hand.

Chuckling, Angie said, "Leave it to you, Jillian, to see the joy in my situation. It's your gift."

"And yours is telling us all the truth. Don't ever stop." With painstaking care, Jillian straightened the collar of Angie's white silk bed jacket, smoothed the sheets, and kissed her forehead. Jillian's normally rousing smile fell, giving her face an expression of despair. "Bye, Luke. Call me anytime. Take care of that little boy. He's a cutie."

"See you."

"Good-bye, Jillian." Angie sounded delicate and distant. "Remind Hank of how lucky he is."

"I will." Jillian left the room almost furtively.

With a tiny smile, Angie watched Luke light a peppermint incense. "Glad you got your boy back."

"Me, too." Filled with love and a sense of rightness, Luke sat on the bed. Sunlight streamed through the window, promising a gorgeous Arizona day of wide sky and balmy air, one of the first since the winter rains had ended.

Angie's sea blue eyes held his for a moment as she touched his cheek. With the faintest of movements, her hand floated down to his open palm. Closing her eyes, she lay still, her pale fingers unmoving in his suntanned hand. With a spasm of panic, Luke glanced at her chest to see if she still breathed.

"Greatest act of surrender..." Angie whispered, the last word almost inaudible. Luke put his ear close to her mouth and heard her say, "Must... surrender. He's come for me."

"Mom?" Luke straightened, tense and alert.

She seemed excited, almost merry. Her eyes darted from Luke's face to the corner of the room. "Can't you see him?"

"Who?"

Her throat rattled as she spoke. "Up there."

Luke looked at the walls, the ceiling, and the open Venetian blinds. "I don't see anything."

"Ty!" Angie sucked in a breath that clicked and stalled in the air.

Time froze.

She never breathed out.

Transfixed, Luke stared at his mother. A wisp of pearly smoke rose from her forehead, leaving her body motionless, still beyond all imagining.

Grief filled him. Tears rolled down his cheeks as Luke raised his palm, bearing her hand to his mouth, and kissed the cool fingertips that smelled of Chanel. She had worn perfume, even on this last day.

Now, Luke understood why he had refused to go to work. Maybe Angie Brock's son would turn out to be psychic, after all. Even Jillian must have sensed the time had come.

Aware within a spacious moment, Angie peered down from the ceiling and saw the back of Luke's head as he bent over her, kissing her hand. She wanted to share her joy with him. "Luke, darling, I'm here. I'm alive. Don't be sad." When his shoulders slumped, Angie called, "I'll always love both of you." She willed her love to fill him and the baby.

Magically, Luke and Aaron glowed. Iridescent light waves streaked out around them. The air shimmered, so beautiful that Angie caught her breath.

Luke saw a presence softly fill the room with Divine white light. It surrounded him and Angie, flowing through them.

Aaron dropped his toy and looked up, waving. "Bye, Mama. Bye."

The baby talk drew Luke's attention to Aaron's happy face. Without a doubt, he saw something. Daring to hope, Luke gazed at the glowing ceiling. Angie's comforting love surrounded him. His throat contracted. "Good-bye, Mom."

The doorbell rang. Although Luke tried to ignore the hateful sound, it rang again. Perhaps Hannah had forgotten her key. Why was she arriving so late, anyway? The doorbell continued to ring, as if someone rocked a finger on it, but Luke did not want to leave his mother.

Angie waved at the baby, her arm light and filled with energy. Someone called her name, and she looked around, just as she had done in the dream reality. Aware that she could see in every direction through the glistening brightness, she moved along a tube-like structure, not

walking or flying, but being firmly pulled forward.
Relaxing, she enjoyed the ride.

Luke heard the doorbell ring once more. Toddling to him,
Aaron pulled at his dad's shirt. With infinite care, Luke laid
his mother's lifeless hand on the sheet. He did not want to
disturb her now. Gathering the baby into his arms, he
hurried downstairs to answer the door.

A delivery boy stood outside, holding a basket of white
flowers. "Delivery for Miz Brock."

"Yes, I'll take it."

The gum-chewing boy thrust the bouquet toward Luke.
"Lillies charged to Luke Brock's Mastercard account."

"Okay. " Adjusting the baby on his hip, Luke took the
flowers and started to kick the door shut.

"Just a minute." The boy dashed to his truck and carried
an arrangement of yellow flowers in a tall vase to the living
room.

"Who ordered these?" Luke felt suddenly exhausted at
having to deal with such details.

Consulting an invoice, the delivery boy shrugged. "No
name on it. Some Navy guy. Paid cash."

"Ty." He really had come for her. Peace filled Luke as he
murmured, "Take good care of Mom for me."

Vibrant and exhilarated, Angie looked down. Only her body
remained in the room. She did not want to look at it, vacant
and tiny. The moment she wondered where Luke and Aaron
had gone, she instantly saw them at the front door.
Someone set a vase of flowers beside Luke. Sunflowers. Ty's
favorite.

A kindly force propelled Angie away, drawing her into
the sky. She watched her roof disappear in a blur of other
houses, palm trees, swimming pools, and highways.
Phoenix grew smaller and smaller beneath her. She turned

toward the whiteness, and the tunnel engulfed her. When she looked back, the Earth had disappeared from view.

In the center of a prism of light, Angie moved, refracting rainbow colors that radiated from her. Feeling blissful in the consummate quiet, she abandoned herself to the loving force that carried her forward. Soon, the energy of the tunnel lessened. She floated to the end and stepped out on emerald grass, velvet soft.

A man stood in the brilliant light beyond, waving to her.

Ty looked wonderful in his white Navy shirt and slacks, the uncontrollable lock of hair curling down his forehead. Ecstatic, she laughed and called out to him as she ran toward him.

Shouting her name, he ran to meet her. They merged in a collision of energy. Angie felt his embrace in every part of her body and mind. Opalescent streamers of light poured out all around them.

Ty gazed at her, love twinkling in his cobalt eyes. "My darling, you kept your promise. You found me again." He picked her up, whirled her around, and kissed her. "Welcome home."

Acknowledgments

Over the years while I have imagined and written the *Alma Chronicles*, many people have influenced my life and thought. Some have given me support, encouragement, and love. I would like to thank these people here and tell them how grateful I am for their presence in my life. Even though a few have died, I trust they know I appreciate them.

Aaron Heathcotte, Annette Lewis, Barby Heathcotte, Betty Joy, Beulah Fesler, Brandon Heathcotte, Brock Heathcotte, Bruce Heathcotte, Bryan Heathcotte, Carol Gibson, Chip Myers, David Perez, Dean Gordon

Emily Heathcotte, Greg Williams, Howard Fesler, Jacque Beatty, Jim Green, Joe Perez, John Bergman, Josh Heathcotte, Judith Lynn-Perez, Larry Crosley

Maggie Perry, Martha Davis, Mary Livingston, Mike MacCarthy, Mike Murphy, Nancy Brehm, Noonie Crosley, Pat Kennedy, Phil Shirley, Rick Aynes, Rick Williams

Rita Heathcotte, Robert Meya, Sharon Atkins, Sonny Crosley, Stephanie Heathcotte, Tearle Dwiggins, Ted Moore, Tom Brehm, Tom Franklin, Tom Larkin, Trena Aynes, Vijaya Schartz

I thank these authors for their books:

Deepak Chopra, Dick Sutphen, Ernest Holmes, Jane Roberts, John Edward, Judith Orloff, Ralph Waldo Emerson, Richard Bach, Walt Whitman

Toby Fesler Heathcotte is both mother and grandmother. A former teacher, she now serves as president of Arizona Authors Association and lives in Glendale, Arizona.

tobyheathcotte.com and outofthepsychiccloset.com

Write to her at toby@tobyheathcotte.com

Books by Toby Fesler Heathcotte

The Alma Chronicles

- *I Alison's Legacy*
- *II Lainn's Destiny*
- *III Angie's Promise*
- *IV Luke's Covenant*
- *V The Comet's Return*

Out of the Psychic Closet: The Quest to Trust My True Nature published by Twilight Times Books

Program Building: A Practical Handbook for High School Speech and Drama Teachers

Seeds for Fertile Minds: Eight Curriculum Integration Tools with Betty Joy

www.ingramcontent.com/pod-product-compliance
Lightning Source LLC
Chambersburg PA
CBHW062140170626
46813CB00002B/767